Praise for JL Merrow's
Hard Tail

"A gripping, fast-paced, and well-written out-for-you story set in rural England...catchy, witty and at times deliciously self-ironic."

~ *Reviews by Jessewave*

"As always with this English author, the main characters are lovable and quirky and the secondary characters are compelling and push the story forward."

~ *Guilty Pleasures Book Reviews*

"...a sweet, engaging tale of a man who has to lose everything to truly find himself... With both emotion and humor, realistic conflicts both internal and external, interesting secondary characters, and a couple of lovable heroes, I couldn't do anything but like *Hard Tail*."

~ *Joyfully Reviewed*

Look for these titles by
JL Merrow

Now Available:

Pricks and Pragmatism

Camwolf

Muscling Through

Wight Mischief

Midnight in Berlin

Pressure Head

Hard Tail

JL Merrow

SAMHAIN
PUBLISHING

Samhain Publishing, Ltd.
11821 Mason Montgomery Road, 4B
Cincinnati, OH 45249
www.samhainpublishing.com

Hard Tail
Copyright © 2013 by JL Merrow
Print ISBN: 978-1-61921-057-8
Digital ISBN: 978-1-61921-039-4

Editing by Linda Ingmanson
Cover by Kanaxa

First Samhain Publishing, Ltd. electronic publication: May 2012
First Samhain Publishing, Ltd. print publication: April 2013

Dedication

To the owner & manager of the real Totton mountain bike shop, Perfect Balance Cycles, whose help and inspiration was invaluable. Keith, I owe you!

Any technical errors that may remain are, of course, my own.

Chapter One

The bell above the shop door tinkled, and Matt Berridge fell into my life.

Literally.

I'd been staring at that glass door, willing someone to come in and stave off the killing boredom before I stuck a bicycle spoke through my neck out of sheer bloody ennui. So when a broad-shouldered, shaggy-headed lad in mirror sunglasses loped into view, I was all eyes. He wore lived-in jeans and a purple Weird Fish T-shirt, with a battered biker jacket over the top. He looked like he'd just got back from a festival somewhere. At least, he looked like I imagined a guy who'd just been to a festival might look. I'd never been to a festival. Too busy with exams and work and getting married to a girl I didn't love.

When he pushed open the door, I barely had time to mentally punch the air—and then he was gone, well-shaped arse over tit.

I'd swear it was nothing but his own feet he tripped over. With a soft cry of "Argh—shit!" he sprawled into the shop on his hands and knees. I didn't realise who he was at first—I just hurried out from behind the counter to help the poor sod up. But when he looked up from under that dark mop of hair, it was obvious. At least, if you had the inside information I did. The sunglasses, which I now noticed were scratched, hung from one ear, and there was a massive, purple bruise around his right eye, which was swollen and half-closed. I winced involuntarily when I saw it, then hoped like hell he hadn't noticed.

"Hi," I said as he staggered to his feet, holding on to my arm. "I'm Tim."

"Oh, right—you're Jay's brother? Good to meet you." He smiled lopsidedly, adding dimples to the freckles already sprinkled on his lightly tanned face. I could easily imagine him as a beach bum somewhere like California, although given the South Coast accent with a hint of a West Country burr, I was guessing Cornwall was probably nearer the mark. "Sorry about that. I'm a total klutz, ask anyone. I'm Matt."

"I guessed." I gestured to the black eye—and then cursed myself for being so tactless. Obviously he was self-conscious about the bruising, or he wouldn't be wearing shades. "I mean, Jay said you'd, er, had an accident. Sorry."

"Oh, yeah. That." He suddenly flashed a blinding grin. He had perfect teeth, except for one on the top left that was endearingly broken. "You don't look like him. Jay, I mean."

If I had a pound for everyone who's ever reminded me that there is one good-looking guy in the family, and I'm not him... I'd still be pissed off about it. "Well, that's the wonders of genetics for you," I said, trying not to overdo the fatalism and come off like a self-loathing loser. "Some kids get the looks. Some get the brains. Me, I got the knobbly knees and the tendency towards early greying."

He peered at me, his good eye narrowed nearly as much as his swollen one, and laughed. "You're not greying!"

"No, but I will be. I take after my dad, and he went grey before he was thirty."

"Yeah? How old are you now?" Matt asked. It was a bit of a weird effect, the cheeky grin on the battered face, but I couldn't help smiling along with him.

"Twenty-eight," I admitted.

"Looks like you've got two years to live it up, then," Matt said, folding up his sunglasses and shoving them in his jacket pocket, adding another scratch with the zip along the way. "Wait—you're married, aren't you? That's what Jay said."

"He did?" Jay talked about me? I wondered what else he'd said. "Um. We're actually not together anymore. Kate and me, I mean."

"Shit." Matt hung his head. "Sorry. Put my foot in it again. I'm always doing that."

"Don't worry," I said quickly. "It's fine—I mean, obviously, it's... Um. We'd grown apart," I finished lamely, trying to reassure him it wasn't as bad as it sounded.

"Oh. Right!" Just like a light switch, the smile was on again. "Right, well, I'd better get to work. Anything new come in?"

I looked at my watch. "Not in the fifteen minutes we've been open, no."

"Right! I'll get out the back, then." And just like that, he was gone.

I'd never have thought a broken leg would turn out to be the most important event in my life. For a start, it wasn't even my leg.

But it still managed to be responsible for moving me from London to Totton. It's all right; you're allowed not to have heard of Totton. It's just a small town near Southampton, out past the Western Docks and across the Redbridge Causeway, over the very tip of Southampton Water. If you keep driving on through, which most people do, in another ten minutes you'll reach the New Forest, home to a million pubs and ponies. It's about as far from London as you can get, philosophically speaking, although it only takes an hour or so on the M3. Particularly if you're bombing down the motorway like a bat out of hell because you've just heard your big brother's in hospital.

Okay, maybe it wasn't just Jay's accident that set things off. After all, I hadn't even heard the news when my marriage broke up.

It happened on a dreary, grey Monday evening, just after Kate had got in from work. I'd been home all day, having recently fallen victim to the merger of my firm, Falstaff & Bird, with a much larger accountancy business. Merger being, of course, merely a polite euphemism for the Falstaff & Bird partners selling the rest of us down the river. Half my department had been made redundant when the two firms combined, and the rest—the lucky ones—forced to relocate to the Williams Way offices in Canary Wharf. Everyone I'd spoken to since the axe had fallen had sounded shell-shocked by the speed of it all and wiped out by the commute.

Kate, being a lawyer, was more or less immune to the slings and arrows of outrageous fortune. Come to think of it, slings and arrows were pretty much her bread and butter. She was home late that day, and looked tired as she dumped her briefcase in the hall. I wondered guiltily if I should have tried to cook something—but then again, if she'd already been having a bad day, it'd be a bit mean to make it even worse. "Want to get a takeaway?" I asked.

Kate didn't meet my eyes. "Just a minute, Tim. I just need to pop upstairs."

"Okay," I said, a bit puzzled—after all, we had a perfectly good downstairs loo if that was what she needed. I wandered back into our tastefully designed living room and closed up the laptop I'd been busy tweaking my CV on, then unfolded the *Financial Times* from the job pages. It wasn't like there'd been anything in there, anyway. Then I sat down on the cream leather sofa and wondered if it'd be worth turning the television on while I waited. The phone rang, and I leapt up to answer it—only to find it had stopped before I got there, presumably fielded by Kate. I sat down again and stared at the bookshelves on the wall by the conservatory. Not much there apart from Kate's collection of modern literary fiction, the books all strictly ordered by binding and most of them unread. She'd deemed my pile of old-fashioned crime paperbacks far too scruffy for the living room.

"Tim?" I jumped a little as Kate spoke, peering around the door as if it might not be safe to come in immediately.

"Expecting someone else?" I quipped weakly, because all this uncharacteristic timidity was starting to worry me.

"No! No, don't be silly—who else would I be expecting?" Kate was still as neat as ever in her pale blue business suit, chosen to match her eyes. She came into the room in little, bird-like steps and perched on the sofa next to me, smoothing down her skirt.

"Is something wrong?" I asked.

"No—well, yes, actually. Tim, I'm so sorry." She was about to cry, I realised with a shock; I could tell by the little sniffs and the way her eyelids were fluttering like a hummingbird on acid.

"Kate, what is it?" I was seriously alarmed now. Had her dad had another heart attack? Had she lost her job too?

"I'm so sorry," she repeated. "But I'm moving out. I'm going to live with—" She hiccupped, and I wondered if I should pat her back. Maybe it would be politer just to pretend I hadn't noticed.

Then I wondered why good manners seemed to be my main concern at a time like this.

"I can't live a lie any longer. Alexander and I have been getting, well, closer—and I'm going to live with him." She looked up at me almost defiantly, but it only lasted a moment. Her slim little fingers kneaded one another savagely, and I noticed she'd taken off her wedding ring, and the engagement ring I'd given her. It had always seemed too big and clumsy for her hands, but apparently that would now no longer be a problem. "You must hate me," she whispered, looking down once more.

"No! No, of course I don't," I said, struggling to work out just how I actually felt. I wasn't sure I felt *anything* right now—apart from a strange disconnect, a numbness spreading out from my core. Hate her? We didn't really do strong feelings like that.

I do hate it when she cries, though. Always have done. I put my arm around her, which turned out to be a big mistake. She burst into huge, ugly sobs and buried her head in my shoulder. I patted her back—I had a fairly good idea pretending not to notice would, in the circumstances, be the polar opposite of good manners. What the hell were you supposed to say in these situations? "There, there," just didn't seem to cut it, somehow. "It'll be all right," was what I went with in the end.

It might have been trite but it had one positive effect—Kate stopped soaking my shoulder and looked up with an expression of outrage only slightly ruined by runny mascara. Thank God I wasn't wearing a favourite shirt. That stuff never comes out. "How can you even do this? God, it's just so unfair! Here you are, *comforting* me—and I'm about to—" She dissolved into tears once more.

"There, there," I said helplessly. Suddenly remembering I had a handkerchief, and it was even reasonably clean, I passed it to her. "Come on, have a good blow."

She blew her nose in that quiet way women seem to manage—I always sound like an elephant attempting the Last Post—and gave me a brave little smile. "It's just—everything's happened at once. You being made redundant, and then,

14

well..."

"Alexander," I supplied, in case all the emotion had made her temporarily forget the name of the bloke she was leaving me for. Alex was a friend of mine, as it happened. Blond, where I was dark; short and chunky, while I was tall and on the lean side; down-to-earth and Northern while I was...not. I wondered if her subconscious was trying to make a point.

I'd always been pleased with how well they got on together.

"I never meant to hurt you," she sobbed, teardrops leaving blotches on her dry-clean-only skirt. I considered sliding the *FT* onto her lap to catch them, but newsprint would only have made a worse mess. Best to leave it.

"You haven't hurt me," I said, not quite truthfully. Let's face it, even if you've accepted that your marriage was a total mistake, having your wife run off with another bloke is going to be bad for the ego. But I didn't blame her for looking elsewhere for what I couldn't give her. I blamed myself for being so bloody determined to keep my head stuck in the sand.

"I hope one day you'll find someone who deserves you," Kate said, sniffing.

I shrugged, wondering bleakly if that would be a good or a bad thing, if it ever happened.

Kate gave her nose one more snuffly little blow and picked up the bag she'd packed before coming back downstairs. I wondered if I should offer to carry it to the car, or if that'd be taken as an insult. It didn't look heavy, so I left her to it. I guessed she'd be back with my dear old mate Alex for the rest of her stuff later.

I thought about dropping some hints as to when I'd be out over the next few days but couldn't muster the energy. Or think of anywhere I'd go, come to that.

She turned her head to give me one last, sorrowful glance

as she stepped through the door, then paused as something struck her. "Oh—and by the way, your mother rang."

It never rains but it pours.

My mother never rings me. Never.

She rings my brother, Jay. I know this, because I asked him once. I ring *her* every couple of weeks or so, because I feel guilty if I don't, but she never seems that pleased to hear from me. Most of the time is usually spent talking about Jay—his latest money-making scheme, his latest girlfriend, whatever. She always finishes up by saying, "Well, at least I don't have to worry about *you*." And then she makes this sort of *tsk* noise under her breath, as if the lack of worry is just one more way I've been a disappointment to her.

So if Mum had rung, it must be something serious. A chill ran through me. Dad's complained for years about pains in his chest, but the doctor's always sworn blind it's just indigestion. What if this time she was wrong? I grabbed the phone and perched on the arm of the sofa to call her.

"Mum?"

"Timothy! It's about time you rang."

I'd only rung her last Thursday. "Mum, is everything all right?" I asked, standing up.

"Well, how can it be? Your poor brother! And it's not like we can get all the way over there every day for weeks on end, not with your father's health—"

"Mum! What's happened to Jay?" I was pacing round the living room by now. Mum often has this effect on me. Thank God we'd gone for the 80% wool carpet.

"What's happened to James?" she repeated scathingly. "Really, Timothy, I do think you might make a bit more effort to keep in touch with what happens to your family. Blood is thicker than water, although I sometimes wonder if you've even heard the phrase—"

"Mum! Just tell me!" I half shouted down the line, cutting her off mid-flow.

There was a brief silence, punctuated by an alarming creak from the plastic case of my phone. I relaxed my grip a bit, although it took some effort. "There's no need to be rude," Mum complained. "Your brother had an accident with his skateboard."

Jay's thirty-one, in case you were wondering. Going on thirteen. "And?"

"He's broken his femur. An unstable fracture, the doctors say. He's almost certainly going to need surgery."

The way she said it, you'd think it was my fault. "But he's going to be okay?" I asked.

Mum sniffed. "Oh, you know doctors. Always telling you not to worry. That woman in the village surgery has never taken your father's heart troubles seriously. Last time he went to see her, she sent him away with nothing but a couple of indigestion tablets! I don't think they train them properly these days. That surgery's never been the same since old Dr. Mallett left, not that anyone ever listens to me..."

She may, admittedly, have had a point there. I tuned her out with the ease of long practice and started making plans to drive down to Southampton next day.

It was only after I'd hung up I realised it hadn't even occurred to me to mention my marriage had just ended.

Chapter Two

Jay's my big brother. Trouble is, he never lets me forget it. He was lying in state in his hospital bed, looking relaxed as ever, propped up on more pillows than I'd had hot dinners. Well, since I'd left home, at any rate. Neither Kate nor I was ever much for cooking. She used to tell me how jealous her friends were that I was always taking her out for dinner. They thought it was romantic. They didn't realise it was the only way either of us would get a decent meal that week.

A couple of nurses were fussing over my brother with big smiles on their faces. Jay was looking pretty pleased with himself too, despite the bandages and the prospect of surgery. If it'd been anyone else, I'd have assumed they'd given him the really good painkillers, but Jay's never been one to worry when surrounded by attractive young women catering to his every whim.

"Tim! Good to see you!" he greeted me cheerfully. "Pull up a blanket and park your arse."

The nurses bustled off, not before giving me that frown I always thought of as the "so which of you was adopted, then?" look. I sat down gingerly on the edge of the bed, the NHS budget apparently not stretching to visitors' chairs these days. "So what happened, then?"

"Oh, it was just bad luck. I was trying to do an Ollie over a park bench, and it went a bit tits-up. I'd have been all right if I hadn't landed right on the edge of it."

"You were doing a *what*?" At least, I assumed he hadn't

meant doing a *who*.

I hoped he hadn't meant doing a *who*.

"An Ollie. It's that trick where you jump with the board, but you don't use your hands. Looks dead cool if you get it right."

"Right... You know, some people would say you make your own bad luck," I muttered. "How are you, anyway? I mean, I talked to Mum, but..."

He laughed. "Has she got you picking out flowers for the funeral already? I'm fine. It's only a broken leg."

"Mum mentioned surgery," I said cautiously.

Jay shrugged, as if it was no big deal. Maybe it wasn't, for him. He's been in and out of hospitals with broken bones since he was five years old—starting with falling out of trees and moving onto falling off mountains. "They're just going to bung a few screws in. I'll be fine."

"Sounds like you'll be off your feet for a while, though. What are you going to do about the shop?" Jay had started up a mountain bike shop around a year ago. From what he'd told me, it was doing okay. From what Mum told me, he was just one step away from world domination, but I'd taken that with a truckload of salt, as usual. "Are the staff up to keeping it afloat for you?"

I should have realised what was coming from the way Jay beamed at me. "Ah, well. That's where you come in, you see? It's perfect timing, innit? You need a job, and I need someone to manage the shop. Perfect!"

"Thank you, Jay. Nice to know someone's happy about me being made redundant." I said it as drily as I could manage, but as usual, sarcasm was lost on him. "Look, I don't know the first thing about running a shop."

"Oh, come on! It's not like you're not used to handling money, for God's sake!" Jay rolled his eyes, as if I were being the unreasonable one.

"The accountancy profession's come on a bit since Bob Cratchitt's day, you know," I protested. "I don't sit in a freezing-cold garret counting money in my fingerless gloves. In fact, I don't think I've *ever* handled actual money in the course of my professional career."

"Well, then, it'll get you back to your roots, won't it? Remind you what all those columns of figures stand for." Jay reached for a glass of water, and I hurried to move aside the enormous flowers-and-teddy-bear arrangement Jay's latest girlfriend had brought in on her way to whatever beauty salon it was she worked in. Olivia, that was her name. I'd passed her on the way in, and in her blinding white tunic and trousers, she'd looked a lot more clinical and professional than most of the hospital staff I'd seen. I certainly wouldn't have hesitated to put the lives of my nails in her hands. She'd said a cool hello to me but hadn't bothered with a smile, presumably deeming me unworthy of risking cracked makeup for.

"Look," Jay was saying, "you know I wouldn't have asked you if there was anyone else."

Never a truer word and all that.

"So stop being a prat. It'll be fine. I'm not expecting a major sales push—just keep the bloody shop open, that's all. Even you can manage that!"

"Thanks for the vote of confidence. But what about your staff?" I was hazy as to the actual number of his employees, but I knew he had some, or one, at least. He'd asked me for advice on PAYE, and I'd put him in touch with a local payroll company. "Why can't they run the shop? Isn't that what you're paying them for?"

"Well, there's only Matt," Jay said slowly. "And he can handle all the repairs and stuff, no problem. But he's, well—put it this way: remember Auntie Pat and her Dulux dog?"

"Big, shaggy, gormless thing that used to jump on everyone and knock over all the furniture?" Now, alas, humping legs and anointing lamp posts in doggy heaven.

"Yeah, well, that's pretty much Matt for you. He's a great bloke, honestly he is, and a wizard at fixing up bikes, but you can't leave him alone in the shop for more than a couple of hours." Jay laughed. "He's got a black eye at the moment. Tripped over his own doormat and landed on his face on the stair rail, the silly sod!"

Great. That was just what I needed when I was feeling my way around a new job: someone who'd likely as not trip me up and send me flying.

"Oh—and I'd better mention it now: he's gay. That's not going to be a problem with you, is it? Tim?" He said my name a bit more sharply than the rest; I guess my face must have given something away. I've always been rubbish at hiding my reactions; sometimes I feel like a TV set with the subtitles permanently turned on. Or maybe if I looked over my shoulder there'd be a little man hovering there giving a sign language translation. "For fuck's sake," Jay went on, "this is the twenty-first century. And don't worry. He's got a boyfriend already, and you are *really* not his type."

"I—" I realised my mouth was hanging open and closed it so fast I nearly broke a tooth. "I'm not homophobic!"

"Yeah, right. You should look at your face in the mirror next time someone mentions the *gay* word. What the hell is your problem?"

He was more bewildered than angry. That's Jay all over. He's so bloody laid-back he can't understand anyone ever having a negative opinion on anything anyone else does. "I haven't got a problem with it, all right?"

"Just as long as Matt doesn't find out. I'm not having you pissing off my staff while you're playing at being a shopkeeper, all right?

How did this happen? How does this *always* happen?

Is there anyone else in the world so good at asking for a favour, and at the same time making it sound like he's *doing* you a favour?

I hope not.

"Anyway, you can stay at my house. Kate won't mind you being away for a few weeks, will she? It'll probably do you both good—absence makes the tart grow blonder, and all that. Not that I'm implying Kate's a tart, obviously." He grinned. "Except when you want her to be."

"She—" My voice caught unexpectedly. I cleared my throat. "Actually, she's left me. Yesterday."

"What? No way! Shit, really?" Jay's face was suddenly so miserable it made me feel bad to look at it. "Tim, listen, I'm really sorry. Do you think she'll come back?"

I shook my head. "No. She's met someone else." I shrugged. "He's a decent bloke. I'm sure she'll be better off with him."

Jay clutched my arm, his big, rough-skinned hand a solid comfort. "She's an idiot, mate. Didn't know when she was well off. Look, if there's anything I can do, anything at all, you tell me, right?"

And that's why I agreed to look after the shop for him.

Because even though he's an arrogant, self-centred layabout and has always taken me—and the rest of the world— for granted, he's my big brother.

And he never lets me forget it.

Jay's house was on the outskirts of Eling. I'd never actually seen it before—I mean, I'd been down to see Jay since he'd moved in, obviously, but we'd always done pub lunches. Just like when he'd been up to see me and Kate, we'd gone out to restaurants. Although, come to think of it, we'd insisted on giving Jay the Grand Tour of the house first. Well, just as soon as we'd got it looking nice. And avoiding the fourth bedroom, about which Kate and the decorators had had a bit of a disagreement and which consequently got left half done.

Outskirts, by the way, are pretty much all there is to Eling, as far as I'd been able to tell on such limited acquaintance with the place. That and the Tide Mill, advertised on brown Tourist Information signs all over town. I'd always assumed it was some kind of watermill except with tides rather than a stream. Now I came to think of it, it seemed unlikely there was an enormous waterwheel sitting there, waiting to be turned twice a day. Maybe I should take a look sometime. It wasn't like I'd be that busy after work. I didn't know a soul down here apart from Jay, and even if any of his friends popped round, I doubted we'd have much in common. Apart, of course, from a difficulty in believing Jay and I were actually related.

Jay bought the house with the money our grandmother left him. Apparently, everyone (by which I mean Mum and Gran) had agreed I didn't need the money, what with the high-flying city career and more letters after my name than were in it. As long as you didn't spell "Timothy" out fully, that was. I inherited the dog-eared complete works of Agatha Christie and the collection of pottery dragons, which Kate had taken one look at and banished to a series of cardboard boxes in the garage.

At least I'd be able to get them out now, I thought, brightening a little.

The hope had been that Jay would use his inheritance to get a more settled lifestyle, and amazingly, it'd actually worked. He'd set up the business, and had money left over for a two-bed ex-council house with a scrubby garden and van-owning neighbours.

I wondered if the neighbours would expect me to be friendly. Like Jay.

Jay had also, while he was at it, embraced a more holistic lifestyle. Which meant misshapen, organic veg and recycling everything. Actually, Jay had started on the path towards all things Green when he was twenty and dropped out of University. He'd gone on the hippy trail to Goa; never mind that he was thirty years too late. He'd come back six months later with a suitcase full of shell jewellery and drug-taking paraphernalia, an all-over tan and an STD. Mum had greeted him like he'd spent the last year and a half starving on a pig farm, not lazing around on a beach out of his skull, and not a word was said about the unfinished degree.

My 2:1 from Durham, meanwhile, was treated with about the same amount of enthusiasm as if I'd just come home with an ASBO and a caution for shoplifting.

After I left the hospital, I drove straight back up the M3. The gorse bushes that lined its southern half were in full bloom, a mass of warm yellow amid dark green. Feeling a bit more relaxed now I knew Jay wasn't actually at death's door, I eased off the accelerator to appreciate the view. Kate and I had never really been into the joys of the countryside. Our holidays together had been spent in cities, perusing museums and art galleries by day and enjoying fine dining and classical concerts by night. Looking at those bushes glowing golden in the late afternoon sun, I started to wonder if maybe there had been something missing. Something simpler.

When I got back to my big, lonely house, I found myself wandering from room to room, just on the off chance Kate might have come back. She had, as it happened—but she'd also gone again, taking the contents of her wardrobe and most of our CDs. Probably a few other things too, which I'd no doubt discover just when I needed them.

Well, two could play at that game. I packed a bag and loaded it into the BMW. Then, on a whim, I went into the garage and picked up one cardboard box marked "Evil Under the Sun" and another marked "Here Be Dragons". I shoved them both into the boot of the BMW and set off back down to Jay's. He'd been keen to have me in the shop the next day. Matt-minding.

The gorse bushes along the M3 were no longer burning bright, and the sky was a rich salmon pink that deepened to inky blue the nearer I got to Southampton. It was only June, but the warm air coming in through the open window tickled my nose with the fecund smells of summer. I sneezed a couple of times, then seemed to grow accustomed to the pollen. I breathed in deeply, while a dozen reckless bugs met a messy end against my windscreen.

As I pulled onto Jay's road, it occurred to me that if the spare key wasn't where he'd said it was, I'd be pretty much stuffed. I knew only one hotel in Southampton, the de Vere one down by the waterfront. The lounge at the front was an imposing pyramid of glass, and though I'd never stayed there, I doubted it'd be cheap. I really ought to start watching the pennies, seeing as Jay's bike shop would put paid to me applying for a proper job for a while. And I'd still have to pay the hefty mortgage on the house in Mill Hill.

Which reminded me, I should probably get in touch with Kate so we could put it on the market. Depression settled on me like a worn-out duvet, lumpy and uneven. Maybe I hadn't been in love with Kate, but we'd been comfortable together. I'd liked the house and enjoyed the experience of setting up a home with someone. Bickering over furniture and experimenting with DIY. (It'd been a short experiment. The guy we'd called in to fix the mess we'd made had visibly struggled not to laugh at our efforts.) And there was just something about a failed marriage that made me feel, well, *failed.*

What with all the pessimistic thoughts, I was mildly astonished to find the key where Jay told me to look, under the third mini-flagstone of the path across the postage-stamp front lawn. It was being guarded lovingly by a large family of woodlice, and I shivered a little as I wrested it from their leggy grasp.

Then I opened up the front door, hauled my bag inside and took a tour around my new, temporary home.

Jay had this knack of furnishing a place on a shoestring and still making it seem cosy and welcoming. The mismatched easy chairs in the living room were squashy and covered with an assortment of bright throws and blankets, and he had one of those L-shaped sofas that seem to beg you to stretch out and make yourself at home. There was a forty-two-inch TV and a small table beside the sofa that was just the right height to park a drink on while you watched. All right, the table was actually an upturned crate, but since it was covered with a stripey Moroccan cloth, who was to know or care?

Something about the room made me feel overdressed. I crossed the tiny hallway to check out the rest of the floor. Downstairs loo: the usual facilities, plus a small shelf of humorous books and a variety of vaguely (and not so vaguely) druggy knick-knacks. I wondered if Mum had ever been for a visit, and if so, what she thought about Jay owning his own bong.

Then I told myself not to be so daft—she probably thought it was some kind of Indian teapot or table lamp or something—and went into the kitchen.

And stopped dead in the doorway. There was a cat in the kitchen. A large, fluffy, ginger cat with an outraged expression on its face when it saw me. It hissed once, then stalked off through the cat flap, tail in the air until the very last moment.

Why the hell hadn't Jay mentioned he had a cat?

Come to that, *did* Jay have a cat? I'd never owned one myself, but didn't they usually come with bowls and litter trays, not to mention sad little rodent corpses on the doormat? There was no sign of anything like that in Jay's cheerfully chaotic kitchen. I checked the cupboards. No tins of Whiskas or anything else with a picture of a cute fluffy kitten on it. There did seem to be a lot of tins of tuna, but that wasn't conclusive.

Even I knew several recipes for tuna. Well, all right. I knew a couple of different sandwich ideas. And the cat flap might just be a relic from a previous tenant.

I decided I'd worry about it if it ever came back. I pulled one of the mismatched mugs off the mug tree and rinsed the kettle out thoroughly before setting it on to boil. Then I looked in the cupboard and sighed. I'd forgotten Jay only drank decaf these days. There wasn't even a decent packet of tea in there—just some green stuff in organic, recycled teabags. I wouldn't have been surprised to find it was made from recycled leaves.

I flicked off the kettle and had a glass of tap water instead.

Then I started writing a shopping list, until fatigue hit me and I realised I hadn't eaten anything since lunch. I idly thought of opening a can of tuna, but there wasn't any bread for a sandwich—at least, none that wasn't cheerfully turning green and furry inside packets proudly (and redundantly) emblazoned with the boast, "No preservatives." And besides, would the cat ever forgive me?

Better safe than sorry, I decided. I hunted around for takeaway menus before remembering what a ridiculous idea that was. By now too tired to bother trying to find somewhere on my phone, I ate some sugar-free, salt-free, taste-free baked beans straight from the can, Mum's voice chiding me in my imagination all the while, then dragged myself upstairs. The second bedroom had been turned into an office, so I crawled into Jay's king-size, unmade bed that still smelt faintly of Olivia's perfume, and slept the sleep of the terminally knackered until morning.

28

Chapter Three

I was woken at seven o'clock on the first day of my new life as a shopkeeper by a cat jumping on my chest. As wake-up calls went, it was fairly effective. I opened my eyes to a mouthful of fangs looking like they were about to take my nose off, which, given the dead-mouse breath coming my way, would actually have been a mercy.

"Gah!" I'm never at my most eloquent when I've just woken up.

The cat hissed back at me, obviously not a morning person either. I shifted position, hoping it would get the hint and bugger off. Too late, I realised the flaw in that plan.

Claws. Twenty of them, or however many cats have—I was a bit busy cursing (all right, screaming like a girl) to actually count them, seeing as they were now firmly embedded in my person. "Off!" I shouted. Or possibly yelped.

The cat hissed at me again, then, mercifully, retracted its six-inch talons and leapt gracefully to the floor. I sat up, wincing, and surveyed the damage. For the amount of pain that had been involved, it was actually relatively minor, but it was just as well Jay wasn't the sort to moan about a few holes and bloodstains in his sheets.

Then I remembered it was his bloody animal that'd done it, so what the hell was I feeling guilty for? I sighed. "Let me guess—that's your way of saying it's breakfast time?"

The cat, which for obvious reasons I decided to name "Wolverine", yawned at me. Maybe it wanted to remind me about the other sharp, pointy things it had in its possession.

"Right, well, I hope you like tuna," I said, sliding my feet into the zip-away travel slippers Kate bought me last Christmas. I'd bought her a new briefcase; she'd seemed quite pleased at the time, but it occurred to me now that these weren't, perhaps, the gifts of a young couple deeply in love. Just how long had the writing been on that particular wall?

We padded downstairs, Wolverine staying at my heels, presumably so he'd be ready to take my feet off at the ankle if I tried to renege on the breakfast deal.

Tuna fish is not my favourite thing to smell first thing in the morning. I'm strictly a coffee-and-that's-it-till-eleven sort of guy. I forked the can into a breakfast bowl while trying not to breathe. Perhaps worried by my show of aversion, Wolverine sniffed at it suspiciously before graciously deigning to eat. Relieved, I switched on the kettle.

Then I groaned, remembering the coffee situation. Was it possible to die from caffeine withdrawal? Why the hell hadn't I driven around last night until I'd found a twenty-four hour Tesco? My preference for sleep seemed utterly absurd in the cold light of morning. In the end, I made myself a cup of organic decaf with three heaped teaspoons, hoping against hope the hippy manufacturer had been too laid-back to bother getting all of the precious pick-me-up out of the stuff.

Eight thirty a.m., I was standing in my boxer briefs in front of Jay's wardrobe with a grumbling case of indigestion brought on by too-strong coffee, wondering what the bloody hell to wear. Obviously I'd brought clothes with me. It was just...none of them remotely resembled anything Jay owned, or seemed in any way suitable for my new career. I'd brought a suit, because— actually, why the hell *had* I brought a suit? I couldn't see that going down too well in a bike shop. I'd packed some other stuff too, chinos and casual shirts—but none of that seemed right, either.

I could have borrowed something of Jay's, I guess, but I'd have looked ridiculous—the jeans were all too short, and everything would be too baggy around the middle. Not that Jay's fat, by any means, just solid and muscular in a way I could only dream of. Growing up (and up, and up) I'd heard all the beanpole jokes I could handle.

I could hear Jay's voice in my head, last time he'd come to visit me and Kate, asking incredulously, "Don't you even *own* a pair of jeans?" and I had to concede, maybe he'd had a point. In the end, I selected an old-ish pair of chinos and my least favourite Ben Sherman shirt.

And made another shopping list.

I got to Knight Rides—that's the name of Jay's bike shop— by nine fifteen, feeling like I'd already been up for half a day. Jay had told me opening time was nine thirty, but I didn't want to be still pratting around trying to work out how to plug in the cash register when the first customers arrived. Turned out I'd been a little optimistic about how keen Jay's customer base was. By the time Matt fell in the door ten minutes late, I'd been sitting behind the counter twiddling my thumbs for the best part of half an hour.

Consequently, when after his dramatic entrance he just disappeared into the back room, I felt cheated. Several people looked in the door or even stuck their heads into the shop before catching sight of me and doing an abrupt about-turn. Why? Did I look that off-putting? Or were they just thrown by not seeing Jay?

I wandered disconsolately around the shop, straightening all the handlebars of the row of a dozen or so bikes Jay had on

31

display and whistling at the price tags. I rearranged the hanging bicycle locks in order of size, then colour-coded the helmets. When Jay got out of hospital, he'd probably kill me for messing up his displays. I checked my email to see if the recruitment agency I'd signed up with had got in touch. No luck there, but there was a tweet from Kate saying she'd be round for the rest of her stuff tomorrow.

I supposed I should be grateful she hadn't broken up with me on Twitter. How would that have gone? *@WhatK8did =>* *@MagicBeanCounter: Am leaving you for @AlextheGr8. Sorry.* *#ItsNotYouItsMe.* Looking at it that way, perhaps it was inevitable they'd ended up together. After all, they both had an "8" in their names.

I was a bit reluctant to leave the till unmanned, but, reasoning that we did, after all, have a door with a bell on it, I eventually meandered out to the back room. Matt's hands were already black with oil practically to the elbow. He grinned up at me from derailleur level. "How's it going? You find everything all right?"

My instinctive reaction would have been to smile back, but it was tempered by a couple of circumstances. For one thing, I hadn't been aware there was anything I was supposed to be looking for and was racking my brains guiltily for any essential duties I might have neglected. For another, I was shocked anew at the way the black eye distorted his boyish, friendly features. "It's a bit slow out there, actually," I said, trying not to stare.

"Yeah," Matt said, his voice muffled as he solved my problem by bending low over the gears he was, presumably, fixing. I was worried his shaggy brown curls would get irredeemably entangled in the chain. "There's never much doing on a Wednesday. Everyone forgets we're open at all, what with the half-day closing."

"We have half-day closing?" I asked stupidly.

Matt looked up, a smudge of grease on his freckled nose. I fought the urge to wipe it off for him, because blokes don't do that for each other. "Yeah, didn't Jay say? We close at one on a Wednesday. I'm surprised he didn't tell you not to bother coming in until tomorrow."

I wasn't. Bloody Jay.

"Oh, well," Matt carried on, "maybe he wanted to start you off gently?"

"What, Jay?" I raised my eyes briefly heavenward. Thinking about my past with Jay often prompted a heartfelt prayer for strength. "Like he did when he thought I should learn how to swim and shoved me off the end of Bournemouth pier?"

Matt laughed. "Did it work?"

"No." I grimaced at the memory. "Luckily there were some anglers there, and one of them jumped in to save me. I was only five."

"Bet Jay got into trouble with your mum, then."

I cast my mind back and hit a blank, apart from a vague memory of Mum telling me I shouldn't have been pestering my brother, anyway. "Doubt it. But the angler gave me a dead crab to take home." I brightened. "Mum must have been horrified, but she just had to smile and say thanks, seeing as he'd just saved my life. And Jay was really jealous." I'd kept the crab in my bedroom for a couple of weeks, until it mysteriously disappeared—by which time the smell had been so rank even I didn't miss it.

Matt sighed. "Must be great, having a brother. Apart from, you know, him trying to kill you and all."

"Er, yes. I think." My turn to sigh. "I suppose I'd better go back and make the place look open." I took a step back toward the door. Matt nodded and bent low over the bike once more, his baggy jeans slipping halfway down his arse to reveal stripey underwear that reminded me of one of the throws in Jay's living room.

I caught myself staring, and shook my head. What the hell was I thinking of? Time to get back to work.

I sat behind that till and counted down the hours to one o'clock. How on earth could Jay make a living doing this? We had only two customers in who actually bought anything—one, a cycle lock for seven pounds ninety-nine, and the other, a pump adaptor for 87p. At this rate, we'd be bankrupt by the end of the week.

As I turned the shop sign to "Closed" I became aware of a sort of shuffling sound behind me. When I turned, Matt was there. "Um. I was just wondering—do you fancy going to the caff for lunch? I mean, it's nothing special, just a greasy spoon sort of place, so maybe you'd rather not..."

"I'd love to!" I said a little too loudly. All those hours with no one to talk to had got to me a bit.

"Great!" Matt enthused—and promptly tripped over the most expensive bike in the shop, which started to topple over towards the next in line. I lunged to catch it, having visions of writing off all Jay's stock in one fell swoop as the domino effect took over. "Shit. Sorry about that," Matt muttered, hanging his dark, shaggy head.

I straightened, breathing hard. "No harm done." Maybe this was how Jay kept afloat. Matt trashed the stock, and Jay claimed the insurance. I wondered how much longer it'd be before they started refusing to pay out for acts of clod.

We made it to the café without further incident, thankfully. Then again, it was only two doors down, past a hairdresser's that wafted out humid fumes smelling of mingled fruit and chemicals. The café was pretty much as Matt had said—linoleum floor, orange Formica tables and a misspelt chalkboard menu that seemed to consist mainly of grease, grease and more grease. Generously seasoned with a sprinkling of misplaced apostrophes. The place was almost full, though, which argued well for the quality of the food, if not for its healthiness. The clientele was mostly male, in a mix of business and casual wear, but there was a group of four women dressed for the office in the far corner. They looked up when we went in, one of them giving me a frankly appraising look that was a little alarming. I broke eye contact and headed over to the free table farthest from their corner, trying to surreptitiously check if I'd spilt anything down my front or left my flies open.

"Does Jay ever come in here—watch out!" I managed to save the vinegar bottle Matt's wayward elbow had knocked off a table on the way.

"Sorry," Matt said, looking mortified. "And, um, no. Not really his sort of place. He usually has something healthy and cold in the shop."

"Would that be Olivia?" I asked archly as we sat at the table. Then I wondered if I'd gone a bit too far with a bloke I hardly knew.

Matt just grinned. "You've met her, then? No, she doesn't come round the shop much. She's not really into bikes."

"Might ruin those perfect nails," I suggested, my cattiness fuelled by relief he hadn't taken umbrage on her behalf.

"Or get oil on those white tunics of hers," Matt added, his unblemished eye twinkling. "We shouldn't diss her, though—she's all right, really. And Jay seems to like her."

As if that was a recommendation. Jay liked *everyone*. A middle-aged waitress in a brown pinny came and asked what she could do us for, so I ordered egg and chips with a mug of coffee (please, God, let it not be decaf), and Matt asked for the same. As we settled down to wait, he started fiddling with the little packets of salt and pepper that were in a cup on the table, and I started making bets with myself on how long it'd be before the table was covered in condiments.

"How long have you worked for Jay?" I asked, curious. Matt talked like he'd known Jay a long time, but then most people tend to do that five minutes after they've met him. Jay's just that sort of bloke.

"Er..." Matt looked like he was *this* close to counting on his fingers. "About eight months now. I knew him before that, though. We go biking together, Thursday nights."

"Just the two of you?" I asked more sharply than I meant to.

"God, no! There's about half a dozen of us. Well, not everyone comes each week—actually, it's been a while since we've seen Adam, I'd better give him a ring and see what's up—but on an average night, there's about half a dozen. You should come along," he added with a lopsided smile.

"I don't cycle," I said a bit shortly. "Haven't had a bike since I was in school," I explained, trying to sound friendlier. "It was a bit hilly where I went to university." Although, if I was honest, a lot of the students had managed with bikes.

Matt laughed, showing that broken tooth again. "You can't run a bike shop and not even own a bike!"

If it had been anyone else, I'd probably have become defensive. But Matt was so good-natured, it just wasn't possible to take offence. "I suppose it is a bit funny," I admitted.

"Why don't you have a look at the stock? Jay always gives a discount to mates; he'd definitely do the same for you."

I had to smile at his innocent assumption that the only thing that had been stopping me from owning a bike up to now was that I hadn't been able to get one on the cheap. "I'll think about it," I hedged and was relieved to see the food turn up—two huge platefuls of eggs with golden yolks and proper chip-shop chips, not the little matchsticks you get in fast-food places.

The next few minutes were spent passing the salt and vinegar—I'd always thought I was a bit heavy-handed with the latter, but Matt absolutely drenched his chips with the stuff—and hunting for the brown sauce in the little cupful of sachets. I noticed with approval that Matt, like me, kept his egg yolk unadulterated and only squeezed sauce on the boring bit.

Then I realised he'd seen me staring at his eggs, so I had to say something to cover my embarrassment. "So, er, did Jay tell you much about me? Apart from that I was married?"

"He said you were posh," Matt said cheerfully, his mouth half full of food.

I gave a nervous little laugh and spread some egg yolk on a chip. "We're brothers. I'm not any posher than Jay is."

"Yeah, you are," Matt contradicted me, gesturing with his fork and nearly taking my eye out. "Sorry. You don't talk like him, for a start."

"I don't?" How did Jay talk, anyway? I tried to think if he sounded, well, more common than me. All I could think of was that he sounded like *Jay*. I ate another chip, this one with a bit of egg white to get it over with.

"Nah. He talks like everyone else."

Great. My accent had social leprosy. "So how do I talk?"

Matt shrugged. "Well. Posh. Didn't you go to Oxford or Cambridge, or something?"

I could feel my face growing warm. "Durham, actually." So I hadn't got into Cambridge, so what? It wasn't like my mother constantly bewailed my failure... Oh. Wait. She did. I took a gulp of coffee, finding the predominant flavour was the salt that had been deposited on the mug by the dishwasher. Still, as long as it had caffeine in, I decided I didn't care.

"Is that where you met your wife?"

I was a bit thrown by the sudden mention. "Kate?"

Matt grinned. "Why, how many wives have you had?"

The furnace in my face turned up to Gas Mark 12. I put my mug down slowly. "Uh, just the one. And yes, we met at Uni." We'd been friends before we were girlfriend and boyfriend. A *long* time before. I think, in the end, it was just that neither of us could think of any convincing reasons to give to people when they asked, yet again, why we weren't going out. So we did, and it had seemed to work all right. The sex hadn't been brilliant, but Kate hadn't seemed all that interested in sex in any case, so that had taken the pressure off quite a bit. We'd been happy enough, I guess—until Kate had started wanting more from life than a husband who was more like a brother.

I'd always wanted a sister, I recalled.

It wasn't a subject I was particularly keen to talk to Matt about, so I tried to shift the focus away from me. "So are you, er, seeing someone?" I asked, cringing internally because when I asked girls this, they always seemed to assume it was a chat-up line.

Matt gave me a wary look. I wondered what Jay had told him about me. "Yeah. Actually, we live together. Um. So do you know the area well?"

I guessed I wasn't the only one for whom it was a touchy subject, although it worried me it might just be that Matt thought I was judgmental. "It's not a problem, you know," I insisted. Matt just looked puzzled, so I was forced to carry on. "You being, well, gay." I cleared my throat, feeling like an idiot. "Do you live in Totton?"

"Oh! Yeah—I mean, no. But I used to. My, um, Steve's place is out in the New Forest." Matt smiled, and his tone got warmer. I wasn't sure if it was for the forest, the house, or for the mysterious and presumably comfortably well-off Steve.

I was already starting to dislike the bloke. "Sounds nice," I said shortly.

"It is—we get wild ponies coming right up to the garden fence, and it's really peaceful out there. The pubs are great too. You should try a few. Most of them do food."

I shrugged. "Never really been that keen on eating out alone."

"We could go to one next Wednesday, if you like. There's this brilliant one I know out towards Lyndhurst—they do a great lasagna. Loads of other stuff too. If it's nice, we could eat out in the garden." Matt made excited gestures with his fork, and a blob of brown sauce teetered but just failed to fall on the table.

His enthusiasm had me sold on the idea even before I'd had time to think it over. "Yes, why not? We could make it a regular weekly lunch date." Matt's eyes went wide, and I cursed myself. "Not that it'll be a date, obviously," I added hurriedly. "Just...two blokes going for a pub lunch. Drinking beer and, um, talking about football. Not a date at all, really. I don't know why I called it that." I took a gulp of lukewarm coffee to cover my embarrassment.

Matt fiddled with one of the little packets of salt that had survived his ministrations earlier. In a belated reversion to form, it came apart in his hands, spilling tiny granules all over the table. "Shit." He sounded miserable, and I felt like a bastard. "Look, Jay said you were a bit—and it doesn't matter, I know some blokes are a bit uncomfortable with the gay thing." Now I felt even more like a bastard.

"It's not…" I stopped. Because it *was* that, and denying it would just make me a lying bastard. I pushed my chair back and stood. "Look, I've got shopping I need to get done. Thanks for lunch; it's been great. I'll see you tomorrow, okay?"

Then I dropped a £20 note on the table and walked out like the coward I was.

Chapter Four

After I'd braved the local Asda—it was a lot larger, busier and generally less user-friendly than the Waitrose I usually shopped at, but it was also cheaper, which, given my straitened circumstances, was a good thing—and cleaned it out of coffee, tea and microwaveable ready meals, I went to see Jay. Obviously, the universe agreed with me that I was due a bit of karmic payback, as Mum was there. She was putting all the get-well cards into a carrier bag and generally looking like she was preparing to re-enact the evacuation of Dunkirk, only on a slightly larger scale.

"Mum?" I said, giving Jay a distracted wave. "Is Jay going home already?"

"Don't be ridiculous, darling. James is far too ill for that. No, the doctors here have admitted he's going to need a further operation, which clearly means the first one wasn't done properly, and I don't think it's good enough. We're having him transferred to the Spire."

"Wait a minute," I said. "Jay, you can't afford a private hospital!" Not on the profits of 87p pump adaptors, he couldn't.

"Don't be silly, dear," Mum said. "He's got insurance."

"He has?" I said stupidly.

"Yeah." Jay finally took part in the conversation. "Mum pays for it."

I stared at her. "What? You've never said anything about getting us private cover."

"Well, I don't, for you, Timothy. There's never seemed to be any need. After all, you don't *do* anything."

"What about the karate?" I sputtered, wounded by her dismissive tone.

"Oh, Timothy." She made a tutting sound with her tongue. "Everyone knows it's all noncontact these days. You're only pretending to hit people. It's not as if it's *proper* fighting."

Way to make me feel good about my shiny new black belt, Mum. "One of the guys at my club broke his wrist a few weeks ago," I pointed out, possibly a little defensively.

"Well, I hardly see how *that* is anything to boast about. Now, mind out, Timothy, I need to carry on packing things up. James, darling, are you sure you're up to the move?"

I didn't stay much longer.

It was only when I got back home to find Wolverine glaring pointedly at the empty food bowl that I realised I'd forgotten to ask Jay if he owned a cat.

It looked like I was going to be down in Totton for a while. Fortunately, I'd packed my *gi*, so all I had to do now was find a karate club to train with. It'd be good to find some new sparring partners, anyway. If you've sparred with the same guys for a while, you get to know how they fight, and you can predict their attacks. Swapping things around a bit would help keep me on my toes.

I did a quick Google search on Jay's computer and came up with a club that met in Totton Sports Centre. They met on Sunday mornings and Wednesday evenings—both times I'd be able to make, with the added bonus I could go along tonight. Cheered by the prospect of an actual social life, even if it was only one predicated on a mutual love of physical violence, I whistled as I shut down the computer.

A quick microwave curry later, I changed into my gi and made my way down to the sports centre, which was a bright, modern building in a quiet cul-de-sac just off the Ringwood Road. As I parked my car, I thought a bit guiltily I probably shouldn't be using it for a journey of only a couple of miles. Maybe I should do what Matt had suggested and take a closer look at the stock tomorrow. After all, if trade was always as slow as today's had been, we could do with the custom.

I negotiated with the chirpy young woman behind the desk until she agreed to let me through the turnstile, then made my way up to what was encouragingly billed as the combat room. The class hadn't started yet, and brown and black belts were milling around, chatting and laughing. I introduced myself to them—figured I might as well get in a plug for Jay's shop while I was there—and they pointed out the Sensei to me.

Sensei Ray Cole was a 5th Dan black guy with a cockney accent and a wide smile, who pumped my hand with so much enthusiasm I was worried it might fall off. "Good to have you here, mate. Just fall in line and give us a shout if you're not sure about anything." He turned away to give a sergeant major's bellow to the class. "Right you lot—line up!"

As I bowed at the entrance of the dojo, the familiar smell of rubber mats and sweat in all degrees of freshness hit my nostrils like a back fist strike. I breathed in deeply. It was good to be home. The remaining tension rolled away from my shoulders as we went through the warm-up before moving on to basics. I suppose it's a bit like meditation, in a way. You're completely focussed on the techniques you're practicing, and it clears your mind like nothing else can. I could feel myself gradually chilling out about the situation with my job, Jay, Kate and—yes—Matt. The problems didn't disappear, but my sense of perspective reasserted itself. Jay would be fine. I'd get another job. Kate and I were never meant to be. Matt...

Okay. That one was a little trickier, and I hadn't quite sorted it all out in my head by the time we moved on to kata, which takes a whole different kind of concentration. Kata, if you're not familiar with the term, is a sequence of around twenty or so predetermined martial arts moves, based on the concept of fighting off a series of attackers. It's a little like a dance, if your idea of dancing involves kicks to the head and strikes to the gonads, which, for all I know, it does—it's not like I've been clubbing much in the last few years.

And then we went on to sparring, at which point a meaty hand descended on my back with bruising force and landed me with the partner from hell.

My local sports centre back in London has a sign up saying "Martial Arts for All". Which is all very well in principle, but in practice, in my considered opinion, there are certain people who shouldn't be allowed within a hundred yards of anything that'll show them how to beat the crap out of people even more effectively. And the bloke I ended up fighting with that night was definitely one of those people.

You can tell them a mile off. They're the ones who, when they go through their basics, give it 100 per cent power *all the time.* They punch the air like it just mugged their granny, and when they *kiai* you need earplugs to avoid permanent damage to your hearing. Their gis are stained with sweat and pulling at the seams over steroid-enhanced muscles. They tend not to be black belts, because a key requirement for passing your black belt is the possession of control.

And you do not want to be stuck with these guys when it comes to sparring. I soon found out my new partner was a vicious bastard, to put it mildly. He might be good-looking and have shoulders half as broad as he was long, but he had a chip on those shoulders the size of the New Forest and a natural ability to channel his fury through his fists and feet. He was supple too, as I found out when he set my head ringing with a snap kick to the left ear. There's not many people who can get their feet up to my six foot two, but we were fairly evenly matched for height. He was half my weight again, though, with legs roughly the girth and weight of tree trunks.

As the pins-and-needles numbness in my ear settled into a dull pain, I backed off a bit, hopping lightly on the balls of my feet. "How about we take it a bit easier?" I suggested without taking my eyes off him for a minute. His hair was thinning noticeably on top, probably a result of all that raging testosterone. He looked a bit like a young Bruce Willis, if Bruce had spent his formative years chomping on steroids and then got really angry about something.

"Not going to learn anything that way, are we?" Bruce countered and lunged in with a jab punch to the solar plexus with his left fist that would have taken out several internal organs if I hadn't managed to block it. I'd swear I felt the bones in my arm vibrate from the impact—I'd have a bruise there tomorrow. I just hoped he wouldn't go for the face, as two members of staff with black eyes wouldn't do the reputation of Jay's bike shop any good at all.

I decided the best form of defence was attack, and I feinted with my left arm before lunging in with a roundhouse kick. It landed just above Bruce's kidney, the impact solid and satisfying. Even though it was barely half power, he was not a happy bunny. His chiselled features twisted in a snarl, and he drove at me like a white Ford Transit van with a red-and-brown stripe round the middle.

I danced to one side, letting all that power and aggression fly uselessly past me; then, when he turned, too slow, I was ready for the roundhouse kick. It was full power and then some, and it was aimed at a point about six inches the other side of my kidney. Message: *I can do anything you can, and I can do it*

45

better.

I sidestepped again and blocked. Even though I only caught the edge of the kick on my forearm, it was a numbing blow—bruise number two on my beleaguered left arm. At the unwelcome return of sensation, I tried not to show how much it had hurt—Bruce was like a pit bull who could smell weakness and wouldn't hesitate to take advantage.

The trouble was, he already had an advantage here. Because, although he was only a brown belt, his technique was at least as good as mine, and he had all the weight and power behind it. And at the end of the day, I didn't want to hurt him—I was the higher belt; I had a responsibility here. Whereas he'd obviously like nothing better than to see me carted off on a stretcher. At which point he'd swear blind he'd thought I could handle it, me being a black belt and all.

Okay. Maybe Mum had a bit of a point about it not being real fighting. But it wasn't like I *couldn't*; I just didn't want to. *Get a grip*, I told myself. *Of course you can handle him.* So what if my black belt was so new it still had folds in it from where it had been in the packet? I felt my resolve strengthen at the sight of the killing rage in his narrowed eyes as we circled each other. This guy needed to be taught a lesson.

Time seemed to slow—and when the next attack came, I was ready for it. I didn't block—just took myself out of his path and let him blunder on by. When he turned, his face had reddened. I hopped lightly on my toes and waited for him to make the next move. It seemed his Neanderthal brain managed to grasp my subtle message that I was ready for anything he could throw at me, as his lips curled in a snarl. Anger made him clumsy, and I easily spotted the feint, blocked it and danced to one side as he steamrollered past.

"Come on and fight, you bastard," he ground out from between teeth so tightly clenched his dentist would probably never forgive me. I braced myself for the next onslaught—and almost jumped out of my gi when Sensei Cole's voice bellowed past my left ear.

"*Mister* Pritchard, change partners, please." Sensei moved into my field of view, bouncing on the balls of his feet like the Duracell bunny with a fresh battery, despite this being his third class of the evening. "Right, Mr. Knight, let's see what you can do." Sensei Cole was the old-fashioned type—everyone in the class, down to the tiniest tots, was Mr. or Ms. Somebody.

Bruce shot me a murderous look and slunk off with the rangy Asian guy I'd already pegged as Sensei's second in command—I didn't know what grade black belt he was, but I reckoned he had to be third Dan at least. He'd probably survive a spar with Bruce, anyway. We shifted over to a vacant space, and Sensei started putting me through my paces.

Sparring with Sensei Cole was a completely different ball game. For a big guy, he was incredibly light on his feet—but it was his control that impressed me the most. He started off slow with me, then upped the speed by precise increments, testing my reactions. Fighting with a guy like that is an incredible buzz. I knew I could trust him not to go too far—and equally, to get himself out of trouble if I misjudged things.

We were both grinning like maniacs by the time the session ended. Sensei patted me on the back. "Very good, Mr. Knight. Very good indeed. Will we be seeing you again?"

I couldn't help a glance over to Bruce, who was glowering in a corner and wiping sweat off his forehead.

Sensei laughed. "He's just a little bit enthusiastic at times, our Mr. Pritchard. Don't worry about it. You'll get used to him." He coughed. "You might want to pick a different partner for a while, though."

As I bowed and walked out of the *dojo*, Bruce glared at me.

JL Merrow

I half expected his foot to shoot out and trip me as I squeezed past his pumped-up physique, but nothing happened.

I hoped that didn't mean he was biding his time for a more satisfying revenge later.

When I got home, Wolverine was in the kitchen glaring pointedly at the empty food bowl. "Who's a cute little pussy-wussy, then?" I crooned, hoping it might wind him up. He didn't even dignify me with a disdainful look. "All right, all right. It's coming." Feeling smug because I'd remembered to get some cat food at Asda, I grabbed a fork and opened up a can.

Ye gods, that stuff hummed. It was worse than the tuna first thing in the morning. "You actually eat this stuff?" I asked Wolverine in disbelief, trying to hold my breath while forking the glutinous mass out into the bowl. He *miaowed* at me. Maybe he was annoyed at me for dissing his dinner.

Then again, maybe not. It turned out Wolverine didn't believe the stuff was edible either. He took one sniff and then backed away hurriedly, turning to me and *miaowing* again, this time with a definite note of reproach. "It's all you're getting," I warned him. He hissed, and it was my turn to back off. Then I felt a bit ridiculous. "If you think you're going to bully me into giving you tuna again, you can think again. I'm going to have a shower," I said firmly.

I escaped upstairs and sluiced off the grime of the day with a certain amount of relief—after all that sparring, I was humming a bit myself. My thoughts wandered, as they do at times like this. There's only so much concentration you can give to lathering up. I wondered how Kate and Alex were doing, and whether they'd had their first row about him leaving the toilet seat up yet. Of course, that wouldn't be a problem for Matt and

48

Steve, would it? Their life was probably one long, happy round of leaving the seat up, drinking beer on the sofa in their underwear, and sharing fart jokes.

I frowned. Did gay guys think fart jokes were funny? Maybe they weren't like that at all. I'd never really known any gay guys all that well—except Graham at Uni, and at the time I hadn't even known he was gay. We'd sort of drifted apart after he got his first boyfriend and came out. But maybe gay guys were different. Maybe they kept their house as neat as Kate did and liked to drink wine and talk about the theatre in the evening?

Common sense reasserted itself forcefully in the form of a vivid, and frankly ridiculous, mental image of Matt sipping Chablis with his little finger cocked. If he had a total personality transplant, maybe. No, Matt was just a regular guy. Which meant that, in all likelihood, Steve was just a regular guy. Right now, they were probably relaxing together on the sofa watching Sky Sports, maybe having a bit of a cuddle...

I turned the tap off sharply. I was clean enough now.

Of course, when I went downstairs again, the kitchen was still full of uneaten cat food and unhappy cat. And the smell... It was like walking into a wall of silage. If I stayed in the room much longer, I'd need another shower. If I left the food here all night, it'd probably follow me upstairs and suffocate me in my sleep.

I sighed. "Look, I'm not giving in, all right?" I said. Wolverine's ear twitched. "I'm merely conceding you may, possibly, have a point here." Twenty pounds of feline bruiser wound their way around my ankles, nearly toppling me as I looked around the kitchen, bowl in hand, wondering what to do with the wretched stuff. In the end, I just dumped it out the cat flap. Something was bound to eat it in the night. This was the countryside. They had foxes, hedgehogs, badgers and...things.

I opened up a tin of tuna and forked it into the newly empty bowl. Wolverine leapt on it like a paparazzo on a celebrity sex scandal. Feeling I'd done my good deed for the day, I went to bed.

Only to be woken half an hour later by what felt like a fur cushion full of rocks and nails sitting on my chest breathing fishy fumes and purring like a buzz saw. I sighed, shoved him off to one side and rolled over. God, I hoped I snored.

Chapter Five

The next morning, my bedmate was nowhere to be seen. "Typical male," I grumbled sleepily, rolling out of bed. Except that wasn't really fair, was it? Over in the New Forest, Matt would be waking up with Steve, all cosy and lovey-dovey, no doubt. I wondered if they'd kiss. God, of course they'd kiss. They were in *love*. Apparently. They'd probably make time for a quickie before work...

God, I needed a coffee.

My mood didn't improve when I walked into the kitchen to a horribly familiar smell and a pretty pattern of cat-food paw prints all over the lino. Apparently, Wolverine had been out and in and out again. Either he'd scared off all the local wildlife or that Asda cat food really wasn't fit for consumption. I wondered if traipsing it all over the floor was his way of making a point.

I put the kettle on, then grabbed some kitchen roll and cleaned up the mess, cursing the entire feline species to Hades as I did so.

Wolverine still hadn't turned up for breakfast by the time I had to leave for work. I worried all the way to the shop.

It was a bit awkward, seeing Matt at the shop after the balls-up I'd made of things in the café yesterday. I obviously wasn't the only one who thought so, as Matt did a near-perfect action replay of the way he'd fallen into the shop the first time I'd seen him.

I made a point of rushing forward to help him up. "Are you okay?"

He smiled up at me a bit uncertainly. The bruising around his right eye had started to yellow, giving that side of his face a sickly greenish tint. "Yeah, I'm fine. Two left feet as usual."

I wondered if it was just nerves or if he'd ever been diagnosed dyspraxic, but it seemed a bit of a personal thing to ask. "I was thinking about what you said," I blurted out instead as he struggled to his feet.

"Yeah?" He sounded a bit cautious. I couldn't blame him.

"About getting a bike," I explained.

"Oh! Right—have you had a look at what we've got?" He sounded relieved we were back in his comfort zone. Two wheels good; two legs bad, I supposed. And since you ask, no, I never did get over reading George Orwell while I was at school.

"Honestly?" I grimaced. "I haven't got a bloody clue what I'm looking for. Or *at*, come to that."

"Well, you've come to the right place to find out!" Matt dusted off his palms on the seat of his baggy jeans, momentarily pulling the denim tight. "What are you planning to use it for?"

"Um, what?" I'd got distracted for a moment. "The bike? Well, cycling."

His brown eyes crinkled at the corners. The right eye was definitely less swollen today, I was pleased to see. "I meant, are you going to ride it on the road or off?"

"Does it make a difference?"

"Er, yeah, just a bit." I could tell he was trying not to laugh at me. "Look at this bike over here."

I followed the sweep of his tanned arm, which for once didn't actually knock anything over. Matt was wearing a lime green T-shirt today. It should have clashed horribly with the orange coral necklace he was wearing, but somehow didn't. Actually, the necklace looked a little familiar—had he been wearing it yesterday? Or maybe I'd seen someone else wearing one... I realised Matt was waiting for an answer. "The black one?"

"The Genesis, yeah. See the tyres? They're wide, with plenty of tread—that's for riding off road, where you need more grip. Road bikes have thinner wheels and not much tread, because what you gain in trail-holding ability and shock absorption, you lose in speed, see?"

I nodded, captivated by the way he seemed to come alive, talking about what he knew so well. I felt a bit of an idiot, though. Well, more than a bit. It all sounded so obvious when he explained it like that. It reminded me of when I took the BMW to the garage, and the mechanics would chatter on about fuel injection and hydraulics, and I'd just have to nod sagely and pretend I understood.

I'd always suspected they'd laughed themselves silly after I'd gone home. I couldn't imagine Matt doing that, though.

"This one's a hard tail—it's only got suspension on the front." Matt pulled the bike out of the rack to bounce it up and down on its front wheel, and I watched as the front forks telescoped gently. He lifted it back into place and selected another. "Now this one's a full susser," he said, giving me another glimpse of that broken tooth. "It's got rear suspension as well. Why don't you give it a try?"

I swallowed. I hadn't been on a bike in ten years or more. At least the karate kept me supple enough that I wouldn't have to worry about not being able to get my leg over.

So to speak.

I sat on the saddle cautiously—but still wasn't prepared for how far it went down under my weight. "Whoa! Is it supposed to do this?" I had a moment's panic. "I haven't broken it, have I?"

"Nah—these bikes'll take someone twice your size and then some. It's just been set up for someone a lot lighter than you; that's why it's so squishy. But I know what you mean. I prefer a hard tail myself."

I flushed slightly as my treacherous brain filled in the *double entendre*. "Can I give that, er, Genesis a go?" I asked, getting off the bike as quickly as I could without totally losing my dignity.

"Go ahead—but you know, if you're only going to be using it on the road, you might want to look at something more like this." Matt loped down to the other end of the rack and pulled out a slimline model with knife-edge tyres and dead-straight handlebars. No question about it, this bike looked more, well, me. It was a city bike, not a trail bike. If the Genesis was an off-road rally car, this one was...a Smart Car.

"I'll stick with the mountain bike," I said firmly, surprising myself with the strength of my gut reaction. Did I really hate my old life that much?

As he pulled the Genesis out of the rack again, Matt grinned up at me like I'd made his day. "You won't regret it. They're great bikes, these." He had the most infectious smile I'd ever seen, and I found myself grinning back at him—even as something seemed to twist inside me.

I realised he was waiting for me to say something, but my mind was a blank—or rather, it was too full of stuff I couldn't possibly say.

Could I? Would it really be so bad if I—

And then the bell above the door jangled, and I was stuck twiddling my thumbs behind the counter while Matt spent the next half hour showing our entire stock to a dithery bleached blonde who chewed her hair and texted constantly.

I was intensely glad to see her tight little shorts wiggle out the door again, despite the fact she hadn't bought a thing—although I wasn't sorry she'd turned up when she did. What the hell had I been thinking of earlier? The confession I'd been about to blurt out to Matt was the sort of thing you couldn't ever take back. And what would have been the point?

"You all right?" Matt asked. Obviously, my little round of self-recrimination had been playing itself out on my face like one of Marcel Marceau's greatest hits.

"Fine!" I said with false heartiness. "Right. Weren't we in the middle of selling me a bike? Should I take a look at some of the others?"

"Well, to be honest, you won't get much better than the Genesis for your first ride. It's a trail bike, so it's versatile, and it's got proper disc brakes."

"Which is good because...?"

"Well, first, they work—not like the rubbish you see on toy-shop bikes—and second, they don't go tits-up in the wet. They're a bit heavier than rim brakes, but I doubt you'd even notice the difference. Anyway, I don't reckon weight's going to be a crucial issue for you, is it?"

"Well, I'm not planning to race it up Snowdon, if that's what you mean."

Matt laughed. "Maybe not in your first week. Nah, the Core 10 is a good, basic model—not too pricey, but it won't fall apart on you either. Why don't you try it out for size?" His enthusiasm, as always, was infectious and hopelessly endearing.

"Hmm. What size do you reckon I take in mountain bikes?" I cocked my head and pretended to study the Genesis critically. "Medium? Large? Extra large?"

"Well, eighteen inches is the most popular size, but this

one's a twenty-inch frame, which I reckon should be just right for you. To be honest, I think that's the only reason it hasn't sold already—we don't get all that many blokes your height coming in."

"So the twenty-inch is the equivalent of an XL, is it?" I pulled the Genesis out of the rack, feeling a totally unwarranted smugness at finding myself above average in this department.

Matt squinted at me and the bike. "More like large," he replied, bursting my bubble. "But you want plenty of clearance over the top tube for those unplanned 'foot down' moments. Trust me, you don't want to be damaging the family jewels out there. That sort of thing can really spoil a ride."

I squirmed internally, both at the unpleasant images conjured up and at Matt mentioning my "family jewels".

"Yeah, looks like that one's about right," he went on, oblivious. "A good rule of thumb is to have the saddle at a height where your leg is straight with your heel on the pedal. Then when you've got the ball of your foot on the pedal you'll have a slight bend in your knee. That means you'll pedal more efficiently and you won't wreck your back."

I swung my leg over the bike and sat down on the saddle. It felt comfortable, if a little insecure—I only had the tips of my toes on the floor. My feet itched to get on those pedals and ride it properly.

"Yeah, that's great." I felt heat rise in my face as I realised Matt's critical gaze was now directed at my crotch.

He nodded, as if satisfied with whatever he'd seen there. "Why don't you take it for a test ride? I mean, it's dry out, so you won't have to worry about marking the tyres if you change your mind."

"Sure you'll be okay?" I asked, already halfway to the door.

Matt nodded, his eyes twinkling. "Yeah, I'll be fine. Unless you're planning a quick run down to Brighton or something?"

"I'll bring you back a stick of rock!" I threw over my shoulder as the door closed behind me.

I had a momentary qualm I might have forgotten how to cycle—after all, it'd been a fair few years—but it turned out it was, as they said, like riding a bike. God, I'd forgotten how much I'd enjoyed this. I bombed down the street, playing with the gears to get a feel for them. The Genesis handled like a dream. It might be an off-road bike, but it didn't seem to mind slumming it for once. Corners—yes, I could see where a road bike would have the advantage there, if you were going for speed. The riding position, too, was different than I remembered from my old racing bike days—much more upright, rather than hunched over the handlebars. It made for a different sort of ride—less head down into the wind, more looking around and enjoying the scenery. Not that there was all that much scenery in this part of Totton, but it gave me a taste of what it'd be like to ride in open countryside.

I whizzed round the roundabout in the centre of town, then reluctantly headed back to the shop. Matt gave a huge grin when he saw me, which I couldn't help returning.

"Okay—you've sold me on it," I said, wheeling my bike back into the shop.

Matt came out from behind the counter. "Do you want me to take it out the back?"

I shook my head. "No—it might as well earn its keep on display until tonight. I'll just put a *sold* label on it."

I disappeared behind the desk to write one out, and Matt headed out back to carry on with the repairs work, leaving me alone with my thoughts.

It underlined neatly just how much of a spare part (pun not intended) I was in this business. It was a bloody good thing Jay wasn't actually paying me—I'd have felt honour bound to give him a refund. Just as I was feeling really down about my lack of success as a shopkeeper, though, a steady stream of customers started to come in. Matt must have been right about the Wednesday effect. I actually took a fair bit of money—and even sold my first bike.

Granted, it had three wheels, was pink and covered in daisies, but the little girl dressed to match seemed almost as thrilled with her new ride as I was to have sold it.

After that, we hit a bit of a lull, which left me with little to do but think. And while I had a lot of things to think about— like whether Kate would want to sell the house or to buy out my share (she could move in there with Alex, wouldn't that be nice?); how long it'd be before I got a letter from her in legalese I no longer had a lawyer living with me to translate; and whether I ought to get a lawyer of my own—for some reason I kept coming back to Matt.

Well, maybe not just him. There were a whole lot of other issues that went hand-in-hand with that can of worms. Not that cans had hands, or worms either, for that matter...

Damn it. I got out from behind the counter and started to pace around the shop, straightening the hanging bike locks (again) and arranging the helmets in order of size this time. Colour-coding them had been a daft idea.

I suppose I was hoping that setting my body in motion might still the whirling of my mind. And in fact the mindless tasks did their usual trick of setting my subconscious free— although not in the direction I'd expected. I suddenly realised where I'd seen that coral necklace Matt was wearing before. Jay. He'd brought it back from Goa.

My throat went tight. Had Jay given it to Matt? Jewellery, in my admittedly limited experience, was what blokes gave to their girlfriends. I'd bought Kate jewellery. Sometimes even

58

when she hadn't asked me to. Was Jay after Matt to be his...boyfriend?

But Jay wasn't gay. Or even bi. Was he? No, he couldn't be. And even if he was, he wouldn't cheat on Olivia—although come to think of it, after a night spent in her chilly company, a bit of time with Matt's warmth would definitely look attractive. But Matt already had a boyfriend, anyway...

I gave a guilty start as the man himself emerged from the back room. "Everything all right?" he called out cheerfully.

"Yes! Yes, of course. Fine. Why wouldn't it be?" I rubbed my hands together nervously. "Sorry. It's been a bit quiet, that's all. Makes me restless."

"Jay usually reads a magazine." There was a stack of old bike mags up on a shelf behind the counter.

"Not really my thing," I said, shrugging. "Although I suppose I might find out a bit more about the business if I look through a few of them."

Matt tightened his lips like he was trying not to smile. "You might want to look at the ones on the bottom first." He reached over for the repairs ledger, dropped it, picked it up again and wandered out back with it, whistling an off-key tune I didn't quite recognise.

I stared after him for a moment—then dug out a magazine from the bottom of the pile and opened it up. And goggled at the assortment of naked breasts and other female parts that leered up at me from the glossy pages. Well, I say assortment, but they were all pretty similar, really, with only minor variations on the general theme of barrage balloons. As far as I could tell, there wasn't even any pretence at being natural—these girls were apparently only too happy to show the world a goodly proportion of their body weight was made of silicone.

The jangling of the shop bell startled me out of my appalled fascination, and I frantically tried to shove the magazine out of sight of the teenage lads in hooded jackets coming through the door. I fumbled, ended up dropping it, and kicked it under the counter as far as I could.

The boys were laughing and joking with each other, and I wondered if they might be trouble. I'd read the *Daily Mail*, so I knew anyone wearing a hoodie was liable to mug me as soon as look at me. But as far as I could tell, they didn't try and shoplift anything, and eventually coughed up the money for a puncture repair kit and another pump adaptor. That made three in the last two days. I wondered where all the old ones were going— was there a pump-adaptor fairy somewhere, maybe living in a brightly-coloured castle built of short lengths of tubing with a screwy bit on the end?

Still, I wasn't complaining. I rang up the sale with a smile. As the lads turned to go, one of them stooped to pick something up and handed it to me solemnly.

"There you go, mate. Dropped your porn."

It was Jay's bloody magazine. Conveniently open to a centre spread of a young lady who'd obviously decided to blow her limited clothing budget on the very last word in depilatories instead. I must have kicked the wretched thing right out from under the counter. "Thank you," I said with as much dignity as I could muster and watched as they left the shop and dissolved into wild laughter outside.

"Bloody, *bloody* Jay!" I fumed, shoving the magazine roughly back under the pile of bike mags.

"Trouble?" Matt's voice made me jump, and I cricked my neck turning back towards him.

"Ouch!" I rubbed the side of my neck, grimacing as the pain and the pins-and-needles gradually wore off.

"Sorry." Matt hung his head. "Didn't mean to sneak up on

you." He turned and started to lope morosely back to the other room.

I stared. What was that all about? "Did you need something?"

Matt spun around. "Oh—nothing important. It can wait."

"Why would it have to?" I frowned.

"Well, you know. You looked a bit..." Matt gestured vaguely. It was lost on me. "A bit what?"

"Um. Pissed off?"

I had to laugh. "Well, maybe. I just inadvertently corrupted a couple of teenage boys, that's all."

One soft brown eye went wide; the swollen one, not so much. "You what?"

"With, I might add, the magazine *you* suggested I read. You might have warned me," I added with a smile. Now the pain in my neck had disappeared, it just seemed like a bit of a laugh. "I tried to get it out of sight and ended up shoving it right under their noses. Does Jay seriously read this stuff at work? Well, look at the pictures, anyway," I amended. Maybe there were articles in the thing, but I'd bet my black belt nobody ever read them. Probably they just printed out the same ones each month.

Matt twinkled. There was seriously no other word for it. "Yep, 'fraid so. I come out of the back room sometimes, I don't know where to look."

"I'd like to say I thought Jay had more taste, but..." I let it hang there—and then laughed as a thought hit me. "You know, I feel sorry for Jay, if he has to get his kicks from this sort of trash. I always assumed that frigid exterior of Olivia's was just a front, but now I'm starting to wonder."

"You bastard." Matt was cracking up. "Next time I see her, all I'm going to think of is Jay with a porno mag."

"And his right hand. Don't forget that very important part of the proceedings." I sniggered. Which, all right, was neither mature nor very brotherly of me, but in my defence, I had spent my whole adult life in the sad and certain knowledge my brother had had more sex when he was still in his teens than I was likely to manage in a lifetime. *And* he'd enjoyed it more.

Just then a customer came in, so we had to straighten our faces and get back to work. It might have been a bit embarrassing if she'd asked what the joke was.

What with her wearing a dog collar and all.

After the Rev had gone off with a new pannier, which I strongly suspected Jay had got in especially for her—after all, it's not exactly something you see on the average mountain bike—we hit another dry spell. I ended up flicking through a magazine again, being very careful to take one from the top of the pile this time. It was full of pictures of blokey men in helmets doing blokey things, most of them covered in mud, and was written in an over-the-top hearty, all-mates-down-the-pub style.

No wonder Jay liked this sort of thing. God, I'd been an idiot, jumping to conclusions about him and Matt. Of course Jay was straight. I was about to close the magazine when a title caught my eye: *What Really Happens During Bonking.* I did a double take and looked around furtively, wondering for a moment if one of the porno mags had slipped inside this issue.

Turned out it was just biker-speak for a catastrophic loss of energy during an endurance race. And they meant catastrophic—apparently bonking can cause dizziness, confusion, heart palpitations and, in extreme cases, seizures and coma. So a bit more serious than just feeling sort of knackered.

I still sniggered as I read the article, with its useful tips on how to avoid a bonk.

The next time the bell jangled, I looked up to see someone who could have stepped right out of the pages of that magazine. He had on baggy shorts and a faded T-shirt and the sort of leathery tan you only get by being out in all weathers. Somebody really should have told him about sunblock and moisturiser. He also had a liberal splattering of mud up his sturdy-looking calves. When he turned to shut the door behind him, I saw the mud extended right up his back, almost to the ends of his over-long ginger hair.

He was probably Jay's dream customer. I could imagine this bloke and Matt talking for hours about *grunts* and *grinders* and other terms I'd picked up from the bike mag but which were still, sadly, all Greek to me. He lingered to cast an eye over the high-end mountain bikes on display, raising my hopes for a moment—those bikes didn't just cost an arm and a leg, you'd probably have to throw in a head and a torso as well; Jay would be seriously chuffed if I managed to sell one—then loped up to the counter.

"'Lo. Matt thur?" he said out of the side of his mouth.

My hopes crashed so far they probably bonked. For all I knew, they grunted and ground too. I pasted on a smile that made my jaw ache. "You must be Steve," I said, shoving a hand out for him to shake.

He took it like this was some arcane ritual never before seen in darkest Totton, and let it go again like it might bite him. "Nuh-uh. 'M Adam. Me 'n Matt 'r jus' mates."

I felt a weird mix of relief and disappointment. "He's just out the back." I found myself pronouncing my words more precisely than usual, as if to compensate for his unclear diction, and hoped he hadn't noticed. "I'll go and give him a shout."

Matt was in his default position: bent over an upside-down bike frame, his rear end pointing at me, baggy jeans for once stretched tight over his arse.

It seemed awfully warm in here. I was surprised he hadn't opened a window. I spoke to him twice before I realised he had his iPod on and couldn't hear me. I didn't think prodding him in the bum would be an acceptable way of attracting his attention so, feeling a bit foolish, I moved around the room until I was in his field of view—or at least, my feet were. Finally, he looked up.

"Tim!" he said a bit more loudly than usual. Then he remembered to pull out the earphones and gave me a goofy grin. "Nearly finished with this one. Need some help in the shop?"

"No—your, er, friend is here."

Matt went utterly, completely still. "Steve?" he said. There was something odd about his voice. Was he embarrassed at the thought of me seeing who he was shagging? I felt myself begin to blush at the thought of Matt and the as-yet-faceless Steve. Shagging.

Alternatively, maybe Matt was just embarrassed at the thought of his lover seeing the clueless idiot he was nominally working under. "No! No, it's, er, Adam. That's who he said he was. Adam. A mate, he said."

"Oh! Adam! Yeah, he's a good bloke. Comes out with us on Thursday nights—you remember I told you about him? Haven't seen him for a while—how's he looking?" Matt chattered away as he stood and wiped his greasy hands on already-stained jeans.

"Er, muddy?" Had Matt mentioned Adam? Maybe he had—when we were at the café, perhaps? I was ashamed to realise I couldn't remember. I'd been too worked up about the whole bloody *gay* thing at the time.

"Yeah, that's Adam all right. Do you want to send him in here?"

I could hardly say no. "All right." I nodded and wondered why on earth I hadn't just done that in the first place. "I'll, um, send him in."

Adam responded to my invitation to go out back with an indecipherable grunt. Or possibly a grind. Then he loped through the door, treating me to another view of his mud-spattered back. I hoped he wasn't planning to lean on any walls.

He was in the back room so long I started to entertain dark suspicions as to what he and Matt might be up to in there. In fact, it began to be getting on for lunchtime, and my stomach started rumbling so loudly I was worried it'd scare off potential customers three streets away. It struck me I didn't even know if we shut for lunch, so I wandered over to the door and had a look at the opening hours on the sign. No help there—it just said nine thirty to six, Monday to Friday, and nine thirty to one on Wednesdays. I dithered a bit about going in to speak to Matt—then told myself firmly that as his (acting) superior here, I was perfectly within my rights to interrupt his conversation with a mate.

I walked into the back room to find them both staring gloomily at a back wheel that, even to my untrained eye, looked a bit bent out of shape. "Is it supposed to look like that?" I blurted out.

It was Adam who answered. "Nuh-uh. 'S buggered." He heaved a heavy sigh and patted Matt on the shoulder. "Gotta go. See y' t'night?"

Matt seemed a bit subdued for some reason, but he nodded and dredged up a smile. "Yeah. See you, Adam." Then he bent his head back down to his work while Adam plodded out through the shop.

Adam's arms were too long for his body, I noticed as I watched him go—his hands were almost down by his knees, and seemed over-large. His legs, in contrast, were short and stubby, and slightly bowed. All he needed was a slightly thicker coat of body hair, and possibly a banana, and the resemblance to an orangutan would be complete.

"He's a good mate, Adam is," Matt said, making me jump a little. Had he noticed me staring at his friend?

"Um," I said self-consciously. "I was wondering, what do you and Jay normally do for lunch? When it's not half-day closing, I mean? Do you close for lunch?"

Matt looked up, his eyebrows disappearing under his shaggy fringe. "Oh, no. I mean, it's a busy time, lunch. Jay always brings stuff and eats it when he can. I mean, I get an hour off, but..." He trailed off a bit awkwardly. "If you want me to stay, you know, that's fine."

"You mean you're willing to sacrifice your lunch hour for the useless newbie? No, don't worry about it—but if you could hold the fort while I go and find some sandwiches or something, I'd appreciate it. Er, any suggestions as to where to get a sandwich around here?"

Matt looked a bit doubtful. "Well, there's Asda... I always make my own."

"I gave up on that years ago. There's only so many days in a row you can stomach cheese and pickle." Plus I'd had an unerring knack of getting the pickle on my tie.

"It's all right if you vary it a bit," Matt said, shrugging.

"Yes? What have you got today?" Maybe I could pick up some tips. Spending a fiver on lunch every day probably wasn't a great idea while I was without gainful employment.

"Carrot and hummus in a wholemeal wrap. With a bit of salad and stuff, obviously. And fruit salad for afters."

"You made all that yourself?" I calculated that must be at least three of his five fruit and/or veg a day. In one meal. I was pretty pleased with myself if I managed one.

"Yeah, it's dead easy, and it's way cheaper than buying food out. I do lunch for me and Steve every day. Course, he's not so keen on the veggie stuff—I had to put chicken in his."

My stomach rumbled. Lucky Steve. "I think that sort of thing's a bit beyond my culinary skills," I said sadly. "I'm still at the 'How to Boil an Egg' stage."

"I could do you too, if you like," Matt said, his soft brown eyes gazing at me.

What? "Er, pardon?"

"Lunch. I could make some for you, if you like. I mean, I'd have to ask for a quid or two for the ingredients, depending on what it was—but it'd be just as easy, making three. And it'd save you going out for stuff."

"I couldn't put you to all that trouble..." I trailed off so he'd know I was only being polite. I was having to hold myself back from biting his oily hand off. In a manner of speaking.

"Nah, it's no trouble. We can start tomorrow, if you like." He smiled. "Or do you want a bite of my wrap first so you know what you're getting into?"

Why did everything he said have to sound like a double-entendre? At this rate, I'd have to nip to the loo and, ahem, adjust myself. "No, that's quite all right," I protested.

"Go on," he encouraged, wiping his hands on a rag. He grabbed a brown paper bag from the side and withdrew a foil-wrapped package, which he started to undress.

Great. Now my treacherous, sex-starved brain had me salivating for a taste of Matt's package. "Seriously, you don't have to—"

Before I could finish speaking, a large, well-stuffed wrap was waved under my nose, mouth-watering smells coming from it. I bowed to the inevitable and tried to judge the size of my bite just right, reckoning that taking too little would seem just as rude as taking too much.

When I tasted it, I wished I'd been a little less restrained. It was delicious. Really, really delicious. Obviously, I'd had carrot and hummus before—Kate and I had sometimes bought packs of crudités from Marks and Spencer and eaten them in front of the telly. But this—this was different. The carrot was crisp and sweet, the hummus piquant and rich. The wrap itself tasted freshly baked, and the whole effect was not so much food as an almost religious taste experience. I had to hold myself back from groaning in a decidedly unseemly fashion.

I swallowed the exquisite mouthful, suffering a pang of regret for its passing. "That's amazing. Seriously, amazing. I'd sell my grandmother for regular lunches of this quality."

Matt grinned. "If it's all right with you, I'd prefer the two quid."

I nodded. "It's probably just as well. I think the authorities tend to frown on unofficial disinterments, anyway. And my mum would kill me."

My sandwiches from Asda tasted like plastic garnished with blotting paper by comparison. I choked them down with the aid of a smoothie—had to get some vitamins in somehow—and prepared for another long, lonely afternoon.

Only to find I was rushed off my feet booking in repairs and services. Perhaps the decent weather we'd been having had prodded people to make sure their bikes were roadworthy—at any rate, I wasn't complaining. I just hoped Matt wouldn't be, seeing as he was the one who'd have to do the actual work.

I hardly saw Matt until it was closing time—just quick words in passing as he brought out bikes people had come to collect and took in others to get to work on them. When the bell jangled dead on six o'clock, I had to stifle a groan—didn't the customers realise we had homes to go to?

On seeing it was only Adam, I gave a relieved smile. "Are you here for Matt?"

"'S right. Goin' f'r a beer." He gave me a long look.

Feeling a bit like a bug under a microscope, I escaped to the back room to tell Matt his friend was back. As he wiped his hands on a greasy rag, the necklace caught my eye. "Matt?" I said without thinking.

"Yeah?" He turned. Smiled.

My stomach flipped over. "Er. Your necklace." I faltered. I couldn't just come out and ask him about it; that would be weird. "It's really nice." I cringed internally but forced myself to carry on. "Unusual. Did you get it on holiday?"

Matt's smile wobbled. His gaze darted over my left shoulder to where I realised Adam had followed me in. "This? Oh—no. I mean, um. I can't really remember. Probably in a shop somewhere. I mean, obviously, it must have been a shop. Cornwall, maybe. Or somewhere else. Probably." He was blushing crimson by the time he finished speaking, and he was looking anywhere but at me.

Shit. Shit, shit, shit.

Why would he lie, if there was nothing to hide?

Chapter Six

After I'd wrangled my new bike into the car and got it home—easier than you might think, as it all seemed to clip together like an expensive bit of Lego—I was itching to try it out. Should I eat first, I wondered? Wolverine hadn't turned up, so obviously it couldn't be dinnertime.

Then again, he hadn't turned up for breakfast, had he? I tried not to worry too hard. Maybe he'd just found someone else to bully into operating a tin opener for him. Maybe he'd even taken up hunting.

Yeah, right. That was about as likely as me taking up pole dancing in a sparkly thong.

I decided to ride first, eat later, so I wheeled my bike into the hallway—after all, it was brand new and clean as a whistle; Jay's carpets had nothing to fear—and went to get changed. Seeing as I was still a bit short of clothes, I slung on a pair of jogging bottoms and a T-shirt I'd already worn once. They hummed a bit and were terminally crumpled from where I'd hung them on the floor last night. I grinned at my reflection in the mirror. Kate would have had conniptions.

Then I ran downstairs to get out my new toy.

I kept away from the main roads and the industrial bit, taking Eling Lane down to a sort of causeway across the river with a tiny toll booth, and stopped for a bit to admire the view. To one side was marshland; to the other, a sailing club, with a forest of white masts bobbing gently on the water. Beyond them lay warehouses, and in the distance, the edge of Southampton docks with a stack of brightly coloured containers like a child's building bricks. People were out walking their dogs, and the occasional fellow cyclist whizzed by. Despite the evidence of busy commerce around me, it felt extraordinarily peaceful.

I crossed the causeway and headed up Eling Hill, which was pretty steep but mercifully short. It wound up past the pretty stone church of St. Mary's on the left, and some equally attractive cottages on the right. It was all very picturesque, but I couldn't shake the feeling it wasn't exactly what the Genesis had been designed for.

As soon as I could, I decided, I was going to find out where the proper mountain bike trails were. Maybe Matt wouldn't mind me tagging along on a Thursday night? I'd definitely have to get in a bit of practice first, though, so as not to look like a total wimp. Going uphill, I could already feel the unaccustomed exertion in my thighs and in my buttocks. Reluctantly, I turned the bike around and headed for home, not wanting to overdo it the first time out and end up walking funny next day. Yes. That was what I'd do: get in a week or two's practice, and then ask Matt if I could go out with him.

In a totally non-date fashion, obviously.

When I got back, I wheeled the bike into Jay's garage for safekeeping. Right next to Jay's impressive tally of three mountain bikes, only one of which was in pieces. I had a bit of a "D'oh!" moment as it occurred to me I could have just borrowed one of them rather than blowing the redundancy money on a bike of my own.

Nah. He'd never liked me playing with his toys. Besides, God alone knew how much he'd spent on these babies, even at trade prices. He wouldn't be too happy if I went out and trashed a thousand-pound piece of precision engineering. Pleased with that little bit of self-justification, I headed into the house.

Wolverine had finally turned up and was sitting in the

middle of the hallway, where he could keep a beady eye on both the front door and the back—just in case I'd tried to sneak in and out without feeding him, I supposed. He *miaowed* impatiently at me. "All right, all right—hold your horses." Relieved to see him safe and sound, I grabbed a can of tuna. He made a beeline for me as I crouched down to fork it into his bowl, sniffing at me and then recoiling hurriedly.

A bit miffed, I gave my armpit a quick sniff and immediately wished I hadn't. "Okay, you're right," I conceded. "I stink worse than that cat food." Looked like my own dinner would have to wait—right now I was putting us both off our food.

I headed upstairs to get cleaned up.

After my shower, I checked my chest for grey hairs (none yet, but it was only a matter of time) and towelled my hair dry. Then I wrapped a towel round my waist and was about to go downstairs when it occurred to me I was alone here. No one to care if I walked around naked; no one to hiss *what if the neighbours look through the window* at me. I blew a kiss at my hazy reflection in Jay's tiny bathroom mirror; already the clear patch I'd wiped was misting over again. After slinging the towel over the side of the bath, I sauntered downstairs, my cock bouncing lightly at every step. Damn, it felt good to be free.

Until, of course, the front door opened when I was halfway down the stairs and Olivia stepped into the house, her eyes exactly level with my tackle.

I did what any red-blooded male would do at this point, which was to cover myself up with both hands and splutter at her incoherently.

Olivia's perfect mask didn't crack. Either she had the world's best poker face or there was a really good staff discount on Botox at that salon of hers. "Tim," she said without lifting her eyes from my hastily hidden crotch. "Jay asked me to pick up a few things for him."

"Right," I said, a bit more croakily than I'd intended. I cleared my throat. "Do come in. I'll just, er, go and…" My hands made vague going-upstairs-with-a-suggestion-of-putting-some-clothes-on gestures, realised they'd abandoned my rapidly shrivelling manhood and scrambled back to bolt that stable door.

"I'll be in the lounge," she said glacially and swept away.

I bolted upstairs and grabbed the first pair of trousers I could find. Then I took them off again because they were Jay's and, as predicted, looked ridiculous on me. By the time I'd made myself decent and got downstairs again, Olivia's perfectly pedicured foot was tapping on the hallway carpet. "Coast's clear," I said with a nervous smile. "No more naked men up there."

She raised a pencilled-on eyebrow. "Should I have expected some?"

"Er, no. Definitely, no," I told her, my face about to spontaneously combust.

She swept past me and disappeared into Jay's bedroom. I tried to remember if I'd left my dirty underwear on the floor and came to the depressing conclusion that yes, I probably had.

There was the distant sound of drawers opening and closing; then Olivia's precise footsteps came back down the stairs.

"Get what you were after?" I asked to justify hovering by the door.

"Yes, thank you." She didn't enlighten me as to what it might have been. Small enough to fit into her handbag, whatever it was. Then again, her presumably fashionable handbag was so large she could have comfortably fit the bed in there. "You know," Olivia said thoughtfully as she turned to go, "we have a lot of male clients at the salon. Have you ever considered a little personal grooming? We do a good deal on male waxing."

I shuddered. "No, thanks."

"Or if you're nervous about pain, you could consider getting your intimate hair dyed. It'd cover up the grey beautifully. It was nice seeing you, Tim."

She swept out again, leaving me standing there, mortified. I had grey pubes? She'd *seen* my grey pubes?

I mentally added tweezers to the shopping list.

And some carpet slippers and a walking stick. They'd go nicely with the pension book I was obviously due for any day now.

I sighed and rummaged in the fridge for a ready meal.

I went to visit Jay after I'd eaten, hoping I'd left enough time for Olivia to be in and out before I got there—I wasn't looking forward to seeing her again in a hurry, in case she started going on about my personal grooming issues in front of my brother. He'd never let me hear the last of it.

The private hospital, it turned out, was only a hop, skip and a jump away from Southampton General. Not, of course, that most of those admitted were up to any of that sort of thing. I supposed Jay might have managed a hop, but skipping or jumping was definitely out. The car park here was free, at least, and the reception was a lot nicer than the NHS one—more like a conference centre than a hospital, really. Visiting hours were a lot more accommodating too—basically they said turn up whenever you want, although I had a feeling they wouldn't be too chuffed about people rolling in after the pubs had closed.

Jay had a private room here, with its own TV and en suite bathroom. He didn't look quite so happy, though—maybe he missed chatting up the NHS nurses. "'Lo," he muttered in reply to my exaggeratedly hearty greeting.

"What's up?"

He shrugged. "Oh, you know. Just bored." He looked out of the window with a wistful expression. There wasn't a lot to see, but I guessed that wasn't the point.

"Missing your usual fresh air and exercise?"

"Just a bit." He turned back to me with a determined-to-stay-cheerful air. "So, how are you getting on at the shop? Matt managing to stay in one piece?"

"Yes, he's doing okay, actually. Hasn't trashed a single bike. His mate turned up today. Adam—you know him?"

Jay cracked a smile. "Bloody hell, how did you cope—alone in a shop with two poofs? Bet you spent the whole time with your hands over your nads and your back up against a wall."

I stared. "Adam's a poof? I mean, Adam is gay?" He hadn't *looked* gay—but then, neither did Matt, did he? "And anyway, should you be using the word 'poof'? I thought it was the sort of thing you could only say if you actually were one."

"Nah, they don't mind. And yeah, Adam's as queer as they come," Jay confirmed, looking pleased about it. I supposed he thought he was striking a blow for tolerance, one bigot at a time. "Single too, last I heard," he added teasingly.

"Very funny."

"You know, I've heard a lot of homophobes are repressed homosexuals—"

My stomach turned to ice. "I'm not homophobic! Bloody hell, Jay!"

I thought I'd been successful in keeping the volume down below a shout, but a nurse passing the open door gave me a sharp look. Jay rolled his eyes melodramatically. "All right, all right—keep your hair on. I was only joking. Don't take everything so bloody seriously."

Right. Yeah. Joking. I tried to breathe deeply without him noticing. "There was something I wanted to ask you about," I said a bit abruptly because I couldn't stand the silence a moment longer. "Are you sure Matt's, well, honest?"

"What? Of course he is!"

"Well, it's just—he's been wearing this necklace—"

"Crime against humanity, is it, blokes wearing jewellery?"

"Shut up. It looked familiar, that's all, and I suddenly realised why. It's that one you brought back from Goa."

"Oh, that. Yeah, that's right. I never wear it anymore, and it seemed like his kind of thing. What's the big deal?"

What was the big deal? "Jay, you can't go giving jewellery to a gay bloke!"

"Why? Last time I looked there weren't any laws against it!"

"But people are going to think—*he's* going to think—"

"What, that we're shagging? I pay him every month too—does that make him a rent boy? Bloody hell, Tim, have you ever listened to yourself?"

"You're not—" I had to clear my throat. "You're not involved with him, are you?"

"Tim, you prick, people are born gay. Or not, as the case may be. You can't catch it. I'm as straight as you are, for fuck's sake."

Well, at least that proved he really had been joking about the repressed homosexual thing. I just hoped my expression wasn't giving me away, that was all. Because I very much doubted Jay was as straight as I was. Mostly because, as it happened, I wasn't. Straight, that is, in case you're confused, which would be understandable in the circumstances. I certainly seemed to have spent most of my life in a state of confusion about my sexuality.

I'd decided a long time ago I didn't want to go skipping down that yellow brick road. I didn't fancy making friends with Dorothy, thought lavender was best left to old ladies, and green carnations made me look bilious. Basically, I didn't *want* to be gay. Mum would hit the roof, Dad would be quietly appalled, and Jay... Well, I'd always had the impression Jay thought I was a bit prissy. Coming out as a man who liked men—my gut clenched at the thought. It'd just be one more way I'd failed to measure up.

So I'd buried those feelings in an unmarked grave and thought that was it. I'd married Kate—didn't that prove I could be normal? Be like everyone else?

Your marriage failed, a treacherous voice inside told me.

So what? Lots of marriages failed. Suddenly I missed Kate so badly it hurt. Life had been so much simpler while we were together. The day we got married, it had felt so right. Like I was finally doing something I could be proud of. Doing things properly.

God, I hated myself sometimes. I'd spent my whole life trying to do things properly and had been an abject bloody failure. Kate deserved more from life than marriage to a loser like me. I hoped she and Alex would be happy together, I really did.

I just wasn't sure I ever wanted to see either of them again, that was all.

I realised with an unpleasant jolt that Jay was looking at me oddly. "What?" I said, a bit defensively.

"Nothing," he said, still giving me the funny look. As if he'd had a glimpse of what was inside my head and was trying to work it out.

God, I was getting paranoid. I coughed. "Right. Well, I'd better be off, anyway." Not that I *really* thought he could read my mind, but sometimes, he seemed to know me a little too well for comfort.

I was already back at my car when I remembered I *still* hadn't asked him about the bloody cat.

Chapter Seven

The next couple of days in the shop were pretty similar to the last, except my taste buds started getting spoilt rotten by Matt bringing me in a packed lunch every day. He wouldn't let me give him more than a couple of pounds a day, either, making his gourmet efforts cheaper than a supermarket packet of sandwiches.

His eye was healing up nicely, I was glad to see—the bruises had faded to yellow already. I'd decided I'd just been an idiot about the necklace. So he'd lied about where he'd got it— so what? He'd probably thought I'd jump to *exactly* the conclusion I had, in fact, jumped to.

Which wasn't that unreasonable, anyway, was it? I mean, if Jay *had* been that way inclined, he'd have been bound to find Matt pretty bloody tempting—the cheeky smile, the readiness to help, the adorable klutziness... I sighed. Time to get those thoughts firmly out of my head, before I totally flipped and asked him out on a date for real.

Saturday, we were both rushed off our feet. It seemed like every five minutes someone was either bringing in a bike for repair or servicing, or coming in to pick one up. By the time six o'clock came, I was more than ready to turn the sign on the door around to "Closed".

"Is it always this bad at the weekend?" I asked a tired-looking Matt.

"Pretty much. It's the time of year, innit? Everyone's getting their bikes out of the shed, clearing off the cobwebs and remembering how the chain fell off at the end of last summer and they never got around to getting it fixed."

"Maybe we should start sending reminders round in February," I suggested as I started to cash up the till. "You know, like the dentist."

Matt laughed. "Can't see it catching on."

He was probably right. "Or…I don't know, offer a discount on winter services?"

"That's not a bad idea. You should suggest it to Jay. Are you seeing him tonight?"

I groaned. The thought of seeing Jay I could cope with. Dealing with Mum after the day I'd had? Not so much. "Think I'll give it a miss tonight. Go home, slump in front of the telly." There was bound to be a *Poirot* on somewhere. "How about you?" I asked, more out of politeness than because I really wanted to hear about all the fun times Matt was undoubtedly looking forward to with Steve.

"Same, probably. Steve's working," he explained.

"Oh? What does he do?"

"He works on the docks."

Steve was a stevedore? I tried not to laugh.

Matt must have noticed my constipated expression. "I mean, he's a supervisor; it's a good job."

"Oh." I was silent a moment, trying to pluck up my nerve. Which was stupid, as this wasn't in any way like asking a girl out on a date. Just asking another bloke if he'd like to spend some time together, that was all. As friends. "Listen, why don't we, er, slump in front of the telly together? Yours or mine, whichever's easiest. We could get a takeaway, a few beers…" What the hell was I saying? I didn't even *drink* beer. It just seemed more of a blokes-together sort of drink than, say, wine. That was a date drink.

And this was most definitely not a date.

Matt didn't seem unduly worried by my dithering and false heartiness. His face lit up like I'd bought him a puppy. "That'd be great! Um. It'd probably be better to go to yours, if that's okay?"

"No problem! Do you know the way? We could go straight there—I'll be finished here in a mo."

Matt nodded. "You're at Jay's, right? I've been there loads of times." He headed off to pick up his battered green Ford Focus that had the back seats permanently down, the better to accommodate bike frames.

I finished what I was doing, locked the shop and drove the BMW back to Eling. As expected, I found Matt on my doorstep, but he was hopping from one foot to another, looking like he'd just ridden three hundred miles on an unpadded saddle. "Everything all right?" I asked.

"I. Um. Sorry. I can't stay."

"Has something happened?" I was a bit worried, he looked so miserable.

"No—no, it's just... I rang Steve, just to check when he'd be in, and he asked where I was going, so I told him, and then he said he'd be home early after all, so I'd better get back."

"Oh. Right." It must have been the exhausting day that was making me feel disappointed out of all proportion to the event. "No—that's fine. I mean, of course you want to be with your... And it's not like we were doing anything special, anyway." I told myself to get a grip, and gave him a smile that hopefully didn't look as fake as it felt. "I'll see you on Monday, okay?"

"Yeah, see you then." Head down, Matt slouched down the path back to his car.

I didn't feel like getting a takeaway just for me, so after I'd grilled some chicken breast for Wolverine—I'd started to worry an unvaried diet of tuna might not really be healthy for him—I nuked a ready meal and sat down with it on the big, empty sofa. Wolverine jumped up beside me, took a sniff at my meal and backed away hurriedly, taking his chicken breath with him. I flicked through the channels until I found something I could bear to watch—some car-crash TV program about embarrassing ailments that fed my inner *schadenfreude* in a misery-loves-company sort of way. "At least I've got you, hey?" I said to the cat.

Wolverine cast me a withering glance and hopped off the sofa to lick at his nether regions.

Sunday found me in more positive mood, but still at a bit of a loose end. It just felt odd, waking up with no one to talk to except the cat. Wolverine was kind enough to wake me at the usual time, so I didn't even get a lie-in. "Your breath's getting worse," I told him as I struggled to focus on the pink nose twitching impatiently only inches from my eyeball. Wolverine yawned. I tried not to gag.

Even though I'd been there only half a week, it felt strange, getting up and knowing I wouldn't be going into the shop. Wouldn't be seeing Matt's infectious grin, or picking him up off the floor after his latest misstep. (Yesterday he'd managed to fall over a customer. Fortunately, the woman had been so embarrassed at thinking she'd tripped him up, she'd felt obliged to buy something.) My mood was curiously flat as I walked downstairs to the kitchen. There seemed to be a funny smell somewhere, but I couldn't locate it and eventually decided it was just Wolverine's breath hanging around, a sort of olfactory equivalent of the Cheshire Cat's smile.

Karate wouldn't start until eleven, so after I'd had a coffee, I decided to take my bike out for a spin. I'd been out with it every night when I got in from work, but the length of my rides had been constrained by the rumblings of my stomach. Today, I wanted to go a bit farther afield, so after passing by the sailing club and going up Eling Hill, I took a country lane down Marchwood way, avoiding the main road.

I pedalled easily past ploughed farmland interspersed with the odd, mysterious-looking spinney until I reached the cosily named Pooks Green. Unfortunately, I was disappointed in my hopes of seeing a hobbit or two ambling by. Perhaps they'd moved out when the railway was built; I had to stop at the level crossing to let a train clatter noisily past. I smiled as I had a flash of memory of doing just this as a child out with my gran— I could almost hear her voice telling me to "Look at the chuffa-train, Timmy!"

Such reminders of civilisation aside, it was hard to remember this pretty, rural scene was only a stone's throw away from Southampton. I turned back when I realised the housing estates I was now cycling through were turning into the outskirts of Marchwood, frustrated I seemed to have run out of countryside already.

I was going to have to get out into the forest, I decided as I sped back to Jay's. Only then would my shiny new bike be able to hold its handlebars up high next to Jay's array of well-ridden cycling hardware in the garage.

But for now, it was time to get my stuff together for karate. Having parked my bike up against the house, intending to get straight back on it and ride to the sports centre, I went upstairs and changed into my gi—only to realise I'd look pretty daft cycling through Totton in bright white pyjamas. Faced with the prospect of having to change back, then find a rucksack to carry my gi in, I ended up abandoning my never-very-strong green credentials and taking the car after all.

The weekend class, when I got there, had a completely

different feel to the Wednesday one. More school kids, with a few who hardly looked old enough for school, their brightly coloured belts wrapped several times around their skinny middles—not that I was one to talk, of course. Unfortunately, my sparring partner from Wednesday was there too. Pritchard— I was damned if I was going to think of him as "Mister" anybody.

He didn't look any happier to see me than I was to see him—he sneered and turned his back deliberately as I approached, effectively blocking me off from the group of brown and black belts standing around having a pre-session chat.

Ye gods, how old was he? Twelve? I started doing a few stretches, and after a minute or two, John, one of the other black belts, detached himself from the group and came over to join me. He was a sandy-haired man in his forties with a cultured voice and impressively toned abs. I'd noticed those last two on Wednesday, although possibly not in that order.

"Don't let old Pit-bull get to you," John said in a low voice. "I think he feels he needs to defend his territory."

I smiled at the nickname. "As long as he doesn't try and pee on me," I murmured, and we both laughed.

I didn't get it, though. What the hell did the guy have against me? Was it my accent—too "posh"? My face? The way I did my hair?

Or was it the other thing? A cold chill ran through me. Could he tell? Maybe there was something in the way I looked at the other guys—without me even realising it? God, could the other guys tell too? A bead of sweat trickled uncomfortably down my back. No, that couldn't be it. No one had noticed anything at my old club—but then, they'd all seen me with Kate at the Christmas do, hadn't they? So if they had noticed anything, they'd have just assumed they'd been mistaken, wouldn't they?

I'd always thought the "gaydar" thing was a bit of a myth, that you couldn't tell just by looking at a guy—but what if I'd been wrong? What if it was just me who was rubbish at it?

"Mr. Knight! Good to see you again!" Sensei's friendly greeting nearly ruptured an eardrum. I spun round to be treated to one of his trademark enthusiastic handshakes. It definitely made a change from the Sensei at my London club, who took his karate very seriously indeed—I think he'd totally forgotten bowing wasn't the normal social greeting in the West, which was a little sad for a bloke called Brian from Billericay.

We all trooped into the dojo—it takes a while when you all have to stop and bow—and lined up. Sensei bounced on the balls of his feet a couple of times, then called out, "Mr. Knight—would you like to do the warm-up?"

I blinked. I hadn't expected this on only my second session here—then again, a warm-up was a warm-up, wasn't it? "*Osu,*" I replied quickly, bowing, and ran out to the front to face a long line of friendly and not-so-friendly faces. Although there was really only one in the last category: Pit-bull Pritchard looked like he'd rather swim naked through boiling lava than have me out the front telling him what to do. "Okay, let's have you jumping on the spot," I began.

I took them through the usual exercises, although I may have put in a few more jumps than usual when I noticed Pritchard wasn't too light on his feet. Maybe he'd had a night on the town last night, and was feeling hungover? I probably shouldn't have enjoyed the thought as much as I did. By the time we finished, he was looking like he thought skinny-dipping in boiling lava was an excellent idea, only it'd be me taking the plunge, not him. I was careful to meet his glare with a sunny smile, after which he looked like he'd decided lava was far too good for me.

Of course, I then had to make sure I avoided Pritchard for

85

the rest of the class, but I'd been planning on doing that, anyway. I managed to keep at least three people between us at all times until the very end, when I had to walk past him to leave.

"Fucking poofter," he muttered as I bowed my way out of the dojo.

I was glad my face was hidden. All I could think of was getting away. Luckily my body was on autopilot and even managed to wave good-bye to the guys as I went. My mind was paralysed, frozen with shock. He'd known. How had he known? What was it that gave me away?

I hadn't been eyeing his tank-like form with illicit desire, that was for sure.

I wondered who else he'd told. I guessed I'd find out on Wednesday, when nobody wanted to spar with me...

Damn it.

I spent Sunday afternoon trying to distract myself by doing mundane but necessary tasks. I threw my dirty clothes in the washing machine, then unpacked all Gran's pottery dragons and arranged them on Jay's shelves. All right, perhaps not strictly speaking necessary, but it definitely cheered the place up a bit. I found the one that looked most like the picture of Puff the Magic Dragon I'd had as a kid and bunged it in the loo next to Jay's bong. It looked right at home. I found myself whistling the song every time I went for a pee.

After that, I drove into Southampton to buy some more casual stuff to wear. It was probably a bit extravagant—I almost certainly had some stuff back in London that would have done, more or less—but I had a nasty feeling Kate and Alex might be there packing up some more of her things this weekend, which would make me turning up a bit awkward. Discretion being the better part of cowardice, I decided to stay away and hit the shops instead. It'd be good for the general economy, anyhow.

I wasn't sure what to buy at first—I tried on some baggy jeans like Matt's, but they just looked ridiculous. In the end, I cast my mind back to what I'd seen in Jay's wardrobe and just bought more of the same. I ended up with two pairs of straight-cut jeans and some longish shorts—summer was coming, after all—plus some shirts that didn't make me look quite so buttoned-up. When I looked in the changing-room mirror I hardly recognised myself. I wondered what Matt would think of the new, casual me.

The boot of my car stuffed with carrier bags, I stopped in to see Jay on the way back. There was a welcome sight waiting for me in Jay's hospital room. "Dad!"

His face lost the vaguely worried look it tends to wear when he's around Mum, and he gave me a bony hug. Dad's built on the same scale as I am, only with even skinnier legs and a bit of a pot belly to balance that out. "Tim, my boy. Wonderful to see you looking so well."

"You too, Dad. How's the, er, you know?" I patted my chest with a furtive glance around in case Mum was watching. Fortunately, she was too busy multitasking to notice: plumping Jay's pillows while giving one of the nurses a ticking off for something or other.

"Ah! Well, between you and me," Dad stage-whispered, not without a furtive glance of his own, "it's been a great deal better since your mother's been too busy coming down here to bother with cooking." Mum and Dad lived in Winchester, which was only half an hour away by road, but, like me, Mum was always glad of an excuse not to cook. "I think Dr. Loving may have been right all along. But you know your mother—she's determined I should have one foot in the grave."

I grinned, more relieved than I wanted to let on. "That's Mum for you—never one to admit she's wrong. How've you been managing, then, with her spending half her time down here?"

Dad put on a martyred expression. "Oh, you know. Surviving. It's not been easy, I can tell you—some days I go hours without hearing a single order to mow the lawn, fix the shelves, fetch something from the attic and while I'm at it, stop *doing* so much, it's bad for my heart." He chuckled and lowered his voice even further. "Don't tell your mother, but I've been having butter on my toast for lunch. And popping to the baker's for the odd eclair."

"On your own arteries be it," I warned semi-seriously. Dad just gave me a mischievous smile and made a *shh* gesture, with a significant look over to Mum.

I thought I'd better say hi to the person I was actually here to visit, so I went over to Jay. Mum had finally got the pillows plumped to her satisfaction but obviously hadn't finished ticking off the nurse yet. From her resigned expression, I guessed the nurse knew she'd be there awhile yet. "So, any news on the leg front?"

Jay made a disgusted face. "Yeah. They've finally worked out which bits they want to pin together and with what, so I'm booked in for surgery." He brightened. "According to the bone guy, I'm the only person under sixty-five who's had a fracture like this in the last forty years. That's why it took them so long to work out how best to treat it. He's planning on writing a paper about me."

Typical. "You know, there are easier ways to get famous. Certainly less painful ones."

"Yeah? Haven't seen your ugly mug on the telly lately. So how's it going with the shop, anyway? Have you managed to stop Matt trashing the place?"

I wasn't sure I liked Jay's attitude. "Matt's been great—you shouldn't be so hard on him. He was flat out yesterday, what with all the repairs coming in and out."

"Putting him up for employee of the month, are you?" Jay grinned. "If I didn't know better, I'd think you'd fallen for his scruffy gay charms."

"Oh, for God's sake—can't I even say something nice about the bloke without you jumping on me like that?" I hoped to God I wasn't blushing; it'd be a dead giveaway.

"Bet you'd be all right with Matt jumping on you—"

My face was burning hot. Maybe he'd blame it on the stuffy hospital room. "Have you ever seen *Misery*? Because I'm quite happy to stage a re-enactment of a certain scene—"

"Timothy!" Mum's voice snapped in my ear. "Would you please try and remember your brother is very seriously injured? We're all extremely worried about his operation."

"Er, sorry." I felt about five years old. "Um, is it really that big a deal?" I asked Jay.

"Nah. They're just going to put a sort of framework in. They said it'll feel a lot better when they've done it, and I'll be able to walk on it sooner."

"*If* he doesn't catch MRSA and lose it altogether," snapped Mum. "Really, the standards of hygiene of some of these young girls—"

"Mum, I really don't think talking about that kind of thing is going to help Jay feel better."

Mum just glared at me.

"God, you two are as bad as each other!" Jay leaned forward, apparently for the express purpose of being able to collapse dramatically back onto his pillows. "You wear me out, you do. Stop *worrying*."

I wasn't sure who was more offended by the comparison—

me or Mum.

"Anyway," Jay went on into the stunned silence, "is Matt okay? In himself, I mean. He seemed a bit low last time I saw him, and then there's the black eye and all."

"Oh, that's nearly disappeared now," I said warmly, glad of the change of subject. "And I don't know what you mean about him seeming low—he's always really cheerful when I see him."

"Yeah? That's a relief. I'd been starting to wonder...so, no more accidents, then?"

"Well, no more visible bruising, if that's what you mean. What did you mean, you were starting to wonder about Matt?"

"What? Nah, it's nothing." He laughed. "Got too much time to think here, that's my trouble."

I nodded solemnly. "You've never really been cut out for that, have you? Thinking, I mean."

Jay threw a pillow at me. It was heading right for my nose, but I blocked instinctively, a perfect *age-uke* that sent it veering wildly off course—straight into Mum's carefully arranged hairdo. Jay cracked up. "Oh, nice shot, Tim! Well done, my son!" Dad and I burst out laughing, and Mum tutted, looking daggers at me as she smoothed down her hair. Although I swear the pillow had just bounced off the lacquer, not shifting a hair out of place.

I wondered why I'd ever moved all the way up to London. It was so bloody good to be with my family again.

By the time I got home, the funny smell in the house had matured into a foul stench that threatened to sear my eyebrows off. A quick search revealed a festering puddle of mostly dried-in cat sick behind the sofa and prompted an even quicker search for a bucket and a gallon of disinfectant. At least the mystery of Wolverine's earlier bad breath was now solved. I'd been planning to get a takeaway, but strangely my appetite seemed to have disappeared. I opened every downstairs window to try to clear the lingering reek and had a couple of slices of toast instead. Then I checked my phone, where I found seven messages from Kate, all saying "Call me!" with increasing degrees of urgency.

I rang her up at once, thoroughly alarmed. Was she ill? Had the house burned down? Had Alex revealed himself as a secret someone-else's-wife-beater and all-round bastard? "Kate, what is it?" I asked as soon as she picked up.

"Tim? Where the hell have you been? I've been leaving messages at the house, at your mum's—"

"I'm at Jay's," I said, frowning. "So what's the problem?"

"Oh," she said, sounding a bit deflated. "How is he?"

"Well, you know—well as can be expected." I was still confused.

"Why? What's happened?" The worried tone was back, and I realised in a flash she didn't know about the accident—after all, why would she? We'd already been history when I'd heard—not, admittedly, by all that long, but still, history.

"He broke his leg," I explained. "That was what Mum's call was about." Naturally, Mum wouldn't have spoken to Kate. I'd never been quite sure why, but they'd never got along all that well. Hence, I presumed, the un-forwarded messages. "So what were you so worried about?"

"Oh—it was just me being silly," she said.

"What do you mean?"

"Well, you weren't at the house any of the times we went back, and you'd obviously not *been* there, and I just thought— but it was just silly of me." She finished up the sentence at top speed, obviously wanting to change the subject.

I was grimly amused. "What, you thought I might have driven off a cliff or something? Don't worry, Kate, I'm fine." Saying it, I realised I was, pretty much. Yes, I'd had my moments of missing her—but speaking to her now, I was stunned to realise I didn't want her back. We should never have been more than friends. "How are you and Alex?"

"Oh, we're fine," she gushed a little too enthusiastically for my liking. "Alex has just been promoted to partner!" Great. Not content with stealing my wife, he had to show me up in the career department too. "How's your job hunt going?"

"It's not. I'm looking after Jay's shop until he's back on his feet."

"Jay's *bike* shop? But doesn't he have staff? Can't they do it?"

"No." It felt weird, and somehow wrong, to talk to Kate about Matt, so I changed the subject quickly. "Anyway, while you're on—what are we going to do about the house?"

"Oh—well, we're planning to stay at Alex's. It's a lot more convenient, really, for work. I suppose I just assumed you'd buy my half—when you get another job, of course. When do you think you'll be getting another job?"

I bit back my initial, impatient reaction. Upsetting Kate wouldn't get us anywhere. "I don't know. I think we should put the house on the market. Who knows," I added, inspiration striking, "I might get a job down here. It'd be nice to be nearer my family."

"Are you sure?" Kate sounded dubious. "I thought you loved London." There was a pause. "This isn't some kind of midlife crisis, is it, darling?"

There was a moment of awful silence, which I rushed in to fill before she could apologise for the accidental endearment, which would have been even more painful than the original slip.

"I'm only twenty-eight! I'm not having any kind of crisis. I'm just taking the opportunity to...re-evaluate a few things, that's all."

"Well," Kate said brightly, "good for you. Um. I think I'd better go now—would you like me to sort out the house, then? Contact an estate agent, that sort of thing?"

"Yes, I think that'd be best." Now I'd said it, it felt like my old life was disappearing at breakneck speed. It was an odd sensation—thrilling but more than a little unnerving. "I'll be up during the week to pick up some more stuff—Tuesday night, probably." I was hoping she still went to Pilates on a Tuesday.

"Good," she said a little vaguely. I wondered if this was as unsettling for her as it was for me. Still, I was sure Alex would help her through it. Bastard.

"Good-bye, then, Kate. Take care."

"You too," she said. Just as I was about to hang up, she spoke again. "Tim?"

"Yes?"

"I really am sorry about all this."

What do you say to something like that? *That's all right* would be letting her off the hook a bit too easily, *Me too* would sound like an admission of shared guilt, and *So you bloody well should be* was way too confrontational.

"Me too," I said in the end and hung up.

Chapter Eight

Monday morning, I got to the shop to find Matt sitting in the doorway waiting for me to unlock it. He gave a big smile when he saw me and unplugged his iPod from his ears while I checked my watch hurriedly.

"I'm not late, am I?"

"Nah, it's me, I'm early." Matt managed to stand up without falling over either foot, although it was a close-run thing. He winced as a stray shoulder hit the doorframe.

"Are you all right?" I asked.

"Yeah! Yeah, I'm fine. Just knocked it yesterday, that's all. Came off the bike," he added, his head down as he brushed off his jeans.

"Have a good day off?" I unlocked the door, and we stepped inside, the bell jangling cheerfully to welcome us.

Matt shrugged, lopsidedly because he only used his good shoulder. "It was all right. You?"

"Oh, you know. Did a lot of boring stuff; went to see Jay."

"Yeah? How's he doing?"

"Great! Well," I amended as honesty kicked in, "actually he's bored out of his mind. He was asking about you."

"Yeah?" Matt looked pleased to be remembered—and a bit guilty. "I meant to go in and see him yesterday, but Steve wanted me to stay at home."

What was this bloke, Matt's keeper? "Well, you can pop in any evening after work. They're very relaxed about it at the

Spire."

"Yeah? Maybe I'll go in tonight, then."

"Trust me, he'll be glad to see you." I had a thought and went over to grab the magazine from the bottom of the pile behind the counter. "Tell you what, you can give him this. A bit of porn ought to cheer him up no end!"

Matt laughed. "Don't know what the nurses'll make of it, though!"

I turned away to hide what was undoubtedly a sly expression.

It wasn't the nurses Jay would have to worry about.

It was Mum.

The morning was fairly quiet—a few customers, a couple of deliveries and a bloke who wanted me to sign up to a directory of local businesses. It seemed reasonable, so I went with it, a little surprised Jay hadn't done so already. During one of the lulls, I ambled into the back room to talk to Matt, finding him, as usual, hard at work. Didn't he ever slack off when no one was looking?

He glanced up from the tyre he was fitting. "Problems?"

"No—just bored," I admitted. I hesitated. "You know your Thursday night bike rides?" Matt nodded to confirm he hadn't been suddenly and inexplicably struck with amnesia. "Well, I was wondering if you'd mind if I tagged along?"

"Yeah—no problem. That'd be great!" Matt looked genuinely pleased at the prospect, and I found myself smiling back at him.

"So how does it work?" I asked, leaning against the worktop.

Matt finished with the tyre and straightened, wiping his

hands on his jeans. "We all meet up where we're going that night—usually around half seven, quarter to eight. Then we go for a ride—that's about it, really. If you give me your email, I'll copy you in on stuff. I mean, we usually decide where we're going to go the week before, then confirm it by email."

"Great! I'll give you my address now." I looked around for a bit of paper and ended up ripping a bit off the back page of the repairs book. "Here you go."

Matt looked at it, then grinned. "*magicbeancounter@gmail.com?*"

"Yes, well. *nicebutdim@gmail.com* was already taken." I cleared my throat. "Now, is there anything I need to bring along?"

Matt pursed his lips. "Well, some of the lads bring along a hip flask of something lethal, but apart from that... Wait, have you got any lights? We're usually out past dark."

"What, even at this time of year?" I was a bit concerned this might be a bit too much for me to handle.

"Well, it often takes a while to get going, and then sometimes we stop at a pub..."

I had a vision of a crowd of lycra-clad mountain bikers crashing through the forest trails getting progressively drunker until the word "crashing" became literally true. "Is that safe?"

"Oh—most of the lads ride out from home, so there's no worry about drunk driving. And it's the New Forest, not the Pennines. If you take a tumble, the landing's usually pretty soft."

That was...not quite as much of a relief as I'd hoped for. I made a snap decision to take the car for at least the first couple of times, so I'd have an excuse not to get wasted. "Okay, so these lights—do I need anything special?" Standard bike lights were more about being seen by cars than casting any actual useful light. I had a feeling cycling down a rough track in the total dark of the forest would require something a little more souped-up.

"Come out the front, and I'll show you." We trooped out to a thankfully customer-free shop—I'd been chatting out the back a little longer than I'd meant to—and went over to Jay's bike light display. "You'll need at least 250 lumens, but best to go a bit higher if you can afford it. The Exposure Toro is good and the 6 Pack is awesome. They'll both do the job, and you won't have to faff about with extra batteries and cables."

Whilst a six-pack had long been on my list of desirable possessions, I'd always envisaged it as a set of really cut abs, not a type of bike light. I chose the Toro, in the end, trying not to wince at the price. Granted, it was bright enough—when I checked it out I saw coloured blobs in my vision for ages afterwards—but when did going for a bike ride get so expensive?

Looking at Matt's enthusiastic smile, though, I couldn't help feeling it was worth it.

I could have done with somewhere to go, Monday evening. Or at least something worth watching on telly. Like Jay, I had way too much time to think—and a vintage episode of *Midsomer Murders* just wasn't enough to distract me.

And like Jay, what I was thinking about was Matt. Although I seriously hoped Jay wasn't thinking the same things I was thinking... No. Jay was straight. He'd said that, and I believed him, because Jay wasn't the sort to lie about it. If he'd been gay, he'd have just come out and said so and assumed everyone would be okay with it. And him being Jay, they probably would have been.

Whereas if it was me... I frowned, scratching Wolverine idly on the top of his head. He showed me those pointy fangs in a tuna-scented yawn, and settled down even more heavily on my lap. At least we hadn't had any repeats of the cat-sick incident, so I'd been able to have a proper meal tonight—if you could call it that when it came in a plastic tub covered in clear film, wrapped in a cardboard sleeve proudly proclaiming it contained one of my five a day. The pasta salad Matt had brought in for our lunch had been orders of magnitude tastier and, I suspected, healthier.

Would it really be different if it was me? Coming out as gay, that was. Was I just misjudging everyone? If I could imagine them accepting a gay Jay, which from the rhyming point of view alone had to be a situation nobody wanted, why couldn't I imagine them accepting a gay Tim?

But what would be the point? My leg was getting pins and needles, and I tried to stretch it out while still weighed down with cat. Wolverine opened one eye and dug his claws lazily into my thigh in warning. I sighed and surrendered to the encroaching numbness as the lesser of two evils.

If I did come out, what would I do? Make a pass at Matt? Try and persuade him to dump Steve and come out with me? Because, let's face it, I was such a bloody catch—still technically married, jobless, and, when the house sale went through, homeless. Not to mention having spent nearly thirty years cowering in the closet. And the grey pubes—mustn't forget those. Oh, yes, he'd definitely prefer my neurotic self to the bloke with the house in the New Forest and hot-and-cold-running ponies.

And anyway, looked at from Matt's point of view, trying to chat him up would actually be kind of insulting. Like I was just assuming that gay men were incapable of fidelity and moreover, permanently up for it with anyone who offered. Even a posh tosser who didn't know his arse from his axle and was standing in for Matt's boss, for Christ's sake. I punched a sofa cushion in frustration.

Wolverine startled awake, ears pricked and tail twitching. I tensed, anticipating multiple puncture wounds in a sensitive area, but he merely fixed me with an exasperated glare and settled back down to sleep. "Are you going soft on me?" I asked, incredulous.

Either that or his stomach was still feeling too delicate for any major bloodbaths right now. I stroked his back rhythmically, all too aware it was more for my benefit than his. Embracing my inner poof would be a stupid idea, I thought with a sigh. Even if I accepted Matt wasn't going to be mine and tried to find another bloke, what did I know about gay relationships? Or pulling a bloke in the first place, for that matter? It'd be pretty bloody ironic if I came out as gay and then totally failed to find a man who was interested in me.

I'd have changed my whole life, exposed myself to ridicule, for nothing.

On the TV, DCI Barnaby pursed his lips as he discovered the incestuous love affair that had sparked the whole sorry series of events in Badger's Drift. Unconventional relationships, he seemed to say, never end well.

Was he right? Would it be madness to risk so much, with so little chance of happiness at the end of it all?

I didn't know.

But at least then I wouldn't have to spend the rest of my life knowing I was a coward and wondering what I was missing.

I woke up late on Tuesday morning after a bad night's sleep with my hair sticking up in all directions and no time for a shower. Well, that solved the Matt question nicely. Clearly there was no chance of him ever fancying me once he'd seen what a god-awful state I woke up in. I flattened my hair down with a bit of water and watched morosely as it sprang straight back up again.

No wonder hats were so popular in years gone by. What I wouldn't give for a stylish trilby or fedora right now. There was a beanie in Jay's wardrobe, but it wasn't quite the same. I pulled it on anyhow, hoping it might flatten my hair down. It made me look like a giant matchstick on legs, but I could always take it off before I went to the shop.

I reckoned I just about had time for a cup of coffee—if I didn't feed the cat. "Nobody should have to deal with a moral dilemma like this first thing in the morning," I groused, stumbling downstairs to the kitchen. Wolverine gave me a smug look as his breakfast hit his bowl, and I set off on my caffeine-deprived drive to the shop, snarling at anyone who dared to hold me up on the way.

I got there just a few minutes after we were supposed to open. Fortunately, there were no queues of impatient customers demanding their right to purchase a pump adaptor on the dot of nine thirty. Matt wasn't there either. I wondered if his timekeeping was this erratic when Jay was around and decided it probably was. Matt didn't seem the sort to take advantage of the boss being away—just the terminally disorganised sort. I smiled just thinking of him—there was something rather endearing about his scattiness.

By the time I'd switched on the till and filled it up with cash from the safe, noting we were getting short of change, Matt had finally arrived. I did a double take as he walked in the door. "Has Olivia talked you into collagen injections? Because I think you ought to ask for your money back."

Matt smiled even more lopsidely than usual. "You mean this?" He touched his swollen lip with understandable caution, then crouched down to re-tie the laces of one of his trainers. "Hit a low branch out in the forest," he explained to his feet.

"You know, they say some people are an accident waiting to happen—maybe you ought to try and work on the *waiting* part?" I said with fond exasperation. "Have you always been this accident prone?"

Still with his head down—how long could one shoelace take to tie?—Matt shrugged and muttered something I didn't catch. Then he rose and disappeared into the back room.

Bugger. I'd overstepped the mark, it seemed. I followed him in there, and he looked round warily. "Sorry," I said. "I keep forgetting we don't really know each other well enough for me to be a bastard to you and expect you to think it's funny."

Matt just stared at me for a moment, an expression on his face I couldn't interpret but which made him look oddly vulnerable. I felt a strange tightness in my chest at the sight. Then he shook his head, shaggy curls flying. "It's not..." Matt paused, then started again. "I mean, I'd get it if you got pissed off about me being such a klutz, that's all. You weren't being a bastard." He gave that painful-looking smile again. "I went to see Jay last night, by the way. Stopped in on my way home from work."

I collected my thoughts, still a bit scrambled by his strange diffidence. "I'd ask how he was, but I imagine he hadn't changed a lot since Sunday."

"Yeah, I guess not. Um, Tim?" Matt seemed troubled.

"Yes?"

"Look, about the necklace I was wearing the other day, when Adam was here..." Matt bit his lip. "Well, I was talking to Jay, and he said you—I mean, it must have looked a bit odd. Sorry. I mean, what I said... You see, the first time I wore it, I was with Steve and Adam and some other lads down the pub, and Steve asked me where it was from..." He thrust his hands into his pockets and walked a few paces away from me, before turning back. "See, it's not his fault, but Steve gets a bit, well, jealous sometimes. So I didn't want to say Jay gave it to me, in case Steve flew off the handle or something. So I said I'd bought it. And then, when you asked about it, and Adam was there, I just sort of panicked, because if I told you Jay gave it to me and Adam went and said something... Anyway, I'm sorry."

"Oh," I said. There was something about this little story that left a nasty taste in my mouth. And it wasn't just finding out Jay, the bastard, had told Matt just how much of an idiot I'd been over one cheap little coral necklace. So Steve was the jealous sort, was he? I was liking Steve less and less the more I heard about him. "Don't worry about it," I said with a forced smile. "Obviously, you wouldn't want your...want Steve to go jumping to conclusions. It's only a necklace, for heaven's sake!"

Matt broke into a relieved grin. "Yeah—that's just what Jay said. I mean, he only mentioned it because he thought it was funny—you thinking he was after me."

"Yes, well, Jay's sense of humour isn't the most mature in the world," I muttered, hoping my face wasn't as red as it felt.

The grin turned wicked. "He told me you and him had a pillow fight."

"One pillow! *And* it was Jay who threw it!"

"How come you didn't throw it back, then?"

"I couldn't! Mum was in the room!"

"Ah, right. Wouldn't want you to get in trouble with your mum." Matt nodded sagely. "I mean, she might stop your pocket money or something."

"Very funny," I said sarcastically, inwardly pleased he felt comfortable enough to tease me like that.

"Must be nice, having a brother," Matt went on, sounding a

bit wistful.

He'd said that before, I remembered. "Are you an only child?"

"Nah—two sisters. Well, stepsisters—my mum was my dad's second wife. They got together when I was little, so he's my stepdad, really. They're way older than me—my sisters, I mean—both married with kids. Haven't seen them for a while, though."

"Live too far away, do they?" I asked sympathetically.

"Bristol—but things are a bit difficult. I mean, it's hard for them to get over here, with the kids and all, and if I go over there, well, we have to be careful my dad doesn't find out." Matt stared at a grease stain on the floor. "It's his generation—he's got some funny ideas about gay blokes. Doesn't want me near the grandkids."

"That's outrageous!"

Matt shrugged awkwardly. "Yeah, well. Maybe it'd be different if I was a blood relative... But he's eighty-three—he's not going to change."

I boggled. "How old's your mum?"

"She died when I was twelve, but she was a lot younger than him, yeah."

I didn't quite know what to say—was it still appropriate to offer condolences for something that happened over a decade ago? But I did feel sorry about it, so I said so.

"'S okay," Matt mumbled.

I was willing to bet it hadn't been. He'd lost his mum and been left with a bigoted old man five times his age just as he was about to reach his teens and, presumably, realise how different he was from most of his mates. It was a good thing he'd at least had Adam. "Do you ever see your real dad?"

"Nope, and I don't want to." Matt said it in an *I don't want*

JL Merrow

to talk about it, end of kind of way, and pointedly grabbed a bike that'd been leaning against the wall, wheeling it into the central work area.

I took the hint and headed back to my till.

Although three separate customers had given me funny looks, it wasn't until a tiny Asian woman walked in and asked me pointedly if it was cold up there that I realised I was still wearing Jay's bloody woollen hat. Indoors. In June.

I tore it off, cursing, and shoved it under the counter.

I didn't see Matt to speak to again until after I got back from a trip to the bank—luckily it was only down the road, so I didn't have to leave the stock in Matt's accident-prone hands for more than a quarter of an hour or so. I went through the *you're-not-Jay* routine with the lady behind the counter and eventually walked back in the shop door newly stocked with change for the till.

Matt was practically bouncing up and down with excitement. "It's here!"

"What is?" I asked.

"The iO single-speed." He pointed to the bike at the front of the row, which I vaguely registered as being a different colour to the one that had been there earlier. "Jay bought it before the accident. It came while you were out."

"What's so special about it?" I asked, crouching down to get a better look. It had a few scratches—obviously second-hand. Then I frowned. "Hang on, is there a bit missing?"

"You mean the gears? Sorry. Shouldn't laugh. That's what single speed means. No gears."

"What?" At this rate, I was going to end up with a permanent line etched across my forehead. "I don't get it.

104

What's the point of a bike with no gears? Especially for..." I glanced at the invoice, which was Sellotaped to the handlebars. "Bloody hell, three hundred quid?"

"Yeah, I know—it's a bargain, innit? Bloke wanted a quick sale. Said his wife told him either one of his three bikes went, or she did." Matt gave the bike a fond glance—then sighed, as if he really wished he could take it home with him. "The frame's steel—makes it nice and springy. Less harsh than aluminium. This one's been fitted with a carbon-fibre fork and handlebars—the Shimano brakes come as standard."

"But..." I was wondering when Matt had stopped speaking English and had moved on to gobbledygook. "Why?" I asked in the end.

He looked at me blankly.

"I mean, why have a bike without gears?"

"Oh—right. Well, some people like it. I mean, they're a lot sturdier—less to damage in a crash—and obviously, there's less maintenance, and they're lighter without the derailleur and all that guff. And round here we've got a lot of single-track trails, and it's not that hilly, so it's perfect terrain for a single-speed. They're supposed to feel more natural, more direct when you ride them." Matt's hand rested lovingly on the saddle.

"Want to give it a try, then?" I asked, amused. I still didn't quite get the point of it all, but maybe you had to be a serious mountain biker to understand.

Matt's face lit up like one of the 900-lumen bike lights I'd been incautious enough to shine in my eyes while faffing around with the stock. "Really? Um, I probably ought to tell you Jay doesn't usually let me test ride the stock..."

"So? He's not here, is he? Go on, have some fun." I'd been about to say, "Knock yourself out," but Matt, being Matt, might have taken me literally. "Just—take care, okay?"

He nodded vigorously, shaggy hair falling over his face, then wheeled the bike to the door, more carefully than I'd ever seen him do anything. There was a warm feeling spreading through my chest at the thought I'd made him so happy.

Of course, if he managed to trash the bike and himself, things would get a mite chillier. I touched the wooden counter for luck and set to emptying out the little moneybags into the till.

When Matt came back, his face was shining, and not just with sweat. "It's brilliant!" he enthused a bit breathlessly, his chest still heaving. "I mean, it's a bit weird 'til you get used to it, and it's harder work uphill, and when you go downhill your legs are going round like buggery, but it's like..." He trailed off, hands waving as they struggled to express what his words couldn't manage. "It's like the bike's just an extension of your legs. Like, you're not so much riding it as being it." He gave me a rueful smile. "That probably sounds like a load of bollocks to you."

"N-no," I managed. My throat was tight, and my vision might even have swum, just a little bit. Matt's smile was broader than I'd ever seen it, he was talking with his whole body, and his enthusiasm wasn't so much infectious as in serious danger of causing a pandemic. He just seemed so...so alive at this moment. As we stood there staring into each other's eyes, I had the strongest, almost painful urge to kiss him.

He'd had me at *buggery*.

Chapter Nine

I ate my lunch (yellow rice salad with prawns; a sort of cold paella that tasted of sunshine and made me yearn for a holiday in Spain) sitting alone at the counter. It was a nice day, so I'd encouraged Matt to go out and get a bit of sun, rather than stay cooped up inside with me. While his well-being had genuinely been a motive, I'd also wanted some time to think things through, and his presence was very definitely a distraction. I couldn't deny it to myself any longer—I was falling for Matt.

Or was I? If I was brutally honest with myself, was I just fixating on the first openly gay bloke I'd ever spent any length of time with? My heart screamed *No!*—but then, what did it know? It hadn't exactly had a lot of experience over the years. I'd never felt this way about anyone—at least, not since my teenage years when I'd had a crush on an older boy that had first clued me in to my not-quite-straightness. I'd seen men I fancied since then, of course—but that had all been about their bodies and yes, all right, their cocks. With Matt... I just kept thinking about his smile, and the way his eyes crinkled up at the corners, and that shaggy brown mop of his that was just made for running your fingers through.

Why the hell did the first bloke I seriously thought might be worth coming out of the closet for have to be unavailable?

Maybe Steve would meet an untimely end, I mused hopefully. Trampled to death by a herd of rampaging New Forest ponies, perhaps. Or gorged to extinction on a surfeit of Matt's gourmet cooking. Perhaps not that—I wouldn't want Matt feeling guilty about it. I sighed and speared a prawn with my fork, wishing it was Steve's body I was impaling on those stainless steel tines... God, what was I thinking? If I really cared about Matt, I wouldn't want him to be unhappy. And I was fairly sure that mourning the untimely death of a live-in lover was likely to be a bit of a downer, at least for a day or two.

Maybe...maybe I should just go for it? Coming out, I meant, not jumping on Matt (*down boy!* I told my libido sternly). Maybe I'd find a bloke who could stop me fixating on Matt. Someone like... I searched my mind for gay men I knew. All I could come up with was a mental image of Adam. He looked even more ape-like in my imagination. At least, I was fairly sure his knuckles didn't *really* scrape the floor as he walked. Yeah, right. Me and Adam. Like that was ever going to happen.

But someone else, maybe? The trouble was, coming out as gay—or even bi; I'd been married to a woman so I could probably pull that one off—was so bloody *final.* A huge, irreversible step: a Rubicon for our times. I couldn't escape the thought that Caesar's crossing of that little dried-up river had technically involved a death sentence. If I couldn't have Matt, was it really worth taking all the risks involved? Worth upsetting my family for, and probably mortifying Kate?

By the time I'd finished my lunch, barely restraining myself from licking the plastic tub clean—it was that good—I still hadn't reached a conclusion, and my head was starting to ache. I was glad when the bell jangled, relieving me from having to think about it anymore—although as it was Matt returning from his lunch break, my thoughts weren't any less confused.

"Had a good break?" I asked, peering at him. "You know, I'd swear you're browner than when you went out. Or you've picked up a few more freckles or something."

He grinned, adding dimples to the already scarily adorable mix. "Yeah, I've been out in the park behind the library. Found a quiet corner and took my shirt off. Got to take any chance you can to get a tan in this country."

I swallowed. My mind conjured up an image of a half-naked Matt that was so detailed another part of me clamoured to give it a standing ovation.

"You know, you should get out sometime," Matt continued, oblivious to my piquant discomfort. "Not tomorrow, obviously, as it's half day—but Thursday maybe? If it's nice, I mean. I could easily mind the shop for you."

"I'm not sure the people of Totton want to be treated to the sight of me with my shirt off in the park," I said drily.

Matt laughed. "Why not? I mean, I wouldn't mind—" He broke off abruptly, probably at the look on my face. "Sorry. That was...sorry." He took a deep breath. "I'll be out back."

I stared after him. Had he meant what I thought he'd meant?

He couldn't have...could he? I looked down at my skinny chest. Underneath my shirt, it was the sort of luminous white the makers of biological washing powders could only dream of.

Matt had probably just meant he could do with a good laugh.

The two men who walked in the door half an hour later were an unlikely pair of friends, I thought. One of them was a bit on the tubby side, wearing glasses and a nervous smile that peeked through his scruffy beard. The other—well, the only reason I could think of for him hanging around with The Beard was to make himself look better by comparison. Except he really didn't need to. He was younger than the other guy; hotter, blonder—well, think of any positive descriptive term you can, and add "er" and you've got the general idea. If he wasn't a model, he ought to be. The only thing I didn't like about him so much was his eyes—they were quick, sharp and icy cold. They made a brief pass over me, then turned back to the bikes, obviously not finding me worth lingering over.

Feeling I needed to be more proactive in the business, I came out from behind the desk. "Anything I can help you with?" I asked. With a bit of luck, they'd just want a pump adaptor. I could manage that, no problem. Hell, if I put my mind to it, I could probably manage to sell them the whole pump.

The good-looking one turned. "You're not Jay," Blondie commented with a business-like smile and a raised eyebrow. If I wasn't mistaken, it held a hint of a challenge.

"Oh—no, are you friends of his? I'm Tim. His brother." I held out my hand, and Blondie shook it firmly. "I'm looking after the shop while he's in hospital—he broke his leg," I explained at Blondie's sharp, interrogatory glance.

"Sorry to hear that—is it a bad break?"

"Pretty bad, as they go. I'll be down here for a few weeks at least."

"You're not from around here?"

"No—London. Mill Hill, actually." I felt like I was being interviewed and rushed to get a question of my own in. "You're locals?"

"We live in Southampton. I'm Luke, by the way. And this is Russell." He turned to indicate The Beard, and his whole manner altered. The hardness disappeared from his eyes, and his smile grew warmer.

"Hi." Russell leaned past Luke to offer me his hand. "Luke's persuaded me to try cycling—I think he's trying to get me fit or something."

"Get out of it!" Luke gave Russell an affectionate shove. "I want you to try it because I think you'll enjoy it, that's all. You're fine—you don't need to worry about getting fit." His gaze lingered over Russell in a way totally unlike the brusque, calculating glance he'd given me—and Russell's response was a shy smile and a long look down at his surprisingly nice shoes. I strongly suspected Blondie's influence there, seeing as the rest of him was clad in M&S jeans and a hand-knitted sweater.

Finally putting it all together, I stared in shock. Were they...? Could they really be...? I blinked as Luke grabbed Russell's arm to drag him over to look at one of the higher-end mountain bikes. They were certainly acting like a couple. "I'll get Matt," I blurted out.

It wasn't the *gay* thing, honest. I just knew they'd need some specialist advice, that's all. Matt came out wiping his hands on a greasy rag and gave the Odd Couple a friendly smile. "Oh, hi, Luke. You all right?"

"Better than you are, by the looks of things," Luke said with a pointed glance at Matt's lip.

"Oh, that—hit a low branch out in the forest, that's all," Matt told his trainers with one of his sudden bouts of shyness.

Luke didn't say anything, but he gave Matt a sharp look before flicking his gaze to me. Not having a bloody clue what he was after, I gave him a weak smile.

It wasn't returned. Apparently, whatever Luke had wanted, I'd failed to provide it.

"You know, you never mentioned this mountain biking was dangerous," Russell said with what was probably meant to be a mock frown, but which unfortunately got lost in the beard.

"Nah, it's just me—I'm a total klutz," Matt said. "So you managed to talk him into it, did you?" he asked, turning to Luke.

Luke waggled an eyebrow as he flashed Matt a brief but blinding smile. "You know me. I've got my methods."

Matt blushed, just in case any straight people in the

vicinity hadn't caught on to exactly what sort of methods he was referring to. I felt like I'd walked into an episode of *Queer as Folk*. Blondie was probably thoroughly enjoying making a heterosexual feel like a minority, I thought. Not that there were, actually, any heterosexuals in the vicinity, but his gaydar obviously wasn't as finely honed as Pit-bull Pritchard's.

It was probably still streets ahead of mine, though.

I retreated behind the counter and watched grumpily as Matt pulled out one bike after another for Russell to look at, sit on and listen to Luke and Matt arguing technical details about. Around halfway through, Russell turned to catch my eye with an expression that said clear as day he didn't have a bloody clue what they were on about either, which made me feel a bit better.

"Have you, er, been together long?" I asked Russell when he was finally allowed up to the counter with his credit card, Luke and Matt still debating the merits of full suspension bikes versus hard tails. (Luke was a full susser fan. I wasn't surprised.) Russell smiled, his beard creasing up at the corners of his mouth. I thought I'd probably like Russell, if we met socially. "Nearly a year now," he said happily. "Amazing, isn't it? Don't know what he sees in me."

There are times when honesty is the only way to go. And this was quite clearly not one of them. On the other hand, there was no way I was about to start complimenting men on their appearance, whether I meant it or not. "I'm sure he's in no doubt," I hedged in the end.

Russell put his card away while I bagged up the helmet, lights and other bits and pieces Matt had managed to flog him. Luke and Matt were still deep in conversation down the front of the shop, although at a lower volume now so I couldn't hear what they were talking about anymore. "Is it difficult?" I blurted out.

"Having a good-looking boyfriend, you mean?" Russell asked.

"Having a boyfriend," I clarified quietly, one eye still on the other two. Luke seemed to be giving Matt a hard time about something.

Russell looked thoughtful. "I suppose I've always been lucky, really," he said. "I never had any trouble with my family—think they were just glad I'd finally found someone." His beard twitched as he smiled. "Luke's had a bit of a hard time of it, though. He's a journalist—it's a bit of a macho culture. Sometimes he gets...comments. But his dad's speaking to him again now."

"But it's worth it?" I persisted.

"Oh, yeah. Definitely." Russell's gaze rested on Luke as he spoke, and there was so much affection in his tone I felt faintly embarrassed, like I'd walked in on them snogging on the sofa. "You're, um, not out, then?"

I flushed. I hadn't realised I'd been quite that obvious. "No." I cleared my throat. "I'm not."

"Maybe you should give it a go," he suggested gently. "While you're down here, I mean. Do a sort of trial run before you have to go back to London."

His words sent a thrill of excitement—and trepidation—right through me. I hadn't even considered the possibility of coming out of the closet on a temporary basis and going straight (hah!) back in if I found the big, wide, gay world didn't suit. But Russell was right. As long as I was careful, I could try things out here, and no one from my old life in London would ever know. No big coming-out drama; no shame if it all went tits-up. "Is there, er, much of a scene here?" I whispered, my gaze darting in all directions as if I thought there might be customers hiding in every nook and cranny, ready to stand up and denounce me as a closet queer.

Russell looked a bit like my eyes were making him dizzy. "Well, I wouldn't go that far, and you're asking the wrong bloke, anyway, but there are a few places—"

"Are we done, then?" Luke interrupted, striding up to clap a proprietary hand on Russell's shoulder.

I spoke up quickly in case Russell hadn't twigged I really didn't want to carry on our conversation in front of the other two. "Yes, I think that's everything."

Russell got the message. He made a little "let your fingers do the walking" gesture where Luke couldn't see it before they grabbed his stuff and said good-bye. I decided I liked Russell a lot—in a totally platonic way. "They seem like a nice couple," I said casually to Matt after the door had finally shut behind them. I thought it might be a good moment to establish my not-your-homophobe credentials.

"Oh—yeah, they are." Matt seemed a bit distracted, staring out the window as the couple in question disappeared from view.

"What was Luke giving you a hard time about?"

He jumped—just a little, but he definitely jumped. "Nothing! No, it was just...it was nothing. I'd better get back out back. Repairs." He was definitely avoiding looking me in the eye as he sidled past the bikes and into the back room.

What the hell?

I went straight to the hospital to see Jay after work. He was supposed to have had his surgery today, so I wanted to make sure it had gone okay. "Where's Mum?" I asked when I got in the door to find Jay, against all probability, on his own.

Then I caught sight of Jay's leg, resting on the blanket, and forgot I'd even asked. "Bloody hell, Jay! What have they done to you?"

The cast was gone, and his leg had...bits of metal sticking out of it. Shiny silver rods and screws, as if some medical student had been given a Meccano set for his birthday and decided to combine his two loves. The rods disappeared into Jay's flesh just above his knee. My stomach gave an uneasy lurch. "Is that supposed to be an *improvement*? When you said they were going to put a framework in, I thought you meant, well, *in*."

Jay gave Frankenstein's limb a cursory glance. "Yeah, it's actually feeling a lot better now. I've got to be careful not to knock it, though."

It didn't look better to me. It looked swollen, painful and frankly nauseating. "Can you walk on it now?"

"Nah. Tomorrow, I'm supposed to start with all that. Be good to get back on my feet."

I swallowed. "So...will you be coming back to the shop soon?"

"Had enough of slumming it down here, have you?"

"Don't be a prat!" It came out a bit more forcefully than I meant it to, and Jay shot me an astonished look. "No—I'm, well, I'm kind of enjoying it, actually. So you don't need to worry about hurrying back. Why not leave it until your leg's healed properly? Take a break. Pun not intended."

Jay was staring at me like I'd announced my intention to start dressing in rabbit skins and living wild in the forest.

"What?" I asked.

"This isn't some kind of midlife crisis, is it?"

Not him as well. "I'm twenty-eight, Jay. I'm three years younger than you are!"

"Yeah, but you've been living life in the fast lane, haven't you?"

"The fast lane? I'm an accountant from Mill Hill, for God's sake!"

"Yeah, but you work in the City. Did work, anyway. And I know you; you never eat properly. Physiologically speaking, you're probably nearer forty."

My jaw dropped—and Olivia glided in just in time to see me standing there like Cletus the Slack-Jawed Yokel. Mum followed in her wake, looking like she was seething over something and would erupt any minute like the apocalypse kicking off.

Olivia gave me a cool smile. "Hello, Tim. Have you given any thought to what I said?"

It was too much. No way was I staying there to be humiliated while Olivia shared the tale of my greying pubes. I squared my shoulders, gathered my dignity—and slunk out of there like a weasel who'd been caught pushing dodgy carrots to little baby bunnies.

By the time I got home, all enthusiasm for going up to Mill Hill that evening had fled. I could live without the rest of my stuff for a little while longer. Actually, to be honest, I could probably live without most of it indefinitely. My clothes were all wrong for down here, Jay had duplicates of most of the decent stuff in my CD collection and as I wasn't planning to enter any tournaments down here, my sparring mitts and pads wouldn't be required.

I wondered if Kate had any plans for the household stuff. Most of it had been wedding gifts from elderly relatives; the kitchen stuff in particular had hardly been used. Was it a bit late now to return the stuff to the original givers? Of course, some of the crumblier great-aunts and uncles had died since then... I thought guiltily of Auntie Pat and her matched set of copper-bottomed pans. Maybe I should have put in a bit more effort to learn how to use them?

Stung by Jay's comments about my diet, I'd popped into Asda on the way back and bought some healthy stuff from their Good For You range, but it was still ready meals. I had a nasty suspicion they still wouldn't be a patch on cooking stuff from scratch.

After all, millions of people cooked food every day—how hard could it be? Feeling inspired, I grabbed one of Jay's cookbooks from the kitchen shelf and flicked through until I found a recipe for something I recognised. Lasagna. That was just pasta, and pasta was easy, right? Trying not to be put off by the list of ingredients longer than my small intestine, I scanned the instructions. *Chop onions...* I could do that. *Brown mince...*trickier but manageable. Probably. *Make a roux in the usual way...* I sighed, shut the book with a snap and went off to make dinner in *my* usual way: pierce film; bung in microwave; wait for bell.

Chapter Ten

Wednesday morning was, if possible, even quieter than a week ago. Odd to think I'd been here only a week; I already felt like my old life in London had just been an unusually long and, frankly, uninteresting dream.

I felt a twinge of guilt at dismissing all my years of marriage this way. But it was only a small twinge, and I seemed to recover from it rather quickly.

Matt seemed a bit distracted—or maybe he just hadn't slept well. Thinking of what he might have been doing instead, I realised from the ache in my jaw I was grinding my teeth. Coffee. I needed coffee. If nothing else, it'd give me something to do with my mouth that wouldn't involve an expensive trip to the dentist.

We—that is, Jay and Matt—kept a small kettle in the back room, together with a jar of Nescafé (Matt) and some dodgy-smelling teabags (Jay). "Fancy a brew?" I asked Matt, interrupting him as he wrote up a repairs invoice in his messy-yet-legible hand.

"Yeah, that'd be great. Thanks. Coffee for me, please," he added as usual. I wasn't sure if it was natural diffidence making him doubt I'd remember his beverage of choice, or if he did occasionally come over all masochistic and have some of Jay's herbal tisane. I wasn't even sure tisane was a word; I certainly wasn't going trust it as a drink.

"Okay. Do you mind if I...?" I waved the coffee jar in Matt's direction. "Sorry—I keep forgetting to bring in a jar of my own."

"Nah, don't be daft. You're welcome to mine," Matt insisted. He still seemed a little subdued, and I noticed, when I handed him his coffee, that he drank it carefully out of the less swollen side of his mouth.

"Are you okay?" I asked.

"Yeah!" Matt stared into his mug. "'M fine."

"I mean, if you wanted to nip down to the chemist's and get something to put on that, or some painkillers, that'd be fine."

"It's okay," Matt insisted, giving me half a smile.

I hesitated—and then the doorbell jangled and I had to get back out front.

It was probably just as well. It clearly wasn't a good moment to sound Matt out about where one might go to experiment with being gay—and anything else I might have felt the urge to say to him right now was probably best left unsaid.

Grown men definitely didn't offer to kiss each other better.

"Right," I said briskly, striding into the back room on the dot of one before Matt could disappear. "Where are we going for lunch?"

Matt turned to look at me sharply, a sort of "you what?" expression on his face. "Lunch?"

"Yes—you promised me New Forest pub lunches, last Wednesday—don't tell me you've forgotten?" I mentally crossed my fingers and prayed for some selective amnesia about my general git-ishness that day.

"Oh! No—no, right. Um. Well, there's the Oak out past Lyndhurst—fancy that?"

"Sounds great," I said heartily. "The Oak it is, then."

Matt looked a bit wary at the prospect, as well he might, based on my behaviour in the café last week. "Er, are we both going to drive?"

I nodded. "Probably best. We'll be going in opposite directions afterwards." Plus, he didn't want to be worrying about getting stranded if I stormed out in a snit again. "Have you got the postcode of the place for the SatNav?"

"Sorry—don't use one."

"Okay—directions?"

Matt looked worried. "Um, well, we start by going to Lyndhurst, but I'm not very good at giving directions—always seem to miss bits out. How about you follow me?"

That was a recipe for disaster if ever I heard one. "Fine," I said and made a mental note to Google the place on my phone as soon as I got to my car.

Of course, when I got to where I'd parked and tried it, I got the little red triangle telling me there was no service around here. Damn it. I'd just have to hope Matt remembered I was tailing him and didn't go shooting off at junctions, like a certain brother of mine I could name tended to do.

A horn tooted, and I looked around to see Matt waving at me from the window of his Ford Focus. I waved back, and we set off in our miniature convoy.

We took the A35 out towards Lyndhurst, where we drove down the one-way system past any number of perfectly nice-looking pubs and restaurants (my stomach grumbling loudly in protest) and then out the other side. It soon felt like we were in the forest proper, the roads bordered by woodland. I was so busy admiring the countryside and trying to remember what little I'd ever learned about identifying trees that I nearly missed it when Matt turned off onto an unmarked side road. There were a few houses here, mostly of the large, expensive variety, with big, well-kept gardens. I wondered if Steve's house was this imposing.

And then we were there. The lane opened out into a Yshaped junction, and right in the middle was the Oak Inn. It was a solid, squarish place, painted white with black window frames, and looked at least a couple of centuries old. To the left, I could see a farm; to the right, a green where a couple of nut-brown ponies were grazing. It was all very idyllic, peaceful and quintessentially English. There was even an old-fashioned red telephone box outside the pub, although whether it was still functional or just there for decoration I couldn't have said. Did anyone ever use phone boxes these days in any case?

I parked the BMW next to Matt's battered old Ford Focus. Matt grinned as I got out. "All we need is a Rolls Royce on your other side and it'll be just like that Frost Report 'class' sketch, only with cars."

I laughed, half surprised he knew the sketch. Neither of us had been born when it had first been broadcast. It was a classic, though—they don't make 'em like that anymore. "Does that mean you look up to me?" I asked.

"Yeah, don't worry—I know my place."

"And apparently it's watching old black-and-white comedy sketches on YouTube," I teased. "Right, are we going to go in and eat before I faint with hunger? You've got me too used to proper food at lunchtimes."

"Yeah? You do realise I've been giving you the veggie options, don't you? Steve reckons that's what proper food *eats*."

To be honest, I hadn't even noticed the lack of meat. "Oh, well—I'll make up for it by having something carnivorous today. Unless that's a problem for you?" The last thing I wanted was to put Matt off his food.

"Nah, don't be daft—like I said, Steve eats meat all the time."

Okay, that was two mentions of Steve in two sentences. I hoped it wasn't going to be like that all through the meal or I could see myself rapidly losing my appetite or, in a worst case scenario, my lunch.

The Oak's interior was in keeping with the outside: bare wooden floors, low beams and wooden furniture. It had a cosy, relaxed feel, but I guessed it really came into its own in winter, when the old wood-burning stove could be lit. We walked up to the hop-festooned bar and ordered our lunch: local sausages with mustard mash and garden peas for me, while Matt just went for a ploughman's. I supposed he'd be cooking tonight in any case.

Once we'd paid for our food, we took our drinks out into the beer garden. The place was pretty busy, even on a Wednesday lunchtime outside school holidays, but we managed to find a table in the shade of, appropriately enough, an oak tree. Well, I was 90 percent certain it was an oak, anyhow. If I came back in the autumn and found it dropped conkers instead of acorns, I'd have to revise my opinion.

I cast a regretful eye at the couple sitting at the table next to us. They were laughing away, each with a glass of white wine beaded with condensation in the warm air. "Seems like there's something missing, having a pub lunch and just drinking Diet Coke."

"You mean like the alcohol?" Matt said, swinging his leg over the wooden bench.

"Not just that. It just seems more relaxed, somehow, having a glass of wine or beer or whatever floats your boat. Like sticking two fingers up at the world and saying *sod it, I have no intention of even trying to achieve anything useful this afternoon, and I'm just fine with that.*"

Matt took a swig of his Coke, and I watched his Adam's apple bob as he swallowed. "So are you?" he asked.

I blinked. "Am I what?"

"Going to achieve anything constructive this afternoon?"

"Oh—very doubtful, I'd say. I suppose I could go up to London and fetch some more of my stuff—we're putting the house on the market; it'll have to be cleared—but I'm out tonight, so it makes the time a bit tight." I shied away, as I had done several times before, from telling him I did karate. It wasn't that I thought Matt would think it was weird or just really not me or anything—but ever since I'd got my black belt, it'd felt like bragging to bring up the subject. Like I was showing off about it. I didn't want him thinking I was that immature. "It'd be a right pain to be stuck in traffic on the M25 and not get back soon enough," I continued, then swatted away an unusually calorie-conscious wasp that had started taking an interest in my Diet Coke. "Thought it was a bit early for these."

"Ah, but you're down south now. We get summer earlier here."

"Bollocks! North London is hardly the Arctic Circle. And the Solent is *definitely* not the Mediterranean."

"Yeah, shame, that." Matt ducked his head over his drink for a moment, then looked up again. "Why'd you move to London—if you don't mind me asking? I mean, you're from around here originally, aren't you?"

I shrugged. "Well, Winchester, so just up the road. London just seemed the place to be—careers-wise, I mean. And it was where Kate wanted to live." Actually, I couldn't remember her ever saying that out loud—she'd just more or less assumed we'd go to London when we graduated, and I'd been happy enough to go along with that.

"Do you miss it? I mean, is it all really slow and boring down here?"

I looked around for a moment at the sunny beer garden, bordered with well-established trees and full of happy people, none of whom were dressed in designer suits or tapping away on their Blackberries. The air was rich with cut grass, beer, hot food and a sort of earthy smell I supposed must be the forest itself. A sparrow darted down not three feet from me to pounce on a crumb left by a previous diner. "God, no. This is brilliant."

The waitress arrived with our food, and I stared in disbelief at half a pig's worth of sausages and a metric tonne of mashed potato. "Are you sure you're a vegetarian?" I asked Matt. "Because I could really do with some help here."

"I'll take some of the mash off your hands," Matt said, not waiting for me to agree but leaning across the table to scoop up a generous portion with his fork. "They do a great mash here."

They did, too. As I tucked in, my taste buds began to regret giving half of it away, although I knew my stomach would thank me for it later.

After the first few forkfuls, I forced myself to get down to business. "So, you and Steve," I said. "Do you, er, go out much? Evenings, I mean. To, you know"—I dropped my voice—"gay bars."

Matt shrugged. "A bit." He ducked his head. "Steve likes to stay in more. Or go out with his mates."

"Where do you go, when you do go out? I mean," I added hurriedly, "are there a lot of gay bars in Southampton? Or, you know, the New Forest?"

Matt looked up again. I hoped I wasn't blushing. "Oh— there's a few. Not that many, but you wouldn't expect it, would you? It's not like Brighton. No, there's a couple of places we go to—when we want to go to that sort of place. There's the Cock in Jeffrey Street, and El Niño in the town centre. But the Cock's a bit cruisey, really, and El Niño's always full of posers." He grinned suddenly. "Luke likes it there."

I supposed "cruisey" wasn't really what you wanted, if you

were in a relationship. Was it what I wanted?

"But Steve likes to go a bit further out—down to Brighton, mostly."

Brighton? That was a long way to go for a pint. No wonder they didn't want to make that trek too often. "Is it pretty lively there?" I'd heard it was the San Francisco of the South of England—but then again, I'd also heard Manchester described as the Venice of the North, so I was taking this one with a pinch of salt.

"Yeah—it's fun, but it's not like going somewhere local, you know? Somewhere your mates go too."

A bit like Southampton was for me, then—although, in my case, that was a selling point. "What are your plans for the afternoon?" I asked, thinking we'd probably spent as much time on *gay* stuff as was safe.

"Oh, you know." Matt made a vague gesture with a bit of bread and cheese, then frowned as his cheese fell off and went through a gap in the slats of the table. "Bit of gardening, bit of food shopping. Nothing exciting. You?"

"Might get the bike out—I probably need to get in some practice before tomorrow night."

Matt brightened. "You're still up for that, then? I told the lads you'd be coming. Adam's looking forward to seeing you again."

"Oh?" I couldn't imagine why. Of course, any enthusiasm expressed by Adam was undoubtedly relative. A word of two syllables, perhaps, or maybe even a distinguishable vowel sound.

I was sorry to leave the pub when we finally finished our lunch. Matt had cheered up no end since this morning, and I felt proud of myself for having in some small way contributed. Possibly.

I could get used to going out places with Matt.

I spent the rest of Wednesday afternoon keeping the shop's books up-to-date. The quarterly VAT return would be due soon, and I didn't want to leave it until the last minute. Luckily Jay had (for once in his life) taken my advice about how to set up his bookkeeping system, so I was easily able to work out where he'd got up to with it all. I tutted as I saw he'd been under-claiming on the input VAT, and corrected his figures with a satisfied flourish. When I had a moment, it looked like it'd be a good idea to go through past returns and see if there was anything we could still claim on.

Still full from lunch, I just had a couple of slices of toast for tea. Wolverine gave me a superior look from his bowl of high-protein fish. I gave him a rude gesture and went off to watch comedy reruns on satellite for half an hour.

My palms were a little sweaty as I got out my gi for karate that evening. Had Pit-bull passed on his *poofter* judgment to the rest of the class? Would I be given the cold shoulder? Or would it be more along the lines of jokes about not letting me get them on the floor? Loaded questions about whether I preferred attacking or defending, that sort of thing?

Wolverine, gorged on tuna, padded into the bedroom and jumped heavily on the bed. He stalked over to the bedside table, where I'd placed one of Gran's dragon figurines. It was a sleek green dragon, smugly holding a sword in its forepaws and with a knight's discarded armour at its feet. The legend on the base read *Tender is the Knight*. Wolverine gave it a suspicious sniff.

"I'd have thought you and that dragon would get on like a house on fire," I told him. Wolverine gave me a look as if to say I'd better not be making fun of him and started to knead the duvet into submission.

126

"Does it bother you that Daddy's a poofter?" I asked him. God, that sounded gay. Although probably not as gay as calling myself "Mummy" would have been.

Wolverine yawned. I hoped the guys at karate, if they'd heard the news, would treat it with the same complete indifference, but I wasn't sanguine about my chances.

When I got there, though, everyone seemed to treat me exactly the same as ever. Did that mean Pritchard hadn't told them? Or they hadn't believed him? It seemed hard to believe that everyone there except him simply found it a non-issue.

Prick-tard himself wasn't actually there, which surprised me. I'd have put him down as the sort of bloke who'd miss his own mother's funeral if it clashed with a training session. It certainly made for a more relaxed evening. Afterwards, I went for a drink at a pub down the road with John, where I studiously avoided all mention of Prick-tard and mentioned my break up as a way of bolstering my shaky straight credentials. John chatted happily about his recent divorce and clued me in on a couple of pitfalls to avoid. All in all, I was feeling pretty mellow when I wheeled my bike back down Jay's drive later on.

Even the discovery that Wolverine had left me a present didn't ruin the mood. It was—or rather had been—some sort of mouse-like creature. As Wolverine had neatly bisected it down the middle and left me only the rear end, it was a bit hard to tell. Especially since I'd discovered its presence by treading on the little beastie.

I got upstairs to find Wolverine had already turned in for the night and was purring loudly in the dead centre of the duvet. I had a quick shower, considered turfing him out, but in the end, reluctant to seem ungrateful for his delightful gift, slipped into the minuscule amount of space under the nearest side of the duvet.

I was asleep within minutes.

Chapter Eleven

Matt was late for work again Thursday morning. He scrambled in with a big smile on his face and his hair all over the place. No prizes for guessing what had delayed him, I thought sourly, my mood already ruined by a bad night's sleep and a stiff neck on waking, courtesy of that bloody cat.

"Sorry," Matt called out cheerfully and disappeared straight into the back room.

I shut the till drawer with a vicious snap. An early customer who'd been browsing around the bike lights looked up. "Cheer up, mate—it might never happen."

"It already did," I muttered. "Probably several times. And that's just this morning."

Later, I wandered into the back. "Have a good evening yesterday?" I asked, keeping my tone painfully neutral.

Matt looked up briefly, then bent back over the brake cable he was working on. "Yeah—it was great. Steve took me out for a meal, and it was brilliant. I mean, he missed training for it and everything."

I wondered what kind of training Steve did but didn't want to get into another conversation about the lucky bastard. Maybe Matt just meant going down the gym—gay blokes were a bit fanatical about their looks, weren't they? One of the many things I liked about Matt was that he didn't appear to have got the memo. He was 100 per cent natural. "Oh? Where did you go?"

"Hotel out towards Ringwood. It was dead posh." Matt looked up again and grinned at me. "You'd have liked it."

He was probably right, but just then I'd have happily seen it burnt to the ground. "Special occasion?" I forced out.

Matt had his head down again. "Nah—we just had a bit of a barney the other day, and he wanted to say sorry, that's all. Are you still on for tonight?"

What's the point? I felt like saying. But that would have been petty. "Yes—of course. Looking forward to it."

Actually, after a day spent rushed off my feet in the shop, I found I really was looking forward to it. I was obviously starting to appreciate the benefits of fresh air and exercise. And it'd be my first opportunity to use the Genesis in the environment it was designed for.

All right, maybe I was looking forward to seeing some more of Matt outside work too. I couldn't remember the last time I'd enjoyed a pub lunch so much as I had yesterday, and it wasn't just because of the sausages.

The arrangement was to meet up in a forest car park. Matt had emailed me the location and thankfully included a map. I deliberately didn't set off any earlier than I needed to. I didn't want to arrive too early and have to hang around like I was hoping for action of an entirely different kind—although apparently there wasn't much of a risk. I'd asked Matt jokingly if there was any danger of unintentional voyeurism on these bike rides. He'd told me in all seriousness that "the dogging car park" was just outside Marchwood and they didn't go around that way all that often.

Of course, sod's law ensured I got held up by roadworks on

the outskirts of Totton and spent the rest of the drive worrying they wouldn't wait for me. I was consequently relieved to swing into the car park and recognise Adam's orange mop of hair. He was standing chatting to a bunch of lads putting wheels back on bikes and adjusting headlights, one of whom I was fairly sure was Matt, although he was bent low over his bike, so I couldn't tell for sure. It definitely looked a lot like Matt's arse.

Feeling slightly embarrassed at the realisation I could pick Matt's arse out of a line-up, I parked next to the group and gave Adam a wave as I got out. He waved back and loped off towards Matt, presumably to tell him I was here. Feeling I shouldn't waste time, I got my bike out of the boot and started clicking it back together before wheeling it over to the rest of the lads.

Matt's mates were a ragtag bunch. I felt positively overdressed in my brand-new cycling shorts and a T-shirt that had neither holes nor stains. Of course, there was every chance that might change before the evening was out. Matt gave a huge grin when he saw me. "Tim! Good to see you. Right—you know Adam." The cuddly orangutan in question gave me a thumbs-up. "And this is Phil, Tel and Andy." They all nodded greetings at me.

Phil was dark and whippet-thin, whereas both Tel and Andy had a slight suspicion of too many Mars Bars around the middle. It was reassuring to see they were just ordinary blokes, not lean, mean, cycling machines. They were both fair-haired, which might have caused me problems remembering which was which, except that Tel had the worst broken nose I'd ever seen. It was practically pointing sideways. Once seen, it was impossible not to stare at, so I cast my eyes around for something else to fix on and landed on the hip flask in Andy's hand. He caught me staring at it. "Fancy a bit of the old muscle relaxant before we set off?"

"Er…"

Adam nudged me. "G'won. 'S good stuff."

Not wanting to seem like a wuss, I took the proffered flask and had a cautious swig. Fire burned down my throat, and my eyes immediately watered. "Bloody hell, what is that stuff?" I choked out, handing the flask back blindly.

There was a general good-natured chuckle. "Some kind of schnapps Andy brought back from Germany," Matt admitted.

"It'll put hairs on your chest!" Andy defended his choice of refreshments.

I winced and wiped my eyes. "More likely to burn them off."

Everyone laughed, and Adam's warm, meaty paw clapped me on the back. I hadn't noticed him getting so touchy-feely with Matt. It was nice of him to want to make the new guy feel welcome, though.

"Right," Matt began. "Tim here's a beginner, so look out for him, okay?" He turned to me. "And if these wankers do something daft, don't feel you have to copy them, all right?"

There was a general chorus of "Who, us? Daft? Never!"

Matt rolled his eyes. "Just remember—follow the track, and if you see a shortcut no one else is taking, don't do what Phil did the other week and assume you know better, all right?"

"What happened?" I asked.

"Turned out there was barbed wire across it. I ended up getting a faceful," Phil told me ruefully.

Now I looked closer, I could see the faint marks. "Nice."

We set off in single file down the narrow dirt drack, with Matt in the front. I'd assumed that, as the newbie, I'd be bringing up the rear, but Adam insisted I go ahead of him.

It was really thoughtful of him to make sure I didn't get left behind, I mused as I pedalled away, my eyes unavoidably fixed on Andy's arse as it wobbled away in front of me.

The trees in this part of the forest were a mixed bunch,

much like the lads. Not that I could have told you what any of them were, but there were tall, spindly ones with delicate leaves, and ancient, gnarled ones that looked like they could have earned a few pounds as extras in *Lord of the Rings*. Broadleaved trees with silvery bark, and tall, scraggy fir trees quite unlike the maypole-like pines I'd seen in European forests. Gran would have known all of their names—I had a sudden flash of memory of walking in a forest somewhere with her when I was little, my small hand in hers, on one of those rare, blissful days Jay hadn't been there to overshadow me.

Or push me face-first into the stinging nettles. All right, he'd only ever done that the once—and Gran had given him a proper tongue-lashing for it—but whenever he'd been around, he'd always managed to be the centre of attention. Jay was always the talker, whereas I was the quiet one, often to be found with my nose stuck in a book. Jay was the one who'd be falling out of trees or coming home from the park with spectacularly bloodied knees from some daft stunt on the roundabout.

I'd be the one who'd be constantly nagged to *leave that, don't climb that, stop running...because you know what happened to your brother.* Conversely, when I decided in my teens I'd like to start karate—mainly, as it happened, because I had a crush on a boy from school who went, but that was neither here nor there—the expected argument totally failed to materialise. Presumably, if Jay wasn't doing it, it couldn't be dangerous.

We soon got to a clearing, where the lads stopped and gathered round what I first took to be some kind of forest sculpture—then I realised someone had built a sort of see-saw out of a tree-trunk and some fallen branches lashed together. From his delighted cries of "It's still here!" I deduced that someone had been Tel.

"Going to give it a go?" he asked Matt.

For a moment, I thought they were actually going to sit on it like kids. Then Matt lined his bike up with the down side and pedalled slowly onto the decidedly unsafe-looking see-saw. I found I was holding my breath as he reached the midpoint and paused to let it tip, but he handled it well and let the bike roll down.

Matt having made it unscathed—perhaps they used him as the mountain-biking equivalent of a miner's canary?—we were all expected to have a go. When it came to my turn, I gamely approached the see-saw, which appeared to have doubled in height since Andy had wobbled his way over.

"G'won!" Adam shouted.

Oh, bloody hell. What was the worst that could happen? Oh, yes—I could end up in hospital with Jay. I glanced at Matt, and he gave me an encouraging smile. Warmth flooded through me.

"Don't be a wuss!" Phil yelled, which turned the thermostat right back down again.

I pedalled my way onto the down side. It was harder than it looked to stay balanced, but I made it to the midpoint, at which my stomach dropped sharply as the see-saw did likewise. "Whoa!" I shouted without meaning to, barely managing to stay upright as it jolted with impact and I zipped back down to earth a lot faster than I'd intended—although fortunately without actually falling off my bike altogether. "Hey, that was fun!"

The others all laughed at my obvious surprise. "Yeah, that's kind of the point," Andy said. "Something from the mini-bar to celebrate?" He had his hip flask out again, and we all took a swig. It didn't burn quite so much this time going down.

We strung out a bit as we went through the forest, the order we rode in changing at every gate (although Adam always seemed to end up behind me, for some reason). It was, as Matt had mentioned, fairly flat, but there were plenty of natural obstacles to negotiate—tree roots, deep ruts left by winter cyclists, horse dung and the odd muddy puddle, some where you'd least expect them. As I whizzed through one and felt mud splatter up my back, I reflected that at least now I'd look the part.

"Reckon I'm dirty enough to be a real mountain biker?" I asked Adam the next time we stopped for a gate and a swig of Andy's "muscle relaxant".

Adam gave me a speculative look. "Y'could get a lot dirtier than that," he said with an odd smile.

He was probably right. There were undoubtedly a lot more puddles to come tonight.

"'Ere, Tim—I wish my wife was as dirty as you!" Andy interrupted. Everyone laughed uproariously at the cringeably old joke, including me. I decided I'd better refuse all offers of refreshments from now on if I didn't want to get done for drunk driving on the way home.

The New Forest, I was beginning to learn, was definitely not one of those places where you couldn't see the wood for the trees. Although a lot of it was, as you might expect, thickly forested, there were also large expanses of grass and heathland. They were great for varying the pace, letting us cruise for a bit before plunging back into the trees, where all the frantic twisting and turning, braking and accelerating kept us on our toes and took a lot more effort.

We passed through a thick stretch of dense gorse—one variety of forest life, at least, that even I could identify—then the view opened up on one side to show a field full of grazing deer, graceful and majestic in the twilight. All too soon we were at the next gate, which led us into enclosed woodland I guessed must be some kind of timber plantation, judging from the uniformity

134

of the trees.

"Y'all right?" Adam asked, coming up behind me.

"I'm fine," I reassured him. "Don't worry," I added, remembering the magazine article. "I'm not about to bonk."

Adam grinned. "Y' sure 'bout that?"

"Well, I don't think so—but you probably know a lot more about it than I do."

"Bet y're a quick learner," he said in my ear.

For a bizarre moment, I wondered if he could possibly be flirting with me.

But that was ridiculous. As far as he knew, I was straight. When had I got so big-headed I assumed every gay guy I met wanted to get off with me? If I hadn't known he was gay, the thought wouldn't even have crossed my mind. Shaking my head at myself, I cycled on, touched by his concern for the new guy and bolstered by his certainty that I was picking things up all right.

From there we passed into another enclosure, but this one was totally different, the trail snaking through a jumble of all kinds of trees that could only have grown up naturally. Darkness seemed to fall early in the forest, and we all switched on our lights. It was while I was following Matt and trying not to let his arse distract me from the trail that I became aware of an altogether furrier rump bumbling along the trail just in front of him. It speeded up as he passed but didn't leave the track, and I passed it in my turn—then looked back to catch a glimpse of a striped black-and-white face, just before it decided it had had enough of life in the fast lane and disappeared into the bracken.

Matt had stopped to take a drink of water—at least, I assumed it was water he was carrying—just up ahead. "Did you see that?" he asked as I pulled up alongside him.

"Yes—I can't believe it! That's the first badger I've ever seen, if you don't count roadkill." I tried not to sound like a kid on his first trip to Disneyland, but I doubt I succeeded. "I suppose you see them all the time," I added.

Matt shook his head as he shoved his drink back in its holder. "Nah—we've been lucky tonight. That's only the second time I've seen one."

"Really?" I was ridiculously pleased I'd been able to share this rare moment with him. For a moment, the darkness of the forest felt like intimacy—as if we were alone here. I took a deep breath—

Then Adam emerged from the gloom and skidded to a halt beside us. "Whassup?"

Matt smiled. "Nothing, Adam. Come on, let's get moving."

The moon was high and almost full as we got back to the car park. I was tired but not exhausted, which made me strongly suspect the lads had been taking it easy tonight for my benefit.

"You enjoy it, then, your first time out?" Andy asked, proffering the now much emptier hip flask.

I waved it away with a smile. "It was great. My arse took a bit of a pounding, though, going over all those tree roots." I rubbed the area in question, wincing theatrically.

There was a warm breath on the back of my neck, and I turned to see Adam behind me. "Y'll get used to it," he said with an odd look on his face.

"Oh, yes, I'm sure I will—if you don't mind me coming back out next week," I said, my gaze sweeping the group.

There was a general chorus of *yeah, course, glad to have you, mate.* Adam leaned in again. "Y' c'n come out any time y' want."

I smiled, pleased to find all Matt's mates being so friendly.

We hung around chatting for a long while before Matt

announced he had to be off, which seemed to be the general signal to start dismantling bikes and bunging them in cars, or simply hanging them on cycle racks and driving off, as the case might be.

I watched Matt's old Ford Focus tootle off with a dull ache of regret.

Chapter Twelve

My legs were a bit stiff as I hobbled downstairs Friday morning, and I nearly tripped over the cat. "Kill me and you don't get fed," I warned him. Wolverine gave a solemn *miaow* to show he understood. Or maybe it was just feline for "Hah! Your corpse will keep me going for *weeks*."

I felt good, though. I'd been out like a light the minute I'd got into bed last night, and if I'd dreamed, my subconscious was keeping the details strictly to itself. I felt refreshed, energised and ready to face whatever the day might throw at me.

Which, of course, it promptly did, just as soon as I'd got in the shop and opened up for the day.

"Er, Tim?" Matt's voice was diffident, almost nervous. "Do you mind if I take tomorrow off? I'll make sure I've done all the repairs that are supposed to be getting picked up. It's just, I never used to work Saturdays, before, and Steve's getting a bit pissed off about it. He wants to go down to Brighton tonight, and we won't get back until really late."

"Oh—yes, of course," I said, trying not to let my disappointment show. It hadn't occurred to me that Matt might have increased his hours since Jay's accident—but of course, Jay would have done some of the repairs too, as well as all the behind-the-counter stuff. "Wouldn't want to be the cause of any domestics." Matt gave me a startled look. Great. I'd put my foot in it again. "Not that you'd—anyway, that's fine. I'll be fine."

Far from being reassured, Matt looked like he wished he'd

never asked. "Are you sure? 'Cause I could always—"

"No! No, I'll be fine. You go and have fun."

"Right." Matt looked more like I'd said "You go and lie down on that rack there, and I'll fetch the thumbscrews." "Thanks," he added unconvincingly and scuttled off out back.

I felt flatter than a deflated inner tube. Okay, so a lot of my time in the shop was spent with Matt in a different room, but he was still *there*. Tomorrow I'd be all alone. No one to talk to; no one to bring me lunch...

Damn. Quite apart from missing Matt personally, I'd got rather used to having at least one decent meal a day.

My depression lifted, however, as it suddenly occurred to me what a golden opportunity this was. With Matt being whisked away for a dirty weekend in Brighton there was absolutely zero chance of bumping into him if I decided to, let's say, investigate the gay scene this evening.

Just as an observer, obviously. I certainly wasn't planning on trying to pull. I just wanted to dip a toe into the water; that was all. Definitely not any other part of my anatomy—no matter how much it might perk up at the very idea. As a couple of customers mooched in, I was glad to be firmly behind the counter at this point.

Anyway, it was a perfect opportunity to test the waters without risking it getting back to my family—and one that might not come my way again for a while, I realised. Thank God for Russell opening my eyes to the possibilities.

Back home that evening, I switched on the computer to Google the places Matt had mentioned. I wasn't sure I could cope with cruisey, so I was about to type in El Niño—then I remembered that was apparently Luke's favourite haunt. Luke was one person I did *not* want to run into when I took my first bumbling steps towards a pinker lifestyle. Cruisey it would have to be. My heart gave a little flutter of excitement at the thought of being cruised—and yes, all right, so did my prick.

There weren't any pictures of the interior of the Cock online, just one of the outside, from which I could tell absolutely nothing. It definitely said it was a gay pub on the website, though—and even promised a drag act on Saturdays. Fortunately, today was Friday. I didn't think I was anything like ready for that level of camp just yet.

I spent the best part of an hour worrying about what to wear. Anything too tight, too sparkly, or designed to show off the nipple piercings I didn't, in fact, have was definitely out, but then neither my wardrobe nor Jay's contained anything remotely like that in any case. It still left the question of whether to dress up or down. On the whole, I decided, *down* was probably safer. I might end up looking like a straight guy who'd wandered in by mistake, but that'd be way better than having obviously made an effort and *still* got it embarrassingly wrong. So I kept the jeans and changed the shirt I'd been wearing all day for an only slightly smarter but, more to the point, fresher one.

Then I had a moment of crippling doubt—maybe the place would have a no-jeans policy? I ditched the jeans and put on some chinos. Great. Now I looked like my mother had dressed me. I sighed and changed back into the jeans. Everyone wore jeans everywhere these days, didn't they? In fact, thinking about it, I couldn't believe I'd managed so long without a pair. Wolverine padded noiselessly into the room and wound his way between my legs, the combination of weight and sheer feline bulk nearly making me do a Matt and land on my arse on the carpet. If I'd kept the chinos on, they'd have been a mess, what with all the ginger fur Wolverine was shedding, but luckily it didn't really show on denim. I decided to take this as the gods' approval of my sartorial choices.

"You'll be on your own this evening," I told Wolverine. "The can opener operator is off for a night out." He stretched and yawned, as if my presence or absence was a matter of supreme indifference to him, which it probably was. So long as I fed him before I left, at any rate.

I thought about taking the BMW, but would the parking by these places be safe? Cars were just as likely to be gay-bashed by homophobic thugs as their owners were, if *Queer as Folk* was to be believed. I squirmed at the memory of the infamous show, which Kate had been given a box set of by a friend and become inexplicably hooked on. I'd suffered agonies on the sofa beside her, trying not to show I was turned on by the naughty bits and dreading she'd notice similarities between me and the characters and guess my secret.

In any case, I was fairly certain I wouldn't make it through the door of a gay bar without a bit of good old-fashioned Dutch courage, or at least the prospect thereof. So I did a bit more Googling and found the name of a taxi firm. When the cab arrived, I cautiously gave the driver the name of a pub Google had helpfully informed me was over the road from my actual destination. "The Ship Inn, Jeffrey Street, please."

He pursed his lips in a manner I swear they must teach them in taxi driver school. "Jeffrey Street? You want to watch out around there, mate. There's one of them pansy bars—well, it's everywhere now, innit? Queers. Run the bloody country, they do. If you ask me"—not that I had, or ever would—"they'll end up making it compulsory one of these days. The only straight people left'll be the bloody rag heads, and gawd help us all when that happens."

It was refreshing to discover he was, at least, an equal opportunities bigot. Unaccountably, though, I quite forgot to tip him when we got to the Ship. He drove off, muttering, "Bloody queers" under his breath, and I looked over the road to the appropriately named Cock Inn.

It didn't look like a queer pub. It looked like a perfectly ordinary English drinking establishment. There were even fewer hanging baskets of flowers out than you'd expect.

Actually, in my admittedly limited experience, the more flowers there are, the rougher the venue tends to be. Perhaps the patrons feel the need to compensate—as if their masculinity has been impugned by all the girly stuff hanging off the place.

Maybe here, the drinkers were pretty enough the pub didn't need flowers. I smiled at the thought, still standing on the kerb like I was waiting for a bus, and a passing bruiser in motorbike leathers gave me the eye. I blushed like a girl and looked away hurriedly. Maybe I should pop into the Ship after all—just for my first drink of the night. Pushing open the heavy door, I stepped inside the pub.

The Ship Inn, which had seemed like such a safe option compared to the Cock, revealed itself to be one of those aggressively macho pubs I normally give a wide berth to. It was a dingy place with a low ceiling and a sort of spit-and-sawdust floor, only without the sawdust. It was deathly quiet, although I could have sworn I'd heard the buzz of conversation as I opened the door. It smelled of stale beer and the sour disinfectant odour you get in public toilets. As I walked in, every eye turned in my direction, and it wasn't so they could smile and bid me welcome. The clientele was exclusively male, the bar staff consisting of a bald-headed man-mountain and a hard-faced woman in a push-up bra wearing clothes that were too tight and too young for her. Also, too leopard-spotted.

There was even a grim, unshaven man propping up the bar with a pit bull at his feet, for all the world a modern-day Bill Sykes. I really hoped I was wrong as to who might be cast in the role of Nancy.

I swallowed. No way could I order a glass of wine in a place like this. It was probably a lynching offence for a bloke.

The dog growled as if in confirmation. I wasn't sure, but I thought I heard its owner growl too.

"You want the Cock—over the road, love," the barmaid said, not unkindly.

"Thank you," I squeaked in tones a three-year-old girl would be embarrassed to own, and fled. Once outside, I checked myself to make sure I still had all my limbs, and leaned against the wall, breathing hard.

Then I checked myself again. Nope, definitely no skin-tight, sparkly disco-wear or even anything remotely rainbow-hued. Did I have "poof" written on my forehead? Or had the patrons of the Ship developed a highly tuned gaydar by virtue of their close proximity to *one of them pansy bars*?

Perhaps I should acquire my own pit bull—that'd confuse them. On the other hand, Wolverine would probably eat it for breakfast.

Right. Time to stop faffing about and get in there. For one thing, there would be safety in numbers. Steeling myself, I took a deep breath and headed over the road—looking both ways first, of course, as it would be the height of irony to escape gay-bashing in the Ship only to be knocked down crossing the road.

As I approached the Cock, a couple of trendy-looking lads who looked barely old enough to drink walked past me, laughing, and disappeared inside. Feeling that if they could handle it, so could I, I pushed open the door to take my first, tentative step into the gay world.

I suppose, subconsciously, I'd expected something off *QAF*—hot, steamy and full of young blond boys with oiled pecs and shiny shorts dancing around poles, that sort of thing. This was—well, it was just an ordinary pub, really. It had ye olde oak beams on the ceiling, a polished wood bar with some nice carved bits, and behind it, all the colourful drinks you could think of and a couple of hundred more besides. Blokes sat at tables, drinking and chatting; others propped up the bar. There were women, too, and not the sort I'd have picked out on the street as lesbians—they had long hair, some of them, and were wearing makeup and nice clothes. One of them even had a skirt on. Everyone looked, well, *normal.*

Just as I was wondering if I'd taken a wrong turning and somehow ended up in a completely different pub than the one I'd been aiming for, I felt a touch on my arm and looked around to see the bruiser in the leathers from outside. He was smiling at me, showing a gold tooth that toned in quite nicely with its nicotine-stained brethren. "'Ullo, 'andsome," he said gruffly. "Buy you a drink?"

I panicked. "Thanks, but...I'm meeting someone. At the bar. Got to go." Flashing him an apologetic and somewhat guilty smile, I scuttled away and started trying to elbow my way into the suddenly dense crowd around the bar. Some of them elbowed back. A frisson ran through me at the thought of being surrounded by—in physical contact with, even—so many gay men. Men who had sex with other men. Men who might even want to have sex with me... Oh, God. Suddenly I needed a drink more than ever.

Eventually I managed to find a square inch of bar that wasn't already occupied. I leant on it, feeling a little flushed, and tried vainly to make eye contact with one of the barmen. I realised I was standing next to a stocky young man with a mop of orange hair that looked worryingly familiar.

The owner of the hair turned to see who was crowding him, and my stomach lurched.

Oh, God. It was Adam.

He gave me a slow smile and a long look up and down, although as we were literally hip-to-hip he couldn't have seen much of me below the chest. "W'nna dr'nk?" Actually it came out even less clear than that, but he helpfully made drinking-up gestures with his hand so I got the picture.

I thought about saying no, I'm fine—but I was leaning over the bar with my wallet in my hand. *Obviously* I wanted a drink. "Er, yes, thanks. White wine."

Apparently effortlessly attracting the attention of a large, tattooed barman with a squeaky voice, Adam bought me a large one. He held up both hands to ward off the fiver I waved in his direction. "'S all right. Come 'n' sit down?"

I took a large swallow of my Pinot Grigio, coughed a bit and followed him like I was marching to my own funeral. What the hell was I going to say to him? If he told Matt he'd seen me here, Matt would tell Jay—and more to the point, Matt would *know*. He'd think I was such a hypocrite—for God's sake, I'd more or less told him the day we met I didn't mind him being gay. As if I was doing him a favour by generously offering not to behave in an overtly bigoted manner.

And God, what if Jay told Mum...? No, he wouldn't do that. Would he? Oh, God. Why the hell did I ever come here? I took another hefty swig of wine.

Adam led me right through the pub and out the back door to a beer garden I hadn't realised existed. It was small and squarish, with high fences and a pergola to disguise the fact it was in the middle of the city. Trailing plants I strongly suspected were artificial hung from the wooden beams, sharing their space with fairy lights. I hoped the irony was intentional. Most of the tables were full, but Adam found one unoccupied in the darkest corner of the place, which suited me. I sat down on the wooden bench. Adam sat opposite me and grinned. "C'mere of'n?"

"No, actually, I've never been here before..." Would he believe me if I said I'd just wandered in by mistake? I took another mouthful of wine to buy some time. My glass was already two-thirds empty, and I was starting to wish I hadn't been too keyed up to eat anything before I came out.

"Saw you lookin' at Matt's arse."

I nearly choked on my wine. That'd probably be a no, then. God, had I really been that obvious? "I'm not—I mean, I was married. To a woman." I gulped down some more of France's finest, hoping it'd either show me some way out of here or kill me quickly.

"Arr." Adam nodded, as if I'd just told him my life story. Then he grinned again and stood up. "C'mere."

"Where?" I yelped.

"'Ere." He beckoned me to him. Hypnotised by his smile— and more to the point, too nervous to let him go off without me—I followed. We ended up in a dark corner around the side of the pub, next to a couple of metal barrels and a passed-out drunk who was snoring gently. "C'mere," Adam said again.

A soft grunting noise caught my attention, and a shape in the shadows resolved itself into two gentlemen getting to know each other rather intimately. I suddenly realised why he'd brought me out here. "I don't think—"

He grabbed me. Where I still had my wineglass in one hand, Pinot Grigiot sloshed over my arm—and possibly the drunk—as I struggled in vain against Adam's lecherous grasp. "I'm not—"

"Yeah, y'are." Adam planted a sloppy, beer-flavoured kiss on my lips, and as his stubble rasped against my skin, I finally admitted to myself that yes, I really was. And maybe he wasn't who I really wanted, but oh, God, he tasted good and his body felt amazing against mine. My arms seemed to be working of their own volition as they wrapped around him and pressed him closer to me—I could only hope the level in my wineglass was low enough by now I wasn't soaking his back. Adam's erection ground into my hip, and God, that wasn't where I wanted it, not at all. My back was solidly against the wall of the pub, but I managed to shift position until our cocks were pressing against one another through our clothes. "Arr, 's right," Adam murmured in my ear before sucking the lobe into his mouth.

Were ears supposed to feel this good? Why hadn't Kate ever—ah—God... I let out an inhuman sound as I felt Adam undoing my flies. And then his hand was on my cock and oh, God...

I was panting like I'd run a marathon and oh, God it felt good. But then he stopped and backed away. "W-what?" I managed.

"Just wait," Adam said enigmatically—and then he dropped to his knees.

Logically, I knew what he must be about to do. But some part of my brain just refused to let the rest of me believe it until it happened, until his mouth opened wide and swallowed me down, and mortifyingly, I came immediately, so hard it was almost painful. Adam just carried on swallowing, as I convulsed and panted and wanted to die.

"God, I'm so sorry..." I gasped out. "I should have—" I should have bloody stayed at home, that's what I should have done.

"'S all right," Adam said, wiping his mouth and smiling up at me. Then he stood. Oh, God—did he expect me to return the favour? I realised I was still holding my wineglass, and miraculously, there was still some in there, so I drank it down in one. Then I wondered if I should have saved some to wash the taste away. Now I was no longer blinded by lust, I so, so didn't want to do this. Another man's penis? In my *mouth*?

Of course, if it'd been Matt's... My treacherous dick gave a feeble twitch, too sated to do more.

I didn't resist as Adam pressed in close and put an arm around my neck, then pulled my hand down to his crotch—and when I realised what he was after, my relief made me respond with a pretty good imitation of enthusiasm. A hand job—I could do that. It wasn't like I hadn't had plenty of practice, although it was weird doing it without being able to feel the results. Adam's cock was thick but short, and I pumped it up and down with gusto. He seemed to appreciate it, judging by the incoherent sounds and the way the veins corded in his neck.

He threw his head right back, and I realised what was about to happen just a fraction of a second too late, as Adam's jizz spurted out all over my shirt and trousers. Were these trousers washable? Yes, yes, they were, so that was all right. Like a drowning man, I clung on to the one positive thing I could think of about this little encounter.

"Sorry 'bout the mess," Adam mumbled through his cheesy grin. He groped in the pocket of his baggy shorts and brought out a grubby handkerchief, which, despite my protestations, he used to wipe me down. He clapped me on the shoulder. "Y'r all right."

Adam was wrong. I wasn't all right. I felt sordid—soiled in more ways than one. This wasn't at all how I'd imagined my first time with a man—or if I had, my fantasies had never ended with me feeling like this. "I've got to go," I said desperately, tearing myself out of his grasp. Damn it, I'd need to call a taxi. I wished I'd brought my car so I could get away from here right now. Plus, if I'd driven, I wouldn't have been drinking, and then I'd never have got into this mess.

Possibly.

I realised Adam was loping along beside me. "What?" I snapped.

148

"Wanna lift?"

"No." I strode to the front of the pub, where a few drinkers had milled out around the door, smoking and laughing. Scrabbling for my phone, I desperately tried to remember the cab firm's number or how to find an alternative. There was a number, wasn't there? Or an app or something, and why the bloody *hell* hadn't I got it sorted before I'd come out?

A hand gripped my arm. "C'mon. 'S just over there."

I gave up and let him steer me toward a shiny red Ford Mondeo parked down a side street. My sense of unreality deepened—this was what Adam drove? "'S my mum's," he explained helpfully.

I sat in silence as he drove me home. Adam turned on the CD player, and we listened to Jessie J exhorting her sisters to "Do it like a Dude." I could have told her that based on my experience, it'd be unlikely to end well. Adam didn't seem to need directions, and a horrible suspicion planted itself in my mind. "Have you and Jay ever...?" I asked, beyond embarrassment by now.

Adam almost doubled up with laughter, which didn't make me feel any safer since he was still driving. "Jay? *Jay?*" He sobered up eventually in the face of my continued refusal to see the funny side. "Nah. 'S straight." He was still chuckling silently as we pulled up outside Jay's house.

I hoped he wouldn't expect an invitation in for coffee, either euphemistically or otherwise. "Thanks for the lift," I said politely, like he hadn't just sucked me off in a pub garden.

"'S all right. See y'round."

Never had the clichéd response, "Not if I see you first!" seemed more appropriate. Not trusting myself to speak, I just nodded, got out of the car and scurried down the path to let myself in the house.

Wolverine was waiting for me. "It's all right for you," I muttered, heading on autopilot for the can opener. "You probably had the snip before you'd even worked out what your willy was for. Take it from me, you're not missing much." As my mind flashed back to Adam's blowjob, my dick jumped up to call me a liar.

"And don't think *you're* getting anything from me after the way you behaved tonight," I told it sternly.

Wolverine *miaowed* indignantly.

I sighed and forked the tuna into his bowl. I should probably have explained I wasn't talking to him, but somehow, I just couldn't find the strength.

Chapter Thirteen

I spent a restless night plagued with excruciating dreams of Adam sucking me off in front of Matt, Jay and my mother. Matt and Jay weren't paying much attention, being too busy excavating each other's tonsils with their tongues, but Mum was staring with folded arms and narrowed eyes, occasionally muttering, "Oh, for heaven's sake, Timothy—show a little enthusiasm!"

Not surprisingly, I woke up headachey, exhausted, and limper than a piece of spaghetti that'd been boiled for a week. Wolverine wasn't on the bed—I supposed all the tossing and turning had been too much for him. I briefly considered taking the day off sick—but I couldn't do that to Jay. Or the customers, come to that—there were at least three people booked to come in and collect repaired bikes today.

It made me realise how cocooned from reality I'd been, in some ways, working for a large firm. Able to take a sickie any time I wanted to, confident there would be other people there able to take up the slack. If Jay—or I, as his stand-in—took a day off, that was a day's sales gone and a dent in the customer goodwill. I was doubly impressed with the way he'd managed to stick it out, with only a day and a half off a week.

I dragged myself in to the shop and spent the morning practising fake smiles for the benefit of the endless stream of customers. Just after lunchtime, the door jangled—and admitted a welcome sight. "Matt!" I could feel my smile splitting my face. "Thought you were taking the day off—shouldn't you be down in Brighton?"

Matt shrugged, grinning back at me. "Nah, we came back last night—well, you know, once the clubs shut. Steve's gone to test drive a new car, so I thought I might as well come in and see how you were getting on."

"Fine, really—but it's great to see you." I realised I was being a bit over-the-top, and tried to tone it down. Thankfully, Matt didn't seem to have noticed.

"Had many new repairs in?"

"Four or five. I tried to be conservative on timescale, seeing as I couldn't really tell what needed fixing." I passed Matt the repairs book, and he gave it a quick scan.

"Looks all right to me—long as the ones in for a service don't need anything major doing, we'll be fine." He smiled as he passed it back, and my heart felt a little lift.

"Are you staying?" I asked.

"Yeah, why not? Might as well make a start on some of these." He didn't head off out back immediately, though. "Did you do anything much last night?"

"No. I, er, stayed in. Watched TV. Something boring, can't remember what it was. Er. Why don't I show you where I put the bikes that came in?" God, why did I have to turn into a babbling idiot every time I tried to tell a lie? I was probably beetroot red as well. And Christ, how had I managed to forget Adam was Matt's best mate? For all I knew, Adam had rung him straight up after our little encounter to give him a blow-by-blow account. So to speak.

It wasn't like it'd have taken him all that long, given my embarrassing performance.

I marched into the back room, avoiding Matt's gaze as if it had the power to turn me to stone, so I couldn't tell if he was giving me a funny look or not. "Here they are—I've labelled them, so let me know if you have any trouble working out which one's which."

Still looking anywhere but at Matt, I hurried back to hide behind the till.

By six o'clock, I'd just about regained my composure. Matt hadn't said any more about last night, or Adam, and he hadn't been acting strangely around me either, so it seemed Adam wasn't the sort to kiss and tell. Not that there had been an awful lot of kissing involved, but *suck and tell* just sounded so, so wrong.

Matt had finished up and emerged from the back room, and I was just about to close up for the night when the bell jangled again. Sighing, I looked round—and froze.

It was Adam.

He loped in casually, hands swinging by his ankles. "'Lo, Matt. All right, Tim?"

I froze behind the counter. What the hell was I going to say to him? Especially with Matt here.

It turned out I didn't have to say anything. To my utmost, cringing horror, Adam casually sauntered on up to the counter, sidled through the gap and, slinging one arm around my neck, pressed a sloppy, chewing-gum-flavoured kiss to my paralysed lips. I was too stunned to even react. As my panicked gaze darted over to Matt, I saw he had the same problem.

"Great night, warn't it?" Adam must have caught sight of Matt's eyes, which were currently rivalling the twenty-nine-inch wheels on the bike he was holding onto, possibly for support. "Got together with Tim at the Cock. He's all right." Having in two short sentences both outed me and damned me with faint praise, he turned back to speak to me. "Wanna go out for a curry?"

"I…" I couldn't speak. All I could do was look at Matt's soft brown eyes, desperate for some sign he didn't think I was an utter wanker. In vain, as he was currently looking at me as if I'd just stripped stark bollock naked and announced my intention to enter for the world puppy-kicking championships.

Then he gave his head an almost imperceptible shake. "That's great. That you've, um, got together. Look, I'd better go. Steve'll be wondering where I am. You have a good time tonight." He hurtled out of the shop, no doubt anxious to get back to the oh-so-perfect Steve.

My stomach twisted at the thought—but I was glad, after a moment, that he'd mentioned Steve. It helped me remember what was going on here. No matter how much I might want him, Matt wasn't mine and in all likelihood never would be. After all, even if Steve fell under a bus tomorrow, would Matt really want to get together with a bloke who'd lied to him? Lied about his night out, about his sexuality—God, Matt probably doubted everything I'd ever told him right now.

I turned to Adam, who was still smiling away obliviously. He wasn't all that bad-looking, really, if you didn't mind freckles and a rather un-evolved appearance. And he was a decent sort of bloke. Plus, although I'd only had a pitifully short time to base my judgment on, he seemed pretty good at sucking cock. My trousers tightened at the thought. I could do a lot worse for my first tentative foray into the world of man-loving.

"Curry sounds great," I said.

I had second, third and fourth thoughts about my date with Adam as I got ready to go out. Did I really want to do this? *Yes*, a certain part of my anatomy told me firmly.

Was I really being fair to Adam? I might like what he did

with his tongue; I might even like him as a friend. But even my overenthusiastic prick couldn't convince me I had any kind of romantic feelings for him. Wouldn't the honourable thing to do be to get out now, before any feelings might develop on his part?

Then again, what if that had already happened? Wouldn't it be worse, in that case, to cancel? Maybe I should go out with him after all. I could let him down gently then. My prick thought that was an excellent idea. *Before* any blowjobs happened, I reminded myself sternly. The burgeoning tent in my boxer briefs deflated like a leftover party balloon.

Then again, who was to say I mightn't feel more for Adam when I got to know him better? I should give him a chance. My prick nodded its agreement.

I wasn't going to bother dressing up particularly—after all, this was Adam we were talking about; his idea of dressing up probably involved a T-shirt that wouldn't show the curry stains. Actually, thinking about it, that wasn't a bad idea. The state my nerves were in, I'd probably spill more than I ate. I quickly changed into a wine-red, tailored shirt I'd bought after seeing *Sherlock* on TV. I hadn't worn it much; people always seemed to stare when I did, and I'd got the impression Kate hadn't liked it much. But Adam, I was fairly sure, wouldn't even notice.

I checked my reflection; hmm. The shirt fit snugly, emphasizing just how skinny I was, and made me look almost vampirically pale. The black jeans completed the picture. It was the closest I'd ever come to flirting with the goth look I'd yearned for, back in the youth I'd lacked the courage to misspend. I was fairly sure I'd passed the point of being able to carry it off now. Still, the ensemble would definitely hide any embarrassing mishaps with the tikka masala. I nodded at myself, gave my darkening chin a quick rub, decided Adam wouldn't give a toss if I shaved or not, and headed downstairs just as the doorbell rang to announce the arrival of my escort for the night.

When I opened the door, Adam just stood there and stared at me for a moment. He was, as predicted, as scruffy as ever in baggy three-quarter-length cargo pants and a faded T-shirt that read, bizarrely, "Archaeologists do it in ditches". Bugger. Was I hideously overdressed?

"Um," I said by way of greeting. "Should I go and change? Have a shave?"

Adam shook his head slowly. "Nuh-uh. *Nuh-uh.* Y're perfect."

I was? "Er, thanks. Do you want to come in? Or shall we head straight off?"

Adam looked torn. Clearly worried by his show of indecision, my stomach rumbled loudly. Adam laughed. "All right. Food first."

The curry was pretty good, as it happened. Adam was quite a fun companion, with plenty of stories about mountain biking mishaps told with his customary economy of words, not to mention vowels, but helpfully illustrated with an impressive collection of scars. Some of them I was amazed he got away with showing me in a public place. Subtitles would have been useful, no question about it, but we seemed to get along just fine.

It was ironic, though—my first ever date with a man, and it felt *exactly* like going for a meal with a mate. I mean, I'd never have taken a woman to this place—it was far too laddish for a date with a girl. But for Adam, it seemed just right. There was no holding hands across the table—I guessed neither of us fancied getting our heads kicked in by the lagered-up rugby players celebrating today's win with a vindaloo and the makings of a killer hangover—and no gazing soulfully into each others' eyes. We just talked, ate and laughed.

Actually, we talked quite a lot about Matt. I got to hear Adam's opinion of the school they both went to back in Somerset ("'S shite"); Matt's mum, who'd died a year or so after they'd started there ("Lovely"); Matt's step-dad ("'S a bastard") and Matt himself ("'S all right"). Hearing that made me feel a bit better about having been described the same way—apparently it was Adam's all-purpose seal of approval.

"Do you know Matt's, um, boyfriend well?" I asked casually.

Not casually enough, apparently, as Adam gave me a knowing smile. Actually, it was more of a leer, but on Adam, the two expressions weren't all that far removed from one another, anyway. Then his face seemed to close off, and he leaned back in his chair and took a long swig of his lager (alcohol-free, since he was driving). "'S not out."

I frowned. "Not out? But I thought they were living together?"

Adam snorted a laugh. "Says Matt's the lodger, anyone asks. Or if they don't. Even charges him rent, the bastard."

At least I seemed to be getting better at speaking Adam. His words were almost totally comprehensible now. "Is Matt all right with that?" I asked. "The hiding, I mean, not the rent." I had to admit, a small part of me—no, not *that* part—could see the advantages. No problems with family, friends and colleagues. Having your cake and eating it.

But it left a sour taste in my mouth, and not just because it was Matt we were talking about rather than a bit of sugar-covered bakery produce. Was that hypocritical of me, given the lie I'd been enthusiastically living all these years?

Adam just shrugged and took another helping of chicken

madras. "Told him to leave the bastard. Won't."

That was depressing. If Matt was prepared to be Steve's dirty little secret even against the advice of one of his best friends, he must really care for him. Love him, even.

I decided I'd better change the subject before I ended up sniffling into my Shiraz. "So, um, do you work?"

"Nah."

Quelle surprise. After all, he was in his mid-twenties and still living in his mum's house, driving his mum's car...

"Studying."

Okay, that was a surprise. I glanced at the front of his T-shirt. "Archaeology, by any chance?"

"Yuh. PhD."

That was definitely a surprise. I scrabbled for something to say apart from an inane remark on how *interesting* that must be. "Er, do you do a lot of digs?"

Adam's eyes lit up, and he pulled out his phone to show me a variety of snaps in various shades of mud. Adam, in a ditch; Adam, standing looking into a ditch. Adam with a skull, presumably ancient and not, say, from his latest acid-bath victim. Adam proudly holding something that was probably a priceless historical artifact but which, to my untrained eyes, just looked like a bit of mud. Adam, with his cock out—*what?*

He grinned sheepishly and turned the phone off. "Din't mean to show you that one," he said, but the way he was looking at me out of the corner of his eye made me wonder just how much of an accident it had been. "You done there?"

I collected my scrambled wits. "Oh—yes, I'm stuffed. You?"

Adam nodded. "C'mon, then. Let's go back to yours." There was a suggestive look in his eye, and I realised now was the time to say something like, "I think we should just be friends," if I was ever going to say it.

I bottled it. Well, there was something about the rough voice and the roguish smile and all right, that last photo that had me thinking, maybe... But basically, I bottled it. Aided and abetted by my treacherous cock. "Okay," I said, my voice suddenly hoarse.

As we sped through the dark lanes in Adam's mum's Mondeo, my mind was a confusing maelstrom of guilt and lust. "Late, isn't it?" I said nervously. "I don't know where the time went."

"'S aright. No work tomorrow."

"Still, lots of things to get done... I never realised how much time keeping a shop takes up." Guilt was winning for the moment.

"Y' gotta have a day off, every now'n'then."

"True, true."

"Enjoy y'self while you're young."

He thought I was young? I was definitely warming to Adam. "Would you, er, like to come in for a coffee or something?" I asked. Guilt threw up its hands in despair and headed off home for an early night.

Adam gave an enthusiastic grunt and reached over to give my thigh a squeeze, presumably to indicate he was more interested in the *something* than in the coffee. I swallowed, suddenly feeling coffee was entirely overrated as a beverage.

As we got out of the car I managed to spare a thought for any neighbours of Jay's who might be watching, and fended off Adam's grabby hands halfheartedly. "Inside," I muttered, my mouth dry with lust. We fell in the front door, and then he was on me, pinning me to the wall with his body, his hard cock doing its best to drill a hole in my thigh. "Oh, God," I gasped, my own prick doing an impressive impersonation of a red-hot iron bar. I humped against him helplessly.

Probably sensing I was about to embarrass myself copiously, Adam backed off a little. "'S a great shirt," he said, running his hands up and down the front. I could feel his calluses through the fabric and hoped distractedly he wouldn't snag the threads. My nipples, however, revelled in the contact, trying to poke right through the material and feel the touch of his warm flesh directly. I opened my mouth to say something, but he beat me to it, sealing my lips with one of his trademark messy kisses. Adam's tongue invaded my mouth as his hands made a recce over my arse, mapping the territory with his clutching fingers.

"Sofa. This way," I blurted when he came up for air. I had a feeling my knees were way too weak to manage the stairs right now. Also, as Wolverine was nowhere to be seen, chances were he'd already claimed the bed. Grabbing Adam's hand, I pulled him into the darkness of the living room. We reached the sofa, and I toppled over onto it with him on top of me. Pushing Adam's T-shirt up, I ran my hands over his broad, strong back. With my eyes shut, I could almost imagine it was Matt I was groping, although he smelt all wrong—earth and coriander, not cinnamon and sunshine...

This was so, so wrong. *Adam*, I told myself firmly. I was with Adam, not Matt.

And when had I noticed how Matt smelled, anyhow?

Adam wriggled around on the sofa until he was lying beside me, not on top of me anymore. I'd have questioned the wisdom of this, but it all became clear when he unzipped my jeans with a practised hand and grabbed me through my underwear.

"God!" I nearly hit the ceiling. "Don't stop!" I added as he promptly did so, probably fearing a repeat of last night's zero-to-orgasm in nought point three seconds.

He muttered something wholly unintelligible and pulled off my shoes. Did Adam have some kind of a foot fetish? Ah, no—

he'd just wanted to get my jeans and underwear off. Very sensible, I thought fuzzily as he swung a leg over my now naked thighs to straddle me, kneeling.

Adam unbuttoned my shirt with infinite care. I struggled up to a sitting position so I could get it off, but he pushed me down again. "Leave it on," he said gruffly.

Okay, so he had a fetish for Sherlock shirts. I could understand that. I lay back down again, wondering vaguely how he'd look in a stripy sweater. Scruffy, I decided, but also cuddly. Matt, on the other hand, would look absolutely adorable... And oh, God, Adam's teeth were biting at my nipple. My hands didn't seem to belong to me any more—they were roaming independently over Adam's shoulders, Adam's hair, and any other bits of Adam they could reach. My cock, meanwhile, was rutting helplessly into Adam's stomach.

It was all so intense it was vaguely terrifying.

"Y' like that?" Adam asked, pulling off my swollen nipple and climbing off to one side of me. "Roll over."

I stared at him for a moment, then did as I was asked. Adam grabbed my hips and pulled at them, and I ended up on all fours. "Put y'r head on the cushion."

It felt vaguely like I was doing some kind of X-rated yoga, all these different positions, but in this matter, at least, I trusted Adam. Even though I felt a bit ridiculous with my arse in the air like that. Were any grey hairs showing? I hoped not.

"Y'r gonna love this," Adam said. And oh, God, I could feel his hot breath on my arse. He grabbed a buttock in each large hand, pulled them apart, and bloody hell, his tongue was running up and down my crack. I made a sound I would have sworn up until then was humanly impossible, a cross between a wolf howling and fingernails on a blackboard. His teeth nipped at my arse cheeks, and then that serpentine tongue of his stabbed at my entrance, prodding and teasing. My legs were trembling so much I thought any moment now I'd collapse into a twitching heap.

The tongue action stopped. "Wanna fuck you. That all right?"

There was a reason we shouldn't do this. I was almost positive there was. But for the life of me, I couldn't, right now, recall what it was. "All right," I agreed dreamily. I heard ripping sounds behind me; the snap of a condom; then felt the cool drizzle of something oily down my crack.

Adam's blunt cockhead pressed against my arsehole, and instinctively I pushed back, trying to draw him inside me. For a moment, I thought I was succeeding—then he gave a strangled cry and the pressure was gone in a waft of cold air on my arse. I twisted to look over my shoulder. "Adam? Are you—oh, bloody hell. Bad cat! *Bad cat!*"

Adam's face was twisted in pain and consternation, and there was a cat hanging off his back. By its claws. Thin trickles of blood had already formed beneath them. I scrambled over, grabbed Wolverine around his hefty, furry middle and hoiked him away. Adam bellowed as the claws tore through his skin one last time.

"Adam? Adam! Are you okay? God, I can't believe he did that! Bad cat!" I scolded my furry burden before dumping him on the floor none too gently. Adam was moaning softly, blood now dripping onto the carpet from his lacerated back. "God, let's get these cleaned up. Are you going to need a tetanus jab?"

His eyes still screwed up, Adam shook his head and grunted something indecipherable. I took it to mean he'd had one recently. I ran into the kitchen, my now thoroughly limp cock dangling sadly between my legs, and ransacked the cupboards for the first aid kit I was sure I'd seen there a few days ago. "Where the bloody hell—got you!"

162

Several handfuls of antiseptic wipes later, it was quite clear the mood had irredeemably altered. Wolverine was curled up on the computer keyboard looking smug, and Adam kept casting him anxious glances. He'd also put his trousers back on. I could hardly blame him—I wouldn't want my delicate bits dangling in front of a cat with maiming on his mind either.

To tell the truth, I wasn't sure if I was relieved or sorry. Both, really. Although part of me was glad I hadn't popped my gay cherry with a bloke I knew I didn't love, another part of me was banging the walls and shouting in frustration, *We were so bloody close!*

Or had I popped my cherry? I wasn't sure how it worked for gay sex. Okay, so there hadn't been any penetration—not by Adam's cock, anyway—but did that really work as a definition of actual sex? Because if so, did that mean lesbians were lifelong virgins? I didn't actually know any lesbians, but I was fairly sure they'd be none too happy at the idea of their sexually active status being dependent on a bloke's bits.

"I'm so sorry about that," I told Adam for the umpteenth time as I pulled on my own trousers. "I don't know what would make him attack you like that—unless maybe he thought you were some kind of rival encroaching on his territory?"

Adam looked incredulous. "What—y'r arse?"

Given that Wolverine had been sleeping in my bed, that was the sort of image of which nightmares are made. "The house, as if you didn't know. Look, I'm really sorry."

He shrugged. "'S all right. Guess I'll be off, then."

"Uh, yes. Sorry."

He left, and as I closed the door behind him, Wolverine came to wind his way between my legs, acting as if butter wouldn't melt in his stinky, befanged mouth. "I ought to kick you out after that shocking display of *cattus interruptus*," I muttered. Then I bent down to stroke him. "What was that all about, anyway? Determined to be the only ginger in the village?"

Wolverine just yawned and batted his head against my legs until I headed up to bed.

Chapter Fourteen

I woke up so late on Sunday morning it barely still qualified as such. My head ached, and the fact I'd been outed in front of Matt—which I'd conveniently managed to forget while blinded by lust last night—came back to haunt me like the ghost of an all-nighter on Russian vodka. He must think I was a coward, a hypocrite—

I sat bolt upright as self-loathing was booted out of play by abject terror. It might not just be Matt I had to worry about. God, what if he'd gone to see Jay last night—or this morning? What if he'd told him the whole story?

I should have asked Matt not to say anything. Bloody hell, I should have got down on my knees and *begged* him not to. So much for my risk-free experiment. Even now, a hysterical Mum was probably being restrained by teams of bulky male nurses...

Usually when I fantasized about bulky male nurses, Mum was nowhere in sight, and a bloody good thing too.

I scrambled out of bed and pulled on the jeans I'd been wearing last night. My first instinct was to dash down to the hospital and find out if my worst fears had been realised—but then what? Either Matt had done it, or he hadn't, and either way, I wouldn't be able to do a thing about it. There was an outside chance, I supposed, of me getting there in the nick of time to stop him blurting it all out, but I had a feeling that bursting into the room waving my arms and shouting, "Don't tell him, Matt!" probably wasn't the best way to keep a secret.

I had Matt's email address, so I supposed I could send him

a message—but God, trying to explain to him why I didn't want anyone to know about my inclinations would be tough enough in person. I really didn't want to attempt it by email, where I'd probably come off like a total prick no matter how many ROFLs and smileys I used.

It was slightly worrying to realise I cared more about Matt's good opinion than about my family's. Doubly so, as there was a good chance Matt's opinion of me was tarnished beyond recovery in any case.

So. No dash to the hospital, then. I looked at my watch. There was barely time to make it to karate, and I seriously considered missing training—but sitting at home worrying wasn't going to do me any good. Better to go and improve my fighting techniques, ready for the first gay-bashing.

Not that I was being unduly pessimistic about the whole bloody mess, of course.

I got there just as the warm-up was starting. Sensei mimed tapping a non-existent watch as I got into line next to John, so when we got onto basics, I was extra conscientious about doing the techniques correctly. It helped take my mind off things, anyway.

"Good night, last night, was it?" John murmured as we waited for the next command.

My stomach lurched—and then I realised, feeling like an idiot, that he'd only been referring to my lateness. "Bit mixed, really," I told him truthfully.

"Oh? I'd been hoping that one of us, at least, had got lucky."

"Luck takes one look at me and runs for the hills," I muttered, just before Sensei bellowed at us again.

I certainly hadn't been lucky enough to have Pritchard miss the class again. He glowered at me from a few places down the line. Not feeling in the mood for a confrontation, when we split into pairs for *kumite* I made sure I grabbed John and dragged him over to the other side of the dojo where we could practice our set attacks and retaliations in peace.

Trouble was, we were told to change partners several times, and each swap seemed to bring me closer and closer to Pritchard. We were almost side-by-side—and then Sensei bellowed at us to get back in line. Breathing a sigh of relief, I turned to head back—only to find myself sprawling to the floor as something took my foot out from under me.

I was pretty certain that *something* had been Pritchard's outstretched foot.

I fell awkwardly and landed heavily, throwing out my right arm to try to break my fall. It mainly succeeded in jarring my shoulder, and I winced at the pain.

"Are you all right?" John asked, reaching down a hand. I took it with my left, and he pulled me up easily.

"You wanna watch where you're going," Prick-tard muttered at me, looking as if he'd have liked nothing better than to give me a good kicking while I was down.

"Are you all right, Mr. Knight?" Sensei bounded over with a look of concern.

"I'm fine," I said through teeth I was trying very hard not to grit. "Just tripped. Not sure what over, though," I added with a look over at Prick-tard that was so pointed it could have etched glass.

Sensei must have seen me glaring but decided not to pursue the matter. Maybe he thought it best to just let things blow over. Or maybe he realised I'd have been a bit more direct in accusing Pritchard if I'd actually had any evidence—even that of my own eyes—that he'd deliberately tripped me.

"What on earth has Pit-bull got against you?" John

murmured in my ear as we got back into line. "Did you sleep with his girlfriend or something?"

Pit-bull Pritchard with a girlfriend... Now that was a scary thought. I wondered what she'd be like. Brash and common? No—someone like that might be tempted to argue with him, and I didn't reckon Prick-tard would go for that at all. No, she was probably small, mousey and timid, too terrified to have an opinion of her own in case Prick-tard disagreed. "Well, he knows about the bike shop. Maybe Jay once sold him a dodgy pump adaptor?"

When the session finished, I made sure I kept an eye on Pritchard in case he was tempted to go for the double. He made do with glaring at me, and I managed to get home without getting into a fight.

I had a quick shower and some beans on toast, feeling positively virtuous at the moderately healthy meal. And I hadn't used the microwave at all.

Then I forced myself to go and visit Jay. Whatever happened, at least I'd know where I stood. For now, at least.

"Hi!" I said brightly, bounding into Jay's room, nervous excitement giving me wings no energy drink could match. "How are you? Feeling any better today?"

Jay looked up from the mountain bike magazine he was leafing through. "I'm all right. You look like you've had a bit too much caffeine, though. Either that or you've been nicking my drugs."

"I'm fine!" I said a bit too loudly. "Um. Have you seen Matt?" I mentally crossed my fingers. Surely if Matt had been in to spill the beans, Jay would have mentioned it straight away?

"Yeah—he came in last night." Jay grinned. "Bit of an

interesting visit."

Oh, bugger. "Really?" I squawked.

"You got a sore throat or something? Yeah, he had to wait until Mum went home, though." Jay laughed. "He told me all about you—I can't believe it!"

I swallowed. "Um..."

"Showing this kind of stuff to kids! You can get in trouble for that, you know!" He turned the bike mag around to show me the magazine he'd concealed inside, and with a sense of relief so profound I nearly collapsed under the force of it, I recognised Samantha, age twenty-three, who apparently liked dancing and looking after the elderly. Although hopefully with a few more clothes on than she was wearing in this particular picture.

"Oh, that!" I froze, hoping I hadn't given myself away, then realised standing there gaping like a dead fish wasn't exactly going to allay suspicion. "That was entirely unintentional!" I finished hurriedly.

"Should bloody well hope so! Now, how's the shop going? Really—I mean, takings and stuff."

Pleased to get back to my area of expertise, I gave him a quick run-down, making it even quicker when I realised his eyes were starting to glaze over. "So in summary, takings are up on the last few weeks, but I assume that's just seasonal. Oh, and I signed you up to a local business directory, and I've been thinking about promotions—there's no reason why we can't spread the servicing work out over the year a bit more, and it'd be good to attract some new customers..." I noticed Jay wasn't exactly looking overjoyed. "What? I thought you'd be pleased I wasn't running the business into the ground."

"Yeah, but..." Jay waved at Frankenstein's leg. "Just feeling a bit useless, that's all."

"Don't worry," I said with false heartiness. "You'll be back on your feet in no time."

Jay brightened a bit. "Have been already, actually, although they told me I won't be able to go home for a while yet." He grinned. "Although I reckon it might be just the hospital trying to get as much money as they can out of the insurers."

"Well, if your doctors are telling you to stay in hospital, I think you should listen to them," I said piously, mentally crossing my fingers Jay wouldn't realise there was an element of self-interest there. "So how did the walking go, anyway?"

"Oh, you know. Stiff, painful—but it was good to get off the bloody bed for a bit."

I gave him a look. "Never thought I'd see you desperate to get out of bed. Usually it's the other way around."

"Tell you what, I'm getting desperate for a bit of that too. Olivia couldn't make it in to see me yesterday."

"Are you telling me you and Olivia have been...here? In the hospital? With your leg like that?" I boggled. "Didn't it, well, hurt? Come to that, is it even possible with all that scaffolding screwed on?"

Jay leered. "Trust me, Olivia's a very inventive girl."

Maybe my mental image of her as the Ice Maiden was a lot further from the truth than I'd thought.

Chapter Fifteen

Monday morning, the coffee in my stomach felt like cement in a mixer as I waited for Matt to turn up to work. God, what was I going to say to him now he knew I'd lied to him—by omission, even if not directly—about my sexuality?

How would Jay handle a situation like this? Simple: he wouldn't get into this situation in the first place. But if he did... I tried to imagine what he'd say: "Oh, Matt? Thought I'd try being a poof for a bit. See how it goes. Yeah, bit of a snap decision. Your mate Adam's a right goer, isn't he? I'm well in there. Right, back to work..."

There was no way on this earth I could say anything like that to Matt—

The door jangled, and Matt stepped through, managing to stay upright this time. He gave me a wary look, and my butterfly-filled intestines tied themselves in guilty knots, no doubt breaking a fair few wings in the process. I took a deep breath. "Matt... I'm really sorry," I said awkwardly.

"What?" Matt frowned, walking towards me. "What for?"

"For, well, lying to you. Saying I hadn't gone out when I obviously had. And, um, the other stuff."

The slight creases on his brow smoothed away instantly. "Hey, it's all right. I get it—you're not out. It's not a problem. And don't worry—I won't say a word to anyone. 'Specially Jay, if you don't want me to." He stared at me earnestly, and I felt ashamed of myself—firstly for lying, and secondly for doubting him. "I know what it's like, okay? I'd never out anyone who didn't want it."

"Matt," I said, the weight of the world slipping off my far-too-narrow shoulders, "you're a star. Thank you."

"Hey, no problem. And, you know, I am glad."

He was glad I was gay?

God knows what my face looked like as he rushed on. "About you and Adam, I mean. He's a good bloke. A good mate. He won't let you down."

I believed him. I wished I could be so sure about myself, however.

Matt disappeared into the back room, and I didn't see him again until lunchtime, when he emerged holding a foil-wrapped package. "Got your lunch, here," he said, holding it out. "Wraps again."

I reached out a bit too eagerly to take it and ended up hissing as my shoulder twinged.

"Are you all right?" Matt asked, frowning.

I rotated my shoulder carefully. "Bit stiff from karate yesterday," I said without thinking.

"You do karate?" There was something about Matt's tone as he asked that made me feel a bit uncomfortable. I was used to people disbelieving me, asking an incredulous *You? Why?*—but this was something different.

"Er, yes. I got my black belt quite recently," I added, feeling a sort of defensive pride.

If I was after congratulations, I didn't get them. Matt didn't even give me the tired old *What, are they giving them away these days?* "Oh," was all Matt said. What was up with him? I couldn't quite put my finger on it—and then it hit me: he was wearing the sort of expression I'd always expected to see on people's faces if I ever announced I fancied blokes.

"What? You don't approve of martial arts?" I asked a bit sharply.

"No—I mean, no, I haven't got a problem with... I just didn't think you were the type, that's all." Matt stared unhappily at his trainer-clad toes, as if they'd just announced they were leaving him to run off with a pair of Gucci loafers.

"The type?" I checked myself. "You get all sorts at karate classes, you know," I went on in a hopefully less defensive tone. "Kids with their dads. Or their mums. Girls who want to know a bit of self-defence. Boys who've been bullied at school and need a bit of physical self-confidence. It's a good sport," I finished a bit weakly.

"Yeah. Sorry." Matt's face was still hidden in a mass of shaggy curls as he stared resolutely at the floor.

"I mean, sometimes you get someone who's a bit of an arse," I admitted. "Take the class I'm going to down here— there's one guy who's the sort who gives the sport a bad name. But we're not all vicious thugs like Prick-tard, sorry, Pritchard."

Matt's head shot up. "Pritchard? Steve Pritchard?"

A hot, uncomfortable feeling spread across my chest. Why the hell hadn't it occurred to me the bastard might be someone he knew? "I don't know his first name—the others all call him Pit-bull," I added, more or less on the principle that blame shared is blame halved.

Then it hit me. "Wait—Steve? *Your* Steve?"

Matt nodded jerkily. "Class down in Totton, right?" He tried to smile. "Yeah, that's him."

I couldn't stop staring at him. Pit-bull Pritchard was Matt's *boyfriend*? "What the hell is his problem?" I burst out. "You know what he called me? A *fucking poofter*! What kind of gay bloke goes around saying that kind of thing?"

"He's...he's just not out, that's all," Matt said, and I hated to see him defending the arsehole. "Like you," he added.

My blood froze in my veins. Then it boiled. "'Pit-bull' Pritchard is *nothing* like me," I snapped. "He's a vicious, bullying thug. Christ, Matt, I can't believe you're with him!" I turned away, my fists clenching of their own accord, and struggled to calm myself.

By the time I'd got my breathing under control and turned back, Matt had disappeared.

Shit.

I made my way into the back room. Matt was leaning against the worktop hugging himself. He didn't even look up when I came in. I felt like the worst bastard in the entire history of bastardry. I'd just been a complete git about the man he— against all laws of common decency, not to mention credulity— apparently loved. "Matt?" I said softly. "I'm sorry."

Matt's head jerked up, and he started to say something, then stopped.

"I shouldn't have said that. It was just a, a gut reaction— Steve and I didn't exactly hit it off." I cleared my throat and wiped my hands on my jeans. "I'm sure he's, um, a lot...nicer...when you get to know him outside karate. Anyway, I'm sorry."

"No—it's all right," Matt said. "I mean—Steve just rubs people up the wrong way, sometimes." It sounded like something he'd learned by rote, as if he'd had to apologise for Steve before.

No surprise there. "Right," I said. "Not his fault." I was lying through my teeth.

"No!" Matt agreed a bit too quickly for my liking. "It's just...how he is."

"Absolutely."

As the conversation seemed to have stuttered to a halt, I muttered something about needing to get back to work and escaped out front again.

I still couldn't believe it. Gentle, sweet, vegetarian Matt was living with Steve Pit-bull Pritchard? I'd always assumed vegetarians were what that bastard ate for breakfast. Maybe…maybe he really was different, outside the dojo?

Or maybe he wasn't. God, how much did Matt have to put up with from Pritchard's bullying ways? Whichever way I looked at it, it was pretty depressing—either Matt was with a bastard, or I'd have to accept Prick-tard had hidden depths. Neither option was particularly appealing.

Too fed up to bother nuking anything for tea that night, I sat on the sofa with Wolverine and ate tuna out of the tin. Having already eaten, he weighed down my legs like a furry cushion stuffed with nails and purred his approval of my dinner choice. "I just don't get it," I muttered, my mood as sour as my dinner companion's breath. "Why the hell would someone like Matt be with someone like bloody Prick-tard? He's a thug, a bully, he pretends Matt's his lodger…"

Then again, was that really so different form me claiming to have had a quiet night in when I'd in fact been experimenting with homosexuality in general, and Adam in particular, down at the Cock?

I put down the tin of tuna, having unaccountably lost my appetite. Wolverine stood, anchored himself briefly with a few well-placed claws, then hopped onto the table to finish my dinner for me.

Chapter Sixteen

When I got to the shop on Tuesday morning, it wasn't just Matt waiting for me in the doorway. There was a large rucksack, a mountain bike and a guitar collectively taking up a lot more space than he did.

"Hey, I didn't know you played guitar," I blurted out before my brain could catch up with what my eyes were telling me about his hunched-over posture and sad eyes. "Bloody hell, are you okay?"

Matt sniffed and struggled to his feet, nearly falling on his guitar in the process. "'M fine."

"No, you're not." For one thing, he was muttering worse than Adam. "Come on in and tell me what's happened. Have you and Steve had a bust-up?" It was hardly a Holmesian effort of deduction, given the luggage and the general despondency.

Matt grabbed his bike and pushed it into the shop. I picked up his guitar in one hand and his rucksack in the other and followed him in. "Matt? Come on, talk to me."

"Yeah. Sorry." He wasn't looking at me. "I've left him," he told his handlebars.

My heart leapt—and then my conscience stepped in to grab it, give it a good shake and slam it back down to earth. I had no business whatsoever being glad Matt and Steve weren't an item any longer. "For good?" I couldn't help myself asking. "I mean, you're sure you won't work things out?"

Matt rolled his bike into the back room and leaned it against the wall. Finally he turned to face me, his shoulders hunched and his hands in his pockets. He shook his head. "Nah. It's over."

"Did...did you have a fight?" I broke into a cold sweat at the thought of Matt trying to stand up to Pit-bull Pritchard.

The shaggy curls shook again. "Not this morning. I just...I just left. I waited 'til he'd gone to work and then I grabbed my stuff and left. I mean, I wrote him a note so he'd know why I'd gone."

"Why?" My blood ran cold. "Is there someone else?"

Matt's face, what I could see of it, turned pink. "It's not that. It's just—it just wasn't a good idea. Me staying, I mean. I thought he'd change—he kept saying he'd change—but he never did."

I wondered exactly what Steve had been doing that he shouldn't. Just being himself would have been ample grounds, in my view, to dump the bastard like a ton of steaming hot manure, but presumably Matt had different views on the matter. If Prick-tard had hurt him... "Are you all right?" I asked again, more urgently this time. My chest ached with the need to go and give him a hug, but distrust of my own motives held me back.

Plus, my arms were still full of Matt's stuff. I put the rucksack down next to the workbench and propped the guitar up against it carefully.

Matt nodded. "Yeah, I'll be fine," he said, his gaze falling to the floor and his uncertain tone giving the lie to his words.

A thought struck me. "Have you got anywhere to stay?"

"Was going to ask if you'd mind me kipping down in the shop for a day or two."

"Don't be daft! Come and stay at Jay's. He won't mind." I gave Matt an encouraging smile. "The sofa's enormous, and it's actually pretty comfortable. It'll be nice to have someone else for the cat to ignore."

He looked up at that. "Jay's got a cat? I didn't know that."

"Well, the jury's still out on whether he knows himself, actually—I keep forgetting to ask him—but the cat seems to think he lives there, so who am I to argue? Anyway, it's settled—you're staying."

"Are you sure? I mean, it's a bit much to ask..."

"Good thing you didn't, then—I offered, remember? Come on, don't worry about it. I'd better go and open up the till out front, but if you need anything..." I trailed off. I wasn't honestly certain what he might need, as such. But I'd make damn sure he got it, anyway.

Matt's smile told me just how relieved he was to have somewhere to go. "Thanks," he said, still sounding a bit awkward. "S'pose I'd better get down to work, then."

I nodded and left him to it.

Unsurprisingly, Matt hadn't provided any lunch today, so I sent him out to get something from Asda. Not that I was feeling particularly lazy or anything like that, but I wasn't sure Matt was really up to dealing with customers on his own, and a bit of a walk in the sunshine would undoubtedly do him good. He came back with a baguette, some French cheese and various other ingredients which he then proceeded to assemble into a simple but delicious lunch. "You know, I'm not saying I don't appreciate this, but an egg and cress on white would have been fine," I mumbled with my mouth half-full of brie.

Still subdued, Matt managed a weak smile. "Yeah, well. I like good food, all right? And it's not healthy, eating a load of packaged crap." He ducked his head. "Sorry. I probably sound like your mum."

"Your mum, maybe, but not mine. Mum hates cooking, always has. She thinks convenience food is the best thing since sliced bread." I looked at the remains of my baguette. "Although I have to say, my opinion of sliced bread has gone right down since you've been doing my lunches."

Matt had a far-off look in his eye. "My mum loved cooking. She was always in the kitchen in her pinny, baking something or other. She used to joke that my stepdad only married her for her sticky buns."

"Oo-er, missus!" I laughed, pleased to see Matt smiling along. "You must miss her a lot," I added more seriously.

"Yeah—it was always just me and her, you know? Even when she married my stepdad—I mean, I was five then, so before that it really was just me and her—but even after, we always spent a load of time together. Dad wasn't really into playing football in the park or any of that stuff—I mean, he'd done all that with his daughters, hadn't he? So it was just Mum and me, 'specially in school holidays. Dad kept working well into his seventies, and he still does the gardening and stuff. He's always hated just sitting around doing nothing."

Matt paused for breath after that little speech, and I nodded. "He'd have been a child in the nineteen-thirties, wouldn't he? I suppose if you grew up during the big depression, you wouldn't want to give up a decent job until you had to."

"Yeah—he was always mad keen on saving money too. Used to drive Mum mad, sometimes. And me." Matt tidied up the remains of our lunch and the various bits of packaging it had come in. "Right. Better get back to work."

"I suppose so," I said, sad our little break seemed to be over.

Matt nodded and headed out back again.

Trade was fairly quiet that afternoon, so as often as I could, I popped out to the back room, where Matt at least was keeping busy with an endless stream of repairs and services.

"I really ought to learn how to do this stuff," I commented as he tightened up the brake cables on an old-fashioned sit-up-and-beg-type Raleigh.

Matt looked up and grinned. "Are you trying to put me out of a job?"

"God, no!" It was a horrible thought. I'd found it bad enough on Saturday without him. "Is this what you've always wanted to do, fixing bikes?"

"Pretty much, yeah. It was one thing me and Dad used to do together, you know? Messing around with bikes and tools and stuff. He's got a garage full of stuff he's built from bits and bobs—there's an old radio with actual valves in, can you believe that? Still works and all."

I frowned. "Valves?"

"That's what they used to have before transistors were invented."

"*Which* century was your stepdad born in?"

"I know what you mean. It's weird, really, how much the world's changed in just his lifetime. When he was young, half the local farms still used horses to work the fields." He made a face. "And being gay got you sent to the nick." He bent his head to his work. "Did you always want to be an accountant?"

"God, no. I don't think there's anyone who's ever grown up wanting to be an accountant." I shrugged. "It just seemed like a good career—decent money, plenty of jobs. Well, back then there were, anyway. Plus, I had a sad lack of any useful skills that didn't involve numbers," I added.

"You shouldn't do yourself down," Matt said earnestly. "I mean, I think you'd be great at running a business, and that's not all numbers. You've got ideas about promotions, that sort of stuff."

"Unfortunately, I also know the statistics for how many new businesses fail in their first year. Jay's done well with this place," I conceded.

Then the bell jangled, and I had to get back out front before I undermined all Jay's good work.

As I unlocked Jay's front door that evening to usher Matt in, it occurred to me a little too late that, given the choice, I'd probably have preferred to get the dragons out of sight before he saw them. Still, maybe he wouldn't notice them at first, and I could shift them while he had a shower or something.

Of course, no sooner had I formed the plan than Matt blew it out of the water. "Hey, I didn't know Jay collected these—they weren't here last time I came round." He picked up the one I'd put next to the computer—it was the one I'd bought Gran just before she died, called "Crouching Dragon, Hidden Tiger". It was a model of a smug-looking dragon crouched on a box, with a tiger's tail protruding from its mouth as if it hadn't quite finished swallowing the beast. "That's pretty cool," Matt said, smiling.

"Oh—it's mine, actually, not Jay's," I said, daftly pleased, as if I'd made it myself. "Well, they used to be our gran's, but she left them all to me."

"You've got more?"

"Dozens. Well, not literally, but there's quite a lot."

"My mum used to like this kind of stuff. Reminds me of her reading me *The Hobbit* when I was little—she used to let me hold one of the dragons, as long as I sat still and listened to the story." Matt stared at the dragon, a tiny smile on his lips. I felt as if I was intruding into a treasured memory and didn't know what to say.

Wolverine, bless his self-centred, greedy little heart, said it for me, choosing that moment to announce loudly from the doorway that it was about bloody time he got fed. Matt turned and, for a heart-stopping moment, almost fumbled the dragon and dropped it, but he managed to set it down safely on the table. "This is Jay's cat, right?"

"Matt, Wolverine. Wolverine, Matt. Better watch out for his claws," I added. I was still looking at Wolverine, but I was confident they'd both realise from the context I was talking to Matt. "He nearly eviscerated Adam last time he was here." My shoulders tensed up. Why the hell did I have to go and mention Adam?

"Oh. Right." Matt studied his feet. Perhaps he was worried Wolverine was about to pounce on them. "Listen, you know, if I'm in the way here, if you want to have Adam round, and all—"

"Don't be daft." It came out a bit more sharply than I'd intended. I felt my face grow hot. Bloody Adam.

Then I reminded myself Adam was Matt's best mate. "Look, it's not a problem for me, having you here, and I'm sure it won't be for Adam."

"You sure? I mean, with him still living at his mum's, it's got to be hard..." He shrugged. "You know. Getting time alone."

The heat spread down my neck and formed a tight band around my shoulders. I really, *really* didn't want to talk to Matt about what I did with Adam. Which was undoubtedly all the more evidence that I shouldn't have been doing it in the first place. Bloody hell, what a mess. Finally, Matt was single, and he was even living in the same house as me.

And somehow, I'd managed to be his best friend's boyfriend, not his.

We ordered in a takeaway for dinner—Matt declared himself more than willing to cook, but he was a guest; it wouldn't have been fair.

Plus, all I had in the fridge was ready meals, so it'd be a bit embarrassing if he went foraging for ingredients. I made a mental note to bin the packaged meals and buy some fresh stuff before Matt had a chance to look inside.

"What do you fancy?" Matt asked. "Indian—oh, wait, you had one of those on Saturday with Adam, didn't you?"

I could have done without him being apparently so determined not to let me forget about Adam. "How about Chinese?" I suggested.

"Sounds great—have you tried Fuchi yet? It's on Rumbridge Street; we could walk there from here. Or I could take the bike and pick stuff up, whatever. They do a great Tofu Macadamia Nuts—or you can have it with chicken, if you don't fancy veggie."

I shrugged. "Well, eating your veggie wraps hasn't killed me—I think I can survive the tofu for one night. It'd be better to get stuff we can share."

"Okay, how about we get the tofu and the Thai prawn curry? And the Quorn chicken in black bean sauce is pretty good, too—"

"Do you know their entire menu off by heart?" I asked with a laugh.

Matt grinned sheepishly. "Only the vegetarian bits."

"How about you just order what you fancy, and I'll eat it? I'm pretty easy-going when it comes to food."

JL Merrow

We both ended up cycling up to Fuchi to collect the food, taking a rucksack because carrier bags and handlebars are not a match made in heaven. "Fancy a bottle of wine?" I yelled to Matt on impulse as we reached the Co-op.

Not that I was feeling the urge to celebrate Matt's breakup with Steve or anything.

Much.

It felt incredibly domestic, chaining our bikes together and walking into the supermarket to do our shopping. Just like Kate and I used to do, except back then it'd been Waitrose, not the Co-op, and we wouldn't have dreamed of taking anything other than the BMW. I couldn't help glancing at the other shoppers, wondering if they thought Matt and I were a couple.

My face must have done its usual job of broadcasting my thoughts far and wide, as Matt leaned in to whisper in my ear. "Don't worry—they'll just assume we're flatmates or something, if they think about us at all."

I turned and pretended to peer at the special offers so he wouldn't see my irrational disappointment.

Chapter Seventeen

The food, when we finally got to eat it, was every bit as good as Matt had promised. If I hadn't already known, I doubt I'd have even noticed it was vegetarian. It went well with the fruity Chardonnay I'd picked out at the Co-op. We were sitting on the sofa afterwards watching an old episode of *Poirot* and feeling pleasantly mellow—at least I was, and I'd assumed Matt was feeling the same way—when Matt dropped the bombshell.

"It was because of what you said," he blurted out. "Me leaving Steve, I mean."

"What?" David Suchet's fake Belgian accent and twirly moustache no longer held my attention.

"You know. When you said you couldn't believe I was with him." He ducked his head. "It got to me, you know? It was like you were disappointed in me. Like you'd thought I was better than that. I hadn't thought about it like that before. I mean, it was a lot like what Luke said, but I s'pose—"

"Luke?" I asked sharply.

"Yeah—when he came to the shop. That was what he was talking to me about, right at the end."

"Luke knows Steve?"

Matt didn't answer for a moment, just stared at his knees.

"Matt?" I prompted.

"He doesn't know Steve, but he said he'd been there."

I was totally confused. "Been where?"

Matt had obviously decided on closer inspection that his

knees needed comforting. He drew them up to his chest, his feet in their stripey socks with the holes in perching on the edge of the sofa, and hugged his legs. "When he was younger. I mean, you wouldn't believe it now, would you? That he had a bloke who used to knock him around?"

All the blood in my veins had apparently been siphoned off and replaced with liquid nitrogen. "He—what?"

Matt shrugged, still hugging his legs in like he was afraid they'd fall off. "You know."

"Wait a minute." I said it slowly, needing to get this absolutely clear. "You're telling me Steve...hit you?"

"It wasn't his fault," Matt said, the words carving themselves into my flesh and leaving bloody scars. "He just gets...frustrated sometimes. You know. Because he can't be out, what with working on the docks and all. He never means to do it."

"Is that what he told you?" I stood up, literally shaking with fury. If Prick-tard had walked in the door right now... Well, he wouldn't have been walking out again, that was for sure. "So all those times you turned up looking battered—Christ, you really had been!"

"Not all of them," he said earnestly, looking up at me as if he was anxious I understand his ex hadn't been a total shitting bastard *all* the time, just, oh, ninety percent or so. "I mean, you know what I'm like."

"So," I began, and it didn't sound like me, not at all. "The black eye? The lip? Why the hell didn't you *tell* someone, for God's sake?"

"He never meant to do it," Matt said, his voice barely a whisper.

"What, his fist just moved of its own accord? Some kind of muscle spasm, was it?"

Matt didn't answer, and I realised with an unpleasant shock that my anger was scaring him. I sat back down on the sofa so at least I wouldn't be looming so much. "Matt... You shouldn't be making excuses for him. That kind of behaviour is totally unacceptable. If he can't control his anger, he doesn't deserve to have a boyfriend." He certainly didn't deserve Matt.

"Yeah, but... I know I wound him up sometimes. I talk too much, and I don't think about what I'm saying, and I'm always knocking stuff over..."

"That doesn't give anyone the right to knock you over!"

Matt took a deep breath. "I know... At least..." His face was screwed up with the effort of trying to articulate whatever was going on inside that shaggy head of his. "He wasn't like that all the time. Sometimes he was really nice, you know? Fun. Caring." He shook his head. "Anyway, I just meant to say, well, it helped, what you said. You know. You believing I was worth better."

"You seriously needed me to tell you that? Matt, of course you're worth better! You're kind, you're good-looking, you're fun to be with—and you're a wizard with the bikes. Anyone would be glad to have you as a boyfriend." I'd leaned forward as I spoke, and when Matt looked up, our faces were only inches apart. My breath caught—his lips were so close to mine. As I watched, they parted, and without even meaning to, I leaned in a little farther—only to see Matt recoil and hang his head once more.

Shit. What the hell had I been thinking of? That he'd welcome a kiss from his best mate's boyfriend? That when I'd said he deserved better than Steve Pritchard, I'd meant a cheating bastard would do just fine?

"Washing up," I blurted out, jumping off the sofa just as Matt mumbled something that sounded like *sorry.* "Need to do the washing up. Chuck away the boxes. Don't want them stinking the place out." I scrambled into the kitchen, where I found Wolverine licking out one of the takeaway tubs. He hissed when I snatched it away. "Tough," I told him. "I'm fairly sure monosodium glutamate isn't recommended for cats, and I don't want you sicking up again."

I rinsed out the tubs and put them for recycling, loaded the dishwasher and looked around for anything else I could reasonably do in the kitchen to avoid having to face Matt again. Did the fridge need a clean? I opened it up and stared at the stacks of colourful little boxes—my secret convenience-food shame.

"Tim?" I shut the fridge door hurriedly when I heard Matt's voice. He was standing in the doorway looking down at nine stripey toes and one pink one that was sticking out through the hole in his sock. "Um, sorry about that," he carried on. "I just... Anyway, I know you're..." The toes curled up tightly. "Sorry."

What? I frowned, trying to make sense of it. He knew I was sorry? Or he knew I was something else, and he was sorry about it? Why was he sorry? And why was my head starting to ache? "Strong wine, that, wasn't it?" I said at last.

"Yeah!" Matt nodded enthusiastically, his shaggy hair bobbing. "Um. Okay if I take a shower?"

"Of course—be my guest. Which, obviously, you are, so... I'll get you a towel." I escaped to the airing cupboard where I got out Jay's fluffiest towel, hanging it on the stair banister. "Here you go," I called down the stairs.

While Matt went up for a shower, I tried very, very hard not to think about the fact that he would soon be naked, only yards away from me. Would be getting into my—all right, Jay's— shower and soaping himself up, lathering all over, maybe paying particular attention to certain areas... I sighed. "Down, boy," I muttered to a part of me that was by now also very, very hard.

When I looked at the clock, I saw it was well after nine. Pritchard must have got home from work some time ago—must have found Matt's note and realised he'd been dumped. If it hadn't been for tonight's little revelation, I might even have been tempted to feel sorry for the bastard. As it was, I couldn't blame Matt for wanting to avoid a confrontation that could land him in the hospital. For the first time, it occurred to me Steve might not feel the same way—might come looking for Matt. Might want to use some very forceful arguments to persuade Matt to come back to him.

I took a deep breath and reminded myself I could handle it if he did—as long as he didn't catch me by surprise, I was confident I could take him in a fight. Of course, Jay might be none too pleased if there was any brawling in his shop. On the other hand, any publicity, as they say, is good publicity... But what if he turned up here? I didn't much like the idea of having to be on my guard constantly. Chances were good he didn't have Jay's address, but it'd be nice to know for sure.

Matt had left his phone charging up on the kitchen counter. As I glanced at it, a text message *kerplunked* through. Should I give Matt a yell? It might be something urgent.

It might be Pritchard, saying he knew where Matt was and was on his way round.

I felt guilty even as I picked it up—but I still checked the message anyway.

It was from Pritchard—at least, I was fairly sure Matt wouldn't have any other Steve texting him *Baby, come back, I miss u.* My stomach lurched. Had I been wrong about Steve?

There were eleven other messages, all from Steve. I opened the second: it was a similar plaintive outpouring of love and hurt. The third: *Im sorry, well work it out.* Guilt twisted painfully inside me. The fourth...I stared at the words, unwilling to believe this was the guy Matt had lived with. Loved. *Ur making a big mistake. Ur nothing without me.* It was like watching a car crash; I couldn't stop myself flicking to the next. *Useles fucking cunt.* Hurried flick. *U no i only say these things cos i love u. Cum bac.* Flick. *Think that posh tossers goin to want u when he finds out how pahtetic ur?*

I shut the phone with a snap and put it down quickly before it slipped out of my sweaty hands. *Posh tosser?* Was that supposed to be me? While I wasn't entirely happy with either part of the description I had to concede I was probably the poshest, well, tosser in Matt's little circle of acquaintance.

Did Prick-tard think Matt, well, fancied me?

Did Matt fancy me?

Maybe...maybe I should tell him how I felt? If there was even the slightest chance he felt the same...

Oh, yes, right. Because of course cheating on his best mate was bound to be the way to Matt's heart. I had to finish things with Adam, I decided. Whether or not Matt liked me was beside the point. The point was, I'd fallen for someone else—hard—and it wasn't fair to either of us to keep messing around with Adam.

I'd call him tomorrow. Get him to come round—or we could go out somewhere, maybe, although that would mean leaving Matt on his own, which I was reluctant to do—and I'd tell him it was over. I hoped Adam wouldn't be too upset. He'd seemed quite fond of me—but we'd never really spoken about what we wanted from the relationship, had we?

It suddenly struck me that tomorrow was Wednesday—karate night. I wondered if Pritchard would go. He really didn't strike me as the sort to sit at home and pine for his ex. I shivered. The thought of Pritchard in fighting mode when he actually had a good reason to be in a foul mood was not a happy one.

Would I go? I felt conflicted. I didn't want to leave Matt on his own—but on the other hand I didn't want to miss training because of Prick-tard, and I definitely didn't want to give the bastard the satisfaction of thinking he'd scared me off. Maybe Adam would stay with Matt, if I asked? Actually, thinking about it, that was a brilliant idea. If Adam was feeling a bit low because of our breakup, Matt would be able to cheer him up. Matt could cheer anyone up.

I was certainly feeling a lot better now.

Chapter Eighteen

When I stumbled downstairs Wednesday morning, the first thing I saw was a tousle-headed Matt, wandering around the kitchen in nothing but his boxer shorts.

I've never had much appetite for food in the mornings, but God, Matt looked good enough to eat. His torso was lean yet defined, just as you'd expect of a cyclist, and those broad shoulders gave him a rangy, powerful look that did interesting things to certain parts of me. "Morning!" I called out a bit too brightly. "Have you found everything you need?"

Matt looked up and stretched, the boxer shorts riding down just a touch to show a teasing glimpse of his treasure trail. I realised I was holding my breath and let it out quickly before my face could turn red. If it wasn't too late already. "Only..." He yawned widely. "Only just got up. What do you normally have for breakfast?"

I swallowed. "Just coffee. But there should be some bread, if you fancy eating something."

"Yeah, I'd keel over if I didn't eat breakfast." Matt looked around and located the bread bin. Fortunately, my prayers were answered: there was indeed bread, and it was in a perfectly respectable condition. True, it was bog-standard white cut-loaf from Asda, but at least it hadn't gone green.

Shoving a couple of slices in the toaster, Matt twisted around to look at me. "Sure I can't tempt you?" he asked.

Toast. He meant toast. Focus, Knight. "Uh—no, thank you. I'll put the kettle on."

Mindful of the strength Matt preferred for his coffee at work, I made his mug with about half as much coffee as I used for mine and added lots of milk. "That's great—thanks," he said, having taken a sip.

I held my mug in both hands and inhaled deeply, my eyes falling closed. Coffee. There's nothing like it, particularly first thing in the morning after a night disturbed by some *very* specific dreams. When I opened my eyes again, I saw Matt gazing at me with an odd expression on his face. I sighed. "Go on, laugh. I know I have a caffeine problem, and I'm just fine with that."

Matt blinked. "Oh—no, I mean, I wasn't going to laugh—" His toast popped up noisily, and he jumped, spilling some coffee on the floor. "Shit—sorry—I'll wipe that up."

"Don't worry about it. Eat your toast while it's hot, I'll get the floor," I insisted. I took a fortifying sip of the brown nectar and grabbed a kitchen towel, only to be beaten to it by Wolverine, who was lapping up the drips as if they were mouse-flavoured. "Scat!" I shouted, shoving him aside and mopping the rest up hastily. I didn't know if coffee was particularly bad for cats, but I was fairly sure it couldn't be actually good for them. And the prospect of Wolverine hyped up on caffeine was not one I wanted to live through.

Assuming survival would be on the cards in any case—I certainly wouldn't have rated Adam's chances if he'd happened to turn up at the wrong moment.

Wolverine stalked away, affronted.

"You know, you've got a weird cat," Matt commented indistinctly, his mouth full of toast.

"Tell me about it," I said in exasperation. "Punishment for my sins, I think."

Matt grinned. "Been a lot of them, have there?"

If lusting after another man when I already had a boyfriend was a sin, I was going straight to hell. I cleared my throat. "Usual amount, I expect. Actually, now I think about it, the number's probably depressingly low."

"Yeah, well—I'm sure Adam'll help you out there," Matt said with a strange sort of tone in his voice. I didn't quite know what to say.

Fortunately, Wolverine chose that moment to stalk into the kitchen and *miaow* at me pointedly. "I wondered where you'd got to, oh guardian of my morals," I muttered as I fetched the can opener.

"You what?"

Bugger. Now I'd have to explain myself to Matt. "I, er—he sort of attacked Adam. At a rather unfortunate moment." I tried not to cringe too visibly.

"Yeah? He looks such a softy." Matt bent down to stroke him. I had a brief moment of panic—besides not wanting Matt to get hurt, how on earth would he do his job with no fingers? But Wolverine just leaned into Matt's touch and purred in ecstasy despite the fact he still hadn't been fed.

"Maybe it really is the ginger thing, then," I mused, having brief and somewhat sadistic fantasies of inviting other redheaded people round to see if Wolverine would go for them the way he did for Adam.

"Doubt it," Matt said. "Cats can be funny, though. What was Adam doing when he attacked him?"

I froze in the middle of forking out the tuna into Wolverine's bowl. What the hell was I going to tell him? *Oh, he was just about to shove his cock in my virgin arse?* I swallowed, and straightened slowly, forcing myself to look at Matt. "I, er, can't remember," I lied, probably excruciatingly badly.

Matt stared at me for a moment. "Oh. Okay," he said and,

looking down, took a bite of his toast.

A few crumbs fell to his chest and were caught in the fine hairs there. I swallowed. If I'd been starving for a month, I couldn't have wanted to lick them off more than I did already. I stared at them ravenously for a long moment—and when I looked up, found Matt's gaze on me. My cheeks were so hot, if I stood there any longer I'd probably give the poor bloke sunburn. "Um," I said intelligently. "Better go and get dressed."

I hoped Matt wasn't anything like as distracted as I was at work that morning, or we'd be sending out bikes with the wrong number of wheels and no brakes. I misheard requests, gave people the wrong change, and more than once had total strangers give me funny looks and ask if there was anyone home. It was a blessed relief to shut up shop at one o'clock.

"Lunch?" I asked, poking my head around the door of the back room.

Matt had already packed up for the day and was looking at his phone with a puzzled frown. "Yeah... I think that wine last night must've been stronger than I thought—there's a load of text messages here marked "read" I don't even remember seeing."

My stomach flipped. "Ah." I cleared my throat as Matt looked at me guilelessly. "I may have accidentally looked at some of your messages. Sorry." I tried to smile, but judging from Matt's expression, it wasn't an Oscar-winning attempt. "Don't suppose you'd believe I mistook your phone for mine?"

"Did you?"

"Er, no." I sighed. "I'm sorry. I swear I won't do it again. I was just worried Pr—Steve might turn up at Jay's, and the phone was just sitting there, and a text came through, and before I knew it, I was checking the messages. I'm really sorry. It was—well, I shouldn't have done it."

"Okay," Matt mumbled. I felt like a total arse. He looked up. "It's not that I mind you seeing them, really... It's just, Steve used to do that sometimes. You know, the jealous thing— sometimes he got it into his head I was seeing another bloke."

God, I was an idiot. "I'm an idiot. Matt, I swear to you on...on Jay's leg, that I won't ever do it again. I'm really sorry."

Matt gave a weak smile. "You know, you could apologise for England. It's okay," he said earnestly. "I know you only did it because of Steve." He shoved both hands in his pockets. "Guess I did the right thing leaving him."

"God, yes!" It burst out of me with possibly inappropriate force.

"Thanks," Matt said. "For, you know, supporting me and all." He wrapped his arms around himself, as if he'd like a hug. I wished, more than anything, I could give him one.

So to speak. "Don't be daft," I said briskly. "Of course I'm supporting you. What kind of a b—of a friend would I be if I didn't?" I crossed my fingers behind my back that Matt wouldn't have noticed the slip. *Not your boyfriend yet, Knight, and he might never be.* "So, er, where do you fancy going for lunch? Pub again?"

"Are you busy this afternoon?"

I shrugged. "Not really. Why, did you have something in mind?"

"Well... I just sort of thought, you haven't been to the beach since you've been down here, have you? So I thought maybe, if you want, we could grab some stuff from Asda and head off down to the coast for a picnic?"

"Sounds great." I felt ridiculously happy at this firm evidence he wasn't mad at me for reading his text messages.

"Do you want to drive, or take the bikes?"

"Depends how hungry you are—it's a fair way, getting on for ten miles, and we've got to shop first."

"Maybe we'll go the lazy route for once, then," I said as my stomach rumbled in horror.

We grabbed a few things from the supermarket—all right, Matt grabbed a few things while I pushed the trolley—and set off down the A326 in Matt's Ford Focus, because the BMW just didn't seem like a seaside sort of car. We bypassed Marchwood and Hythe, then skirted the edge of the oil refinery at Fawley, a cyberpunk forest of chimneys belching out (hopefully clean) smoke and steam into the air next to Southampton Water. One or two showed flickering flames on top, like candles from a giant's birthday cake.

"Russell works there," Matt commented, nodding in that general direction. "He's a chemical engineer."

"Oh?" I said intelligently. "How do you know those two—is it from, um, gay bars? Or just from the shop?"

"Bit of both, really—saw them in the pubs and recognised them when they came in to buy stuff, so we sort of got talking. It's great, what they have together," he added a bit wistfully.

I nodded, gazing out of the window as Matt turned off the main road, leaving the chimneys of progress behind us and heading once more into the countryside. Open fields soon gave way to housing developments and local shops; then we were out of the town and back into the country again. The lane narrowed and became enclosed by trees, their dappled shade producing a sort of strobe effect with the June sunshine. With the view obscured, it was my nose more than my eyes that told me when we passed a pig farm.

"Nearly there now," Matt said, and all of a sudden, we rounded a curve in the road, and I could see the sun glinting off the sea ahead of us. We parked in a car park right on the sea front, overlooking a narrow shingle beach.

I breathed in deeply as I got out of the car. The air smelled like summer, and everything looked naggingly familiar. I did a slow turn, taking in the grassy parkland, the line of straggly evergreens, and across the water, the low, misty shape that had to be the Isle of Wight. "You know, I think my gran and grandad used to bring me down here," I said with dawning wonder. "Grandad used to skim stones across the water, but I was always rubbish at it. But then, I can't have been more than ten. And Gran used to pack a picnic..." I turned to Matt, a huge smile on my face. "I can't believe you brought me here—I didn't even know I remembered it until now."

Matt answered my smile with one of his own, and my heart stuttered, my whole body filling with warmth that had nothing to do with the sunshine. We stood there for a moment, and maybe I just imagined it, but Matt seemed to hold his breath while I struggled to find the words to tell him how I felt... But no—it was too soon. I had to speak to Adam first. It was the only decent way to do things. I swallowed. "How about that picnic, then?" I asked in a voice gone husky.

It was as if Matt woke from a trance. He started and shook himself. "Yeah—course. I'll get the stuff."

We sat on the shingle looking out to sea, eating sandwiches Matt made up there and then using rye bread, Roquefort cheese, smoked salmon and guacamole in various indescribably delicious combinations. We had the place almost to ourselves— just the occasional old couple strolling past, or shrieking children too young for school, who quickly dragged their young mums off to the playground. Boats sailed past and gulls cried out mournfully, probably because we refused to share our sandwiches with them.

"You get windsurfers here, at the weekend," Matt said.

"Ever tried that?"

"No, but it always looks like fun. You?"

Matt laughed. "Who, me? You know what I'm like—I tried it once, but I spent more time falling off the board than I did on it."

"Doesn't everyone at the start?"

"Well, that's what the instructor said, at first. By the end of the hour, he was begging me to try sailing instead—like he said, you can do that sitting down."

I swallowed my last bite of the tangy Roquefort. "Is it an inner-ear thing?" I asked, hoping he wouldn't think I was being too personal. "Or something like dyspraxia?"

"Diss-what-sia?" Matt shrugged. "Nah. I'm just a klutz, that's all." He smiled and picked up his Diet Coke.

"Cheers," I said, clinking bottles with him. "Here's to klutzes everywhere."

As we finished, the breeze coming in off the sea seemed to pick up—or maybe it was just so long sitting still that made me feel a bit of a chill. I stood, wrapping my arms around myself. "Want to skim some stones? Bet you manage to get more bounces than I do."

"Bet I don't," Matt said cheerfully, scrambling to his feet.

He won that bet. Matt was unbelievably, awfully, spectacularly bad at skimming stones. Most of his efforts just plopped into the water and sank like, well, stones. I, on the other hand, seemed to have finally got the knack. "Yes!" I shouted after one particularly good effort, punching the air for good measure. "Did you see that? Nine bounces! We have a winner!"

"Right, that does it. I'm conceding defeat." Matt clapped me on the back in congratulation, and even that casual contact was enough to derail my mental processes completely. "Fancy a bit of a walk? We could go round the coast a bit."

I collected my scrambled thoughts. "Sounds good."

As we crunched through the shingle, Matt nodded to the Isle of Wight. "Ever go over there?"

"Just once—Gran and Grandad took me for a day trip." I frowned. "I think Jay was in hospital then too—broken collarbone; I can't remember how he did it. Anyway, all I can really remember is being disappointed you couldn't walk all round it in half an hour. It didn't seem like a proper island."

"Yeah, it's about seventy miles around the outside." He must have caught my look of surprise that he knew it that exactly. "There's a round-the-island cycle race every September. Jay and me and some of the lads go down most years. You should try it—might want to get a bit of training in, first, though."

"Just a bit," I agreed. "If I tried it right now, I think my legs would fall off."

"Actually, there's worse things you've got to worry about on the long-distance routes. Phil had a bit of trouble last year—things got a bit, um, twisted."

I winced as I realised just what *things* Matt was referring to. "Ouch."

"Yeah. His wife was well miffed about it and all." Matt grinned. "Race you to the concrete bits!" He set off along the beach, hurdling the low wooden breakwater, and I scrambled after him, my feet slipping and crunching in the shingle. He was faster than he looked, and it took me almost until the "concrete bits" he'd mentioned before I overtook him with my longer legs.

"Hah! Beat you!" I gasped, bending over to rest my hands on my legs while I got my breath back. "What are these things, anyway?" I asked, looking around at the low concrete blocks that lined the shore. "Did there use to be something here?"

"It's to do with the D-Day landings," Matt confirmed, his face flushed from the run. "They built these huge concrete boxes here and towed them out to France... It's all on a board over there. And you see the big bars of chocolate?" Startled, I followed his pointing finger with my gaze and saw a sort of concrete flooring laid on the beach that did, indeed, resemble giant bars of chocolate. "They were so the tanks wouldn't sink in the sand when they drove them onto the ships."

We wandered over to the board, which told us Matt's "huge concrete boxes" had been *caissons*—or basically, huge concrete boxes—which were constructed here on the beach and towed across to Normandy for D-Day. They'd formed part of a floating harbour the size of Dover, needed to handle supplies for the 160,000 Allied invasion forces who'd landed in France. It must have been a staggering undertaking—I could hardly believe the six-thousand-ton behemoths would have even floated.

I stood and stared out to sea, shading my eyes from the sun with one hand. What must it have been like for those men, I wondered, leaving English shores and not knowing if they'd ever return? "If we'd been born sixty years earlier, that could have been us going off to fight," I mused. "Sort of puts your own troubles into perspective, doesn't it?" I suddenly remembered who I was talking to. "Shit. Sorry—didn't mean to—"

"No—No, you're right." Matt said. He bit his lip. "I really was daft to stay with him so long, wasn't I?"

I hesitated, then put a hand on his shoulder to reassure him. I tried to ignore the effect the physical contact was having on me as I spoke. "When you're right in the middle of a situation, it's often hard to keep your perspective." I looked at my watch. "We should probably head back now."

We walked back along the shingle, me with my hands shoved firmly in my pockets because I wasn't sure I could trust them not to stray back over to Matt if I didn't keep an eye on them. Matt did the same, but I didn't flatter myself it was for the same reason.

"You know, it's weird," I said, struggling to formulate my thoughts even as I spoke. "All this time, I've been thinking that this—me being down here, I mean—was just a sort of interruption. Normal service will be resumed shortly, that sort of thing. But now I'm not so sure." I took a deep breath, the smell of the sea filling my lungs. "Now—coming back to this place—I think maybe this is my normal life. Or should have been. It was living in London that was the aberration." As we reached the car park, Matt fumbled in his pocket for his keys, his gaze not leaving my face for a second. "Maybe...maybe I had to go away to learn to appreciate it—but I stayed too long, and I forgot it instead. But now, it's all coming back." I frowned. "Does that make sense?"

Matt nodded. "You know what? You couldn't pay me to live in London. All those people crammed in together, all breathing the same air."

"It's not as bad as you think," I said, wondering if I really believed it myself. I sighed. "But it's not like this."

We got back into the car, and I batted fondly at the furry dice hanging from the rearview mirror. When they settled back into position, both sixes were facing me. It felt like an omen, and I smiled.

"You're not going to karate tonight, are you?" Matt asked as we washed up after dinner that evening. We'd picked up a few ingredients for veggie pasta when we'd been shopping earlier, which Matt had cooked up with my dubiously helpful assistance. It had all seemed so simple, I'd wondered what on earth I'd been making a fuss about all these years.

"Why?" I asked. I'd been looking forward to going to karate, as it happened.

"It's just—if Steve sees you, he'll ask where I am."

"You think I'd tell him?" I was hurt he'd even consider it.

"No—course not. It's just... Look, don't take this the wrong way, but I think he'll be able to tell if you're lying." Matt gave me a nervous look, apparently worried he'd offended me.

In fact, I was grateful for the timely warning—my Judas face would have given me away in the next thirty seconds. I turned to the sink and pretended to scrub the coffee stains out of a mug. "Actually, I, er, I thought I ought to go and see Jay tonight. See how that leg's getting on." I mentally crossed my fingers Matt wouldn't invite himself along. "But I don't like leaving you here on your own. How about I call Adam?"

Matt gave a weak smile. "What, to babysit?"

"Yep. I'll tell him he's to tuck you in bed nice and tight and read you a bedtime story." I frowned. "And not a dirty one, either."

"Spoil all my fun, you do."

"Maybe I'll—" I coughed. Now was not a good time to blurt out how much I'd like to tell him some dirty stories of my own. "I'll give Adam a call," I finished.

As I grabbed the phone, it occurred to me that Adam did, after all, have a life and might not actually be sitting at home waiting for my call. Luckily for me, it seemed Wednesdays were his life's night off. He picked up his phone with an "Uh-huh?" and declared himself willing to come over and Matt-sit with his usual economy of syllables.

When I opened the door to him half an hour later, I felt an odd pang in my chest. It was almost like regret—no, scratch that; it *was* regret. I might be doing the right thing here, but, well, for a moment I almost wished things had been different.

That I'd been able to feel for Adam what I felt for Matt.

Hearts. Who'd have one? "Come in, Adam," I said, half expecting to be grabbed and forcibly snogged, and perversely disappointed when no predatory lips came my way.

"All right?" he said, holding up a six-pack of lager. "'S for Matt."

"I hope you're not planning to get him drunk and have your wicked way with him," I said, and immediately wished I'd engaged brain before opening mouth. The last thing I wanted to do was put ideas like that into Adam's head. Particularly as I was about to split up with him.

Fortunately, Adam laughed. "What, me'n'Matt? Nah. We're just mates."

The hallway only seemed half so big with Adam taking up space in it, and when Matt appeared to say hello to his friend, there was barely room to swing a cat.

Of course, any attempt to swing Wolverine was likely to prove fatal to the person doing the swinging, so that was probably just as well.

"Adam, can I have a quick word? Sorry, Matt," I added, feeling awkward.

I led Adam into the kitchen and shut the door. He looked around a little nervously, for Adam. "Where's y'r cat?"

"Wolverine? Oh, he's out at the moment. Don't worry—if you keep the kitchen door shut after I've gone, even if he comes in he won't be able to bother you." Or, as it might be, rend poor Adam limb from limb.

Adam looked relieved that blood transfusions weren't, after all, in his immediate future. I breathed a silent prayer that Wolverine wouldn't take it into his furry head to come back in the house in the next five minutes. "Look," I began awkwardly. "I...I don't know how to say this, but..."

Adam's freckled face creased into a smile. "'S all right."

"You don't know what I'm going to say."

Adam shrugged, still smiling. "I seen the way you look at Matt. 'S all right. Seen th' way he looks at you, 'n' all." He loped over and hugged me with those ape-like arms. "Good luck."

"I... Thanks," I said, stunned—and if I was brutally honest with myself, just a tiny bit hurt. *Obviously,* I hadn't wanted Adam to be devastated, but he seemed to have found it remarkably easy, breaking up with me. I shook my head. *Get over yourself, Knight.*

Adam was standing there, looking at me with a shrewd eye. I gave a rueful smile, and hugged him back with genuine affection. "You're a great guy, Adam. Thanks for everything. And I'm sorry it didn't work out."

"No, y're not," he contradicted me good-naturedly. "G'won. Get on out of 'ere."

I'd had it all rationalised; how it'd be good for me to go and train. Get the aggression out of my system.

I'd been lying to myself. The real reason I'd gone, I realised as I bowed my way into the dojo, was so I could find an excuse to beat the crap out of Steve Bloody Prick-tard. He was there as usual, just chatting away with the other brown belts as if nothing had happened, as if Matt didn't even now still bear the marks of his violence. Time seemed to slow. It'd be so easy to just stride over there, grab him by the front of his gi and punch that vicious, cowardly face into a bloody pulp.

My hands were curling into fists, and I actually took a step forward—then Sensei came toward me with a friendly smile, breaking the spell. I forced myself to calm down and return his greeting.

Training didn't work its usual magic, though. Even after the warmup, after basics, I was still tense. All the time I was watching the guy out front demonstrating the moves, at least half my attention was on Prick-tard, three men down the line from me. And God, he knew it. Every time my eyes flicked his way, he was glaring at me. When we went on to sparring, I couldn't tell you who made the first move, but we marched straight up to one another.

"You've got a fucking nerve, turning up here tonight," he snarled, the menace in his face matched by his belligerent tone.

"I could say the same about you," I countered, fighting to keep my own voice level. God, I was ready for this. I could picture myself, standing victorious over his battered body, every bruise a revenge for what he'd done to Matt. Payback for every downcast look, every hurt he'd ever suffered.

But then I heard Sensei's voice behind me. "All right there, Mr. Knight?"

It was enough to bring me to my senses. God, what the hell had I been thinking of? I hadn't become a black belt so I could solve all my problems with my fists. Hell, wouldn't that make me just as bad as Pritchard? Yes, I hated that bastard, but I hated the way he made me behave, made me think, even more.

"Fine," I managed to Sensei, and he moved on to another pair, giving us an assessing glance as he went.

I turned to Pritchard and spoke in a low, intense voice, for his ears only. "I'm not going to fight you, you bastard. I don't want to have to look at you that long, and I certainly don't want to have to touch you." I turned away, but he grabbed my arm. Furious, I twisted out of his grasp. "Just leave me the fuck alone—and if I ever, *ever* see you within a hundred feet of Matt, I'll bloody kill you, understood?" I hissed.

Pritchard's face twisted. "Yeah? You and whose army? I

could take you with one hand behind my back, you little ponce."

I barked an incredulous laugh. It was loud enough that the pair sparring nearest to us turned to look. "Enough with the gay insults, all right? We both know how bloody hypocritical you're being."

"You shut your fucking mouth," he spat. "Or I'll shut it for you. Permanently." A vein was standing out on his forehead; I spitefully hoped it would burst.

"Worried someone's going to find out your dirty little secret?" I couldn't resist taunting him.

"Like you're not just the same," he sneered.

Enough was enough. I was damned if I was going to let him say that about me. "As it happens, no, I'm not. Not anymore. I'm gay," I said in a louder voice. "And if anyone's got a problem with that, well, it's their problem."

Pritchard stood there, stunned. "You stupid fucking—"

"Just leave me and Matt alone, all right?" I said tiredly and walked away. It was a breach of etiquette, leaving the dojo without Sensei's permission, but I hoped he'd forgive me. Or be glad to see the back of the floor show, more likely.

I walked down the stairs and out of the sports centre, waving good-bye to the receptionist as I went, then made my way through the car park. As I got out my car keys, I was still, to be honest, a bit light-headed from having just announced my homosexuality to the world—or at least, the two or three people in the dojo who'd actually been near enough to hear me.

Then a pile-driver punch slammed into my side, just above my kidney.

Winded, I staggered a few paces, then spun around gracelessly. If I'd been in the mood to be scared of Pritchard, I'd have been bloody terrified. His face, in the twilight, was purple with rage, and his teeth were bared, his lips pulled back in a ferocious snarl.

"Come on, you coward. Fight me, you fucking poofter!"

It was the last insult, more than anything, that made me punch him back. He was such a piece of filth. I don't know if I was fighting for me, for Matt, or for all the other poofters he'd slagged off—and probably beaten—in the past. Perhaps it was the reminders of World War Two I'd seen earlier, spurring me on to fight for what was right. Maybe I was just fighting what I could see of myself in Pritchard: the cowardice; the hypocrisy; the wanting to have all the benefits with none of the responsibilities.

Maybe it was just because he was such a hateful piece of shit.

As I leapt past him, catching him on the ear with a backfist strike, a warm drizzle started to fall. "Call that a fucking *uraken*? There's girls with white belts who could do better than that."

Casual misogyny apart, he was right. My knuckles didn't hurt as much as they should have—I was still pulling my punches.

"Think you're so fucking special, don't you?" Pritchard sneered. "You and that fucking slag Matt. Think I'm stupid?"

It was probably just as well he didn't leave a pause for me to answer.

"I know you were fucking him in that bloody shop," he snarled.

What? "Look, Matt and I aren't—"

He lunged at me again, feinting with a jab punch and following it up with a side thrust kick that could have knocked several internal organs clean out of my body had it connected. I retaliated with a kidney punch of my own. It landed a little off target, and I felt my knuckles bruise against his ribs.

I wasn't sure, but I thought I felt a rib cracking under the force of my blow.

Pritchard swore and came straight back at me, feet flying in a series of kicks. I dodged and blocked instinctively—not thinking, just reacting. The ground was getting slippery, and I had the vague impression of people around us. I thought I heard a police siren in the distance.

As a roundhouse kick came in, I made a sweeping block, putting him off-balance. I danced out of reach and retaliated with a textbook *uraken* to his temple.

He dropped like a stone.

I stood there, panting, staring down at him as he lay on the ground in the rain—and then I felt a hand on my shoulder, and Sensei was there.

For the first time since I'd met him, he wasn't smiling.

Chapter Nineteen

It felt like a lifetime later when I pushed open Jay's front door. Matt was on me before I'd even kicked my shoes off.

"Tim? What the hell happened? It's two o'clock!" He caught sight of my face—and of my gi, now crumpled and stained with blood and dirt. "You didn't go to see Jay, did you? You went to karate. To fight Steve..."

"You should see the other guy," I said weakly, trying to smile.

"Are you hurt?" he asked urgently, his hands reaching out as if to check me over for broken bones.

I shook my head and immediately wished I hadn't as pain flooded me behind the eyes. "I'm fine. They had a doctor look me over—there's nothing major."

"They?"

"Um. The, er, police."

"Shit, are you in trouble?"

"Um," I said again. "Probably. Sort of depends on your Steve."

"He's not my Steve!" Matt's tone was furious, and I stared at him. He took a deep breath and ran a hand through his already tousled hair. "What happened?"

"Well, ironically enough," I said, untying my belt, "I decided I didn't want to fight him. So I left the dojo."

"He came after you." It wasn't a question.

I nodded, hanging my belt over the stair rail. "Threw a

punch at me before I'd even noticed he was there. The girl on reception saw us fighting and called the police before she told Sensei what was up."

"What happened?" Matt took a deep breath. "Did you—was Steve badly hurt?"

I'd known he would ask, however much it galled me to see his concern for the bastard. He'd been living with him up until a couple of days ago—of course he still had feelings for him. "Concussion, I think. Maybe a couple of cracked ribs. I think I must have lost it a bit. Sorry."

"What? He attacked you! You don't have to apologise for hitting back."

"I'm a black belt. I'm supposed to have more control." I realised I didn't have a clue what happened to black belts who got convicted of assault—did they lose their karate licence? Get ceremonially stripped of their belts? All of which, of course, would pale into insignificance if I ended up in jail.

God. How would I cope if I went to jail? I'd never even been to boarding school.

Matt ran his hand through his hair again, looking as worried as I felt. "Have you been charged with anything? What did Steve say about it—is it his word against yours?"

All very good questions. "I've been released on police bail— no charge yet. They're, um, waiting to talk to Steve. He sort of ended up unconscious." I couldn't look at Matt. "I'm sorry. He kept on coming at me, and I just sort of lost it—he was going on about poofs, and after what he did to you..."

"He had it coming," Matt said so viciously I stared at him in shock. "Shit, Tim, I'm the one who should be saying sorry. If it wasn't for me, he'd have left you alone."

"Well, to be fair I think there was a fair amount of personality clash going on too—"

"It was my fault!" He spun away from me, then whirled back. "Monday night—I asked him about karate, about if he'd seen you there—I mean, if he'd known who you were. He said he'd known since the first time you went—that was the day we met, wasn't it? He said...he said a lot of stuff about you too. That's when we had the fight."

"The fight?" I struggled to think—Matt hadn't had any new bruises in the last few days, had he? After all, I'd seen him in just his boxers only this morning, and it wasn't like I hadn't been paying attention to detail. "Did he hurt you again?"

"He..." Matt took a deep breath. "He didn't hit me that time. He just sort of shook me, and then he slammed me into the wall. I hit my head a bit hard and blacked out—only for a minute," he reassured me hurriedly. "But that's when I realised...I had to leave him."

"Matt..." I couldn't bear it. I wanted to grab hold of him and never let him go—except for the hour or so I'd be spending beating Pritchard into a bloody pulp. Maybe I'd make it two hours. I was feeling generous. "Did you see a doctor?"

"Nah, just took a couple of paracetamol and went to bed in the spare room."

"Matt! That's incredibly dangerous. You could have had a concussion. Promise me you'll never do anything like that again."

"It's all right—I know what a concussion feels like."

He probably did, but still... "Matt, just humour me, okay? Go see a doctor next time." I let out a long, shuddering breath. "Let me see it."

"There's nothing there, honest. It didn't even bleed," Matt protested, but he still turned around and parted his hair away from the back of his head.

There wasn't, in fact, a lot to see—just a bit of bruising. I prodded it gently with a finger.

"Ouch!"

"Sorry. Just checking." It had seemed fine—no ominous squashy bits. I reluctantly conceded Matt's self-diagnosis had probably been correct—after all, it'd been forty-eight hours since the injury; anything bad that was likely to happen would probably have done so already.

"Anyway," he said, turning back around, "if you need me to, I'll go down the police station and tell them he knocked me around, okay? So they know what he's like."

"Thanks," I said. As the last of the adrenaline drained away, I leaned back against the banisters and closed my eyes, weary to my very bones. "You know, I don't understand why you didn't go to the police before. When he hit you. Why would you just let him get away with it?"

There was a long silence. I opened my eyes, worried I'd crossed a line.

Matt was slumped against the opposite wall, his hands in his pockets. "I know. I—I just felt... I don't know. He was always so sorry once he'd calmed down. Always swore it'd never happen again. And I just—well, it's not a very manly thing to own up to, is it? That your boyfriend's been beating you up."

"Matt..." I sighed. "You're not the one who should be ashamed about it."

"Yeah. Maybe. But it still didn't seem right, doing anything that'd out him. He was so paranoid about anyone finding out about us."

"So why was he even going out with you?" I caught myself. "Um, that probably sounded a bit uncomplimentary—"

Matt managed a half laugh. "'S all right. See, that was the other thing. I mean, it was my fault—I mean, I was only supposed to be the lodger. It wasn't like he went looking for a

213

boyfriend or anything."

"But it got to be a bit much for him, seeing you wandering around the house in your boxer shorts?" For the first time, I felt a sneaking sympathy with Pritchard. For, oh, about a nanosecond or so. "Okay, so he was confused about his sexuality. That still doesn't give him the right to take it out on you."

"No, but..." Matt shrugged. "And it wasn't like I was even his first or anything... But it still didn't seem right, giving him away when he didn't want anyone to know about us."

"He was an idiot," I said without thinking. "If I was your boyfriend, I'd want everyone to know about it." I pushed myself upright and took a deep breath. "Look, don't worry about work, tomorrow. The shop's doing fine—the business isn't going to fail if we don't open up for a day. I think we could both do with catching up on our rest. I'm going for a long, hot bath. You get some sleep."

Matt nodded, his face hidden by his hair.

I trudged upstairs, ran the bath water as hot as I could stand and lay in it until it went cold. My mind was blessedly blank, too numbed by tonight's events to muster a single thought. When I finally climbed out, I craved a coffee and went downstairs in my dressing gown to see if I could dredge up some of Jay's decaf.

"Matt?" I asked, blinking at the figure leaning on the kitchen counter, his hands wrapped around one of Adam's cans of lager. "You should be asleep."

He shrugged. "Wasn't feeling like it. Not just yet." He looked up at me with a twisted smile. "And anyway, Adam's hogging the sofa."

"Adam's still here?" I realised guiltily I'd completely forgotten about Adam.

"Yeah—he said he'd stay till you got back, but he was asleep by then, so I didn't want to wake him." Matt put down his lager, the thud of the can on the counter suggesting most of the contents were still inside.

"Why didn't you say? Look, you'll have to share the bed with me." I could feel my face heating up. "There's plenty of room." And I'd probably end up lying awake all night, just to make certain I wouldn't molest him in my sleep.

Matt looked up, his face pale in the harsh fluorescent light. "Are you sure? I mean, if you're injured…"

"I told you—there's nothing serious. Just a bit of bruising."

"Bad?"

"Not sure—but that kidney punch left its mark." I opened my dressing gown to try to have a look, but the twisting involved was a bit too uncomfortable right now. "Can you see anything?"

Matt gave a sharp intake of breath as he stepped toward me. "Just a bit."

"Make a right pair, don't we?" I said without thinking. Matt's face fell so far it was practically in Australia.

"'M sorry," he said, turning away.

I grabbed his arm. "Sorry for what? Matt, none of this is your fault."

"It's my fault Steve had it in for you." He ran a hand through his shaggy curls as he stared at the fridge. "I—well, I said some stuff about you, the day I met you—and he… I think he kind of got the idea I, well…that I liked you."

Everything went so still I thought for a moment time had stopped altogether. "Was he right?" I asked, my voice hoarse.

Matt didn't speak for a moment. "Adam…Adam said you two'd split up," he said, turning back to face me at last.

Maybe it wasn't an answer to my question—but God, I

215

hoped the *yes* I'd managed to read between the lines wasn't just wishful thinking. My heart was beating so hard I worried for my ribs. "Yes," I said managing not to let my voice crack on the word. "You know...you know there was never anything serious between me and him, don't you?"

Matt nodded slowly.

"And you know I... If it hadn't been for Steve, and then Adam—you know I, well..." That time my voice did crack. I hadn't known how to finish that sentence anyhow. "Matt..." Failing for a second time, I gave up on words and put my hands gently around his waist. He didn't immediately shake them off, which I hoped was a good sign. "Do—" I cleared my throat. "Do you think you might...?"

Empires rose and fell. Stars burst onto the night sky, then fizzled out to nothing. A whole season of *X Factor* came and went, the winner rocketing from obscurity to number one, gabbling excitedly about living the dream, then disappearing to stack shelves in Tesco.

Finally, Matt nodded. "Yeah. I mean, I do."

"Thank God," I breathed and kissed him.

His arms were warm and trembled slightly around my neck, and he tasted of lager and salted crisps and relief. Funny how I'd never liked the taste of lager until now. I explored his mouth hungrily, memorising its contours, tracing his broken tooth with my tongue. I couldn't hold him tightly enough; there were clothes in the way, for a start. Matt's work-roughened hands slid from my neck to my chest, bared by my open dressing gown.

"I can feel your heart beating," he whispered.

A hundred corny clichés quivered on my tongue but, thankfully, died unspoken. "Let me feel yours," I said instead, tugging at his T-shirt. Matt pulled it over his head in one easy motion, and I pressed against him, revelling in the feel of his skin on mine, cool after my overheated bath. My hands roamed over his back and dropped down to slide inside his blessedly baggy jeans and reach his arse. It was firm and tight from all the cycling he did, and I kneaded it gently through the cotton of his boxer shorts, hardly able to believe this was finally happening.

Matt ran his hands over my chest, rubbed his thumbs over my nipples. My grip on his arse tightened involuntarily. "Ah— sorry," I gasped, breathing hard.

"Don't be," he said, looking up at me with wide eyes. I wanted desperately to kiss him, but I needed to look at him more, to burn the sight of his face into my memory so that maybe, finally, I'd believe he was mine.

Was he mine? He was obviously—very obviously— interested in having sex with me, but did that mean anything, really? "I don't want a one-night stand," I said in a rush, worried I'd bottle out before finishing the sentence otherwise.

Matt looked at me for an interminable moment. "Me neither," he said at last.

I closed my eyes for a moment in sheer, blessed relief. When I opened them again, he was smiling at me.

"What?" I asked, paranoia rising.

His smile widened. "Nothing. Only—you're not like a lot of blokes I've known."

"In what way?" I asked suspiciously.

"Oh—it's just, most blokes only seem to care about getting their end away, you know?" His smile wobbled for a moment. "It's nice to meet someone who's not like that."

I had a brief but strong urge to demand names and addresses. "Matt, you know it's never been like that for me. Not with you," I added, in a sudden burst of honesty. "Not that I don't want to—you know, but that's not what it's all about." I took a deep breath. "If that was all I cared about, I'd have stayed with Adam."

It was mean of me, and I'd probably burn in hell for it—God knows, I deserved to—but I was glad when Matt flinched at the mention of my ex.

"But I'm here with you now," I carried on. "And that's the only place I want to be."

Matt seemed to melt in my arms. I pressed my lips to his, kissing him with a passion I hadn't even known I possessed. He answered, his arms tightening about me and his mouth devouring mine, invading it. Our erections pressed against each other with heat that seared even through our clothes. "God, I want to get you naked," I breathed as he released my mouth to gulp in air. I ran my hands up and down his back, then let them creep down to their favourite resting place, Matt's arse. "Is this too soon?" I asked, humping against him. "I mean, we've both just come out of relationships—"

"Yeah. Probably," Matt muttered, sucking on my left earlobe. "Maybe we ought to take things a bit slower." His hand slid down the back of my boxer briefs, which were all I was wearing under my dressing gown. Which, by the way, was beginning to feel way too hot.

"Be sensible about it. Don't try to—ah!" I gasped as Matt's finger slipped into my crack. "—walk before we can run."

"Take it easy," he breathed, nibbling a way along my jawline.

"Or," I suggested, grinding myself into him, "we could just fuck like bunnies and worry about it later."

"Sounds good to me." I felt Matt smile against my neck. "And anyway, you're the boss."

"I hope that doesn't mean you're going to throw me over for

Jay as soon as he gets out of hospital."

"Nah—no offence to Jay, but he's really not my type." Matt nibbled at my collarbone. "Why would I want to swap when I've already got the best-looking one in the family?"

"Flattery will get you everywhere," I muttered weakly, overcome. "Can we take this upstairs?" I felt more than a little uncomfortable at the thought of getting up to anything—all right, anything more—in the kitchen with Adam snoozing in the next room. Plus, I hadn't seen Wolverine since I'd got back—he hadn't been on my bed—which meant he might slink through the cat flap at any moment. I wasn't anxious for a repeat of what had happened the last time I'd tried having sex in front of him.

"Yeah. Sure." Matt seemed to be having trouble speaking as we disengaged from our embrace. My prick strained obscenely at the front of my boxer briefs, a clear wet patch at its tip.

Matt reached down to give it a gentle caress, and my eyes fluttered shut. "Upstairs, now," I begged.

As we got to the bottom of the stairs, I took a quick peek into the living room, my dressing gown pulled shut just in case. This was really not the time to be sending mixed messages to Adam.

The man in question was flat out on the sofa, snoring gently while Wolverine purred in counterpoint from his lap. It looked like my ginger theory was a bust, anyway.

God, I hoped Wolverine hadn't really been defending my arse. Maybe I'd better lock the bedroom door, just in case.

There seemed to be twice as many stairs as usual, or maybe it was just that we couldn't keep our hands out of each other's clothes, which tended to hinder our progress a bit. When I finally shut the bedroom door behind us, I leaned on it for a moment in sheer relief, then let my dressing gown fall to the floor with a soft towelling thud. "Jeans. Off," I said succinctly.

Matt scrambled to comply, fumbling at his zip until it gave way. His baggy jeans slid easily to the floor, and I grabbed his hand as he stepped out of them. This would be the worst possible moment for him to trip and brain himself on the bedpost. It also made it easy to pull him back into my arms.

Matt was careful to avoid my major bruises as he returned the embrace, but I still winced as he put pressure on a sore patch of rib. "Fuck—sorry." He backed away from me with a look of concern. "Are you sure you're up for this?"

I gave a pointed glance down to my groin. "If I was any further up for this, I'd be coming already. I'm fine. Just—just don't stop," I begged. "And can we lose the underwear?"

Matt hooked his thumbs into his boxer shorts and gave a little wiggle as he pushed them down. It was so unbearably cute I couldn't wait to kiss him, so I grabbed him and pulled him tight against me, our lips pressed together and his naked cock burning a hole in my boxer briefs. Mindful of the fire risk, I held Matt with one hand and pushed them down with the other, fumbling a bit as the elastic caught over my erection.

"Oh, God," he breathed as our cocks finally got to say hello to each other. It was a fair comment. I wrapped a hand around us both, my whole body aflame and my head reeling.

I wanted him in so many ways, my mind was an unholy mess of pornographic images.

"Do you want me to suck you off?" Matt asked, and the images blurred and refocused into one, very specific picture.

"No," I said and dropped to my knees to take him in my mouth. The saltiness of his precome swept over my tongue like a tsunami. His cock seemed a lot bigger than it had in my hand, stretching my jaw wide, the head of it bumping the roof of my mouth. My only regret was that I couldn't fit even more of him in. Matt groaned. I wondered if it felt anything like as good for him as it did for me, just knowing who it was I had in my mouth. I swirled my tongue around Matt's cockhead and poked the tip into the slit.

"Fuck!" Matt exploded, thankfully not literally, and I sent a silent *thank you* to Adam for ensuring I wasn't totally ignorant when it counted. I alternated licking along the length of him with sucking at the tip, the musky male scent of him filling my lungs and intoxicating my mind, and when the pressure in my own groin became unbearable, I took myself in hand. "Oh, God, yeah... Oh, fuck," Matt kept repeating. I'd thought it was pretty damn good, receiving a blowjob. It had never even occurred to me that giving one could be even better. And this was Matt I was sucking. To have him inside me like this—the intimacy of it was overwhelming. Next time, I thought hazily, maybe we could try sixty-nine, but right now I was way too close to even suggest it.

"Oh, God, Tim, I'm going to—Tim!" I resisted all Matt's efforts to pull away with an iron grip on his left bum cheek, and he jerked and spurted and filled my mouth with salty, viscous fluid.

I swallowed it all. The thought of his come inside me, becoming part of me, was so hot I couldn't hold back any longer. I came too, ecstasy tearing through me in an unstoppable tide. "God—Matt—" I gasped as pearly white streams shot up his legs, and then I all but collapsed, panting, against his hip. He held my head and stroked my hair as I came down from that high.

We were both a bit sticky when he finally helped me up so we could stumble into bed. I grabbed a handful of tissues from the box on the bedside table—thoughtful of Jay to be so well prepared—and we wiped ourselves down and lobbed the used tissues in the general direction of the bin. When we'd finally made it under the duvet, I clasped Matt in my arms and held him tight, plastering come-flavoured kisses on his lips and navigating his mouth lazily with my tongue.

As I negotiated his jagged tooth for the umpteenth time, I broke the kiss, feeling suddenly sick. "Did that bastard do that?"

"What?"

"Your tooth. Did Steve fucking Prick-tard break your tooth?"

"Oh—nah. Green Day album."

I stared. "Did someone dare you to try eating it?"

Matt grinned, and I was so busy feeling my heart melt at the sight I nearly missed his next words. "I had it in a carrier bag on my handlebars. Only it sort of swung into the spokes, and I went arse over tit and landed on my face on the ground."

I winced. "Ouch."

"Yeah, I got a right bollocking from Dad about it."

I stroked his hair. "Guess he did care about you, in his way."

We were silent a moment, just enjoying the closeness, and I was starting to drift off when Matt spoke again. "You know—what I said before, about why I left Steve?" Matt said, then hesitated.

"Go on," I encouraged him.

"Well, it was true—but it wasn't the only reason." I waited. "It was partly, well, seeing you with Adam. It just made me realise—well, if you could come out for him, then if I hadn't been with someone else, maybe I'd have been the one you'd have come out for. I mean, I didn't really think I would have been—but there'd have been a chance."

My mouth was dry, and my heart ached for him—for us

both. "You were the one I came out for," I said hoarsely. He looked at me, startled. "If it hadn't been for you—seeing you in the shop every day—realising what I was missing out on by hiding—"

"That's just how I felt," Matt burst in. "Like, it was my fault I didn't have anything better, because I didn't have the guts to end it with Steve."

"We're a right bloody pair, aren't we?" I wrapped my arms around him so tightly anyone trying to separate us would have needed a crowbar and possibly high explosives. "We should get some sleep," I whispered. "It's been a long day."

And tomorrow, I'd find out just how far-reaching its effects would be.

Chapter Twenty

I woke up slowly, which was probably just as well. Wolverine appeared to have migrated in the night from the duvet to my chest, his fur tickling my nose. Startling him could easily have resulted in multiple lacerations. Except...wasn't that fur the wrong colour? I blinked, blearily. If that was Wolverine on my chest, then whose arm was around my waist?

My heart gave a leap as events washed back into my memory. It wasn't Wolverine; it was Matt, and he was finally mine. I blew gently on the curls tickling my nose, and Matt stirred, making a "Mmmmph" kind of noise. It was easily the most adorable thing I'd ever heard in my life. I shifted around until we were lying on our sides, chest to chest, with my arms holding him tight. Matt still wasn't more than half awake—at least, most of him wasn't. Part of him was very definitely bright-eyed and bushy-tailed.

So to speak.

I kissed the top of his head, and he mumbled again and shifted until his lips met my neck. As we nuzzled, our cocks got busy saying good morning to each other, and Matt managed to get a hand down between us to help them along, obviously more awake than he'd appeared. He pumped us together in a sleepy rhythm that was far more effective than it ought to have been. I could feel my orgasm building rapidly. "That's...God!" I gasped.

"Mm, yeah..." His strokes speeded up, getting harder as they got faster.

"Matt!" I shouted as my climax thundered through me. His

eyes sprang open as if I'd just shouted *Fire!* "Shit," I panted. "Sorry—did I put you off?"

Matt grinned. "Nah, just made me jump. But, you know, not in a bad way." He let go of our cocks, mine now very deflated and frankly grateful not to get any more stimulation, but his still hard as a rock.

"Do you want me to take over?" I asked, kissing along his stubble-rough jawline and down to his neck.

"God, yeah," he whispered right into my ear.

I slid my hand down and, on a whim, slathered it liberally with the mess I'd just made before wrapping my fingers firmly around Matt's cock. "Oh, yeah," he murmured, his eyes dropping shut again as I pumped him up and down. "That's...yeah. God, don't stop."

"Not planning to," I promised, speeding up a little. The look on his face was incredible, and my heart melted, full of love and fierce possessiveness. Matt groaned incoherently, and when I slithered down in the bed a bit so I could suck on his nipple, he bucked once, twice—then came, hot liquid spurting up onto my shoulder.

He grabbed hold of me and pulled me up to kiss me, apparently not bothered by my no doubt appalling morning breath—after all, I'd never got around to cleaning my teeth after sucking him off. Ye gods, my breath must have hummed. By a weird process of association my thoughts strayed to Wolverine and from there to Adam. "Do you think he's still here?" I wondered.

"Who?" Matt asked sleepily. "Oh—Adam? What time is it?"

I struggled round reluctantly to look at the clock. "God— eleven o'clock. We'd better get up."

"Thought you weren't opening the shop today?"

"No, but we probably ought to put a notice up. *Closed due*

to *family emergency* or something." And there was the other thing, but I couldn't face breaking the mood just yet.

"I can do that, if you like," Matt offered. "It won't take a mo to cycle round."

"Okay—but have some breakfast first," I insisted.

After all, it was in my vested interest to keep his strength up.

We pulled on some clothes and plodded downstairs to find Adam still dozing on the sofa, although Wolverine had abandoned him to glare pointedly at his empty bowl. I gave Adam a gentle shake as Matt did the important stuff, i.e. feeding the cat.

"Whassup?" Adam muttered drowsily.

"Adam? It's eleven o'clock. I thought I'd better wake you," I said.

He blinked at me, his eyes gradually focussing. "Tim! You 'n' Matt all right?"

"Yeah," I said, with probably the world's soppiest smile on my face. "We're all right."

Adam grinned. "I better bugger off, then." He swung his legs off the sofa and stood up, stretching his unfeasibly long arms out wide. "Look after 'im," he said and loped off, pausing only to direct a cheery wave at Matt in the kitchen on his way out.

"Thanks, Adam," I said. "Thanks for everything."

It was late enough that when Matt cooked up some eggs, even I was keen to demolish a plateful and mop up the last of the yolk with some bread and butter. While I washed up, he nipped off to the shop to hang up the sign. My phone rang while he was out, but on seeing it was Mum, I switched it off guiltily. I really couldn't face talking to her with all this hanging over my head. As predicted, Matt was back within half an hour, his face shining and his hair tousled from the ride.

All I wanted to do was hold him, but it was time to broach a possibly uncomfortable subject.

"Matt, I'm afraid, ah, Kate's coming round later. You know, my, er, wife." I winced as I said the *W*-word. "She's coming to help me out with the legal stuff." I'd rung her last night from the police station—just to ask about lawyers down here—but once she'd heard the story, she'd insisted on coming down herself, probably to check I hadn't gone completely round the bend.

I wondered what conclusion she was going to come to about that once she'd heard the full story.

Matt looked wary. "Oh, okay. You want me to disappear for a bit, then?"

"No—no, of course not. I'd, um, like you to meet her." I mentally crossed my fingers behind my back at that last bit. While there was no way on earth I was hiding Matt away like some shameful little secret, it had to be said I wasn't actually looking forward to the great revelation. "I mean, I haven't told her about, well, us, but I'm going to."

"Are you sure? I mean..." Matt stared at his feet. "I'd understand if you wanted to keep a low profile for a bit. I mean, it's not like that many people ever knew about you and Adam."

"Matt," I said, sliding my arms around his waist and feeling a ridiculous thrill, even now, at being able to do so. "I'm not hiding how I feel about you. And, well, I think I owe it to Kate to be honest with her. Finally."

He smiled, putting his arms around my neck. "You know what? I think you do love her. No—not like that," he said in answer to my barely articulated protest. "Like a sister or something. It's nice."

God, I loved him, I realised with a rush that felt like I'd just drunk a whole bottle of champagne. Through a straw. "Maybe you're right. But..." I hesitated. It was too soon to say it, I knew. The last thing I wanted was to scare Matt off. "I'd rather be with you," I said instead, pulling him closer.

We kissed, slow and gentle.

"Look, Matt," I said when we paused for air, our foreheads resting together. "Just so you know, I'm not going back to London. We're selling the house, and I'm going to look for a job down here. Something with reasonable hours and no long commute, so I'll have time for other things. Like mountain biking and being with people I love." I cleared my throat and carried on. "I'm sure Jay will let me sleep on his sofa if need be, when he finally gets back home."

"Yeah—course he will." Matt paused. "And, well, I'll be needing to look for a place. Maybe...maybe we could think about getting somewhere together. I mean," he added quickly, "as, well, flatmates, or something. You know."

"Of course," I said, feeling so full of happiness I was probably about to rupture something. "Because it'd be way too soon, obviously, to really move in together. But flatmates... That'd be good."

The doorbell rang, and the sudden lurch of fear in my belly came as a stark reminder I might not have to worry about accommodation for the next three to five years, or whatever they gave you for GBH these days. "That'll be Kate," I said, disentangling myself from Matt with reluctance.

He nodded. "I'll be upstairs, then. If you need me."

Kate stood on the doorstep, looking cool and elegant in a short-sleeved navy wrap dress I didn't think I'd seen before. "Oh, Tim!" she said, her lip wobbling.

I gathered her up in a huge hug—at least it seemed huge

compared to the size of Kate; I'd forgotten just how tiny she was. "Thanks for coming," I said, standing back with a smile splitting my face. I was incredibly glad to see her. Had she put on a little bit of weight? If she had, it suited her. Made her look...more relaxed. Happier with herself. She probably wouldn't thank me for mentioning it, though.

"Well, of course I came! Look, I know things didn't work out with us, but I meant it when I said I hoped we'd always be friends."

"Of course we will," I said, meaning it. "It really is good to see you—and not just because of this mess I'm in. Come on in, don't stand on the doorstep."

She nodded, turning brisk and businesslike as she stepped over the threshold. "Right, well—first things first. You said you were waiting to hear whether the other party would corroborate your story?"

"Yes. Look, come on into the living room and sit down. I'll put the kettle on—you've come a long way. Coffee?"

"Mm, please," she said, ignoring the living room in favour of following me into the kitchen.

"Black, no sugar?"

"Of course. It's only been a few weeks."

"Ah, but I thought Alex might have been a bad influence on you." Alex liked his coffee with cream and two sugars, and why was I sparing a thought for the man who'd stolen my wife?

Probably so I could remember to send him a thank you note, I thought cheerfully. Although perhaps that might not be well received. "How is old Alex, anyway?"

"He's...fine."

She sounded so uncertain I looked up from the coffee mugs. "Kate? Is something wrong?"

"No! No, we're fine, it's just, well, you. Don't take this the wrong way, please—but you just seem so awfully chirpy."

I put down the teaspoon. "Ah. Well." I cleared my throat. "Actually, I've got something to tell you. But it might be better if we sit down first."

"Whenever anybody says something like that, I start to worry even more," she said darkly as I handed her a mug of coffee.

"It's nothing to worry about, honestly." After I'd said it, I realised she might have a different point of view. "At least, I don't think it is."

"Tim, will you please just *tell* me?"

I glanced regretfully at my steaming coffee, swirling enticingly and tantalising me with its aroma, and put down my mug. Then I took a deep breath. "There's a part of me I've been hiding. All this time." I swallowed. Suddenly this didn't seem so easy. "I'll always think fondly of what we had. But I think you know, deep down, we were never really in love. Look, I realise this may be hard for you to accept—God knows, it was hard enough for me—but I'm, well, I'm gay."

The world seemed to stand still for a moment. Kate stared at me, her mouth half-open, and my heart pounded uncomfortably as I waited for her to speak.

"Oh, thank God!"

Okay, that wasn't *exactly* what I'd been expecting. "You're...pleased?"

"Of course—don't you realise, I thought all this time it was me? I thought—God, I thought I'd failed to be a good enough wife; I left you because it wasn't working and then I *still* made you mess up your life." She gave me the soppiest smile I'd seen in years. "It all makes so much sense, now. I didn't...I didn't make you unhappy; you just *couldn't* have been happy with me."

Guilt stabbed at me as I grabbed both her hands. "I didn't...I had no idea you felt like that. God, I'm so sorry. It was *never* your fault. It was mine, all along."

"Rubbish! You can't help being gay."

"No, but I didn't have to bury my head in the sand and hope it'd go away. I should have been more honest—with you, with myself. But I just kept thinking—God, I was stupid." I shook my head. "I thought if I didn't *let* myself be gay, I wouldn't be."

"Oh, Tim." She let go of my hands—and wrapped her arms around me, squeezing me tight.

I hissed, Wolverine-style, at the sudden pain in my bruised ribs.

Kate sprang back as if I'd electrified her. "I'm so sorry! God, how thoughtless of me. Does it hurt very much?"

"It's all right—I'll live."

"Can I...see?"

I raised an eyebrow. "Any excuse to get my kit off, eh?"

Kate looked affronted. "As your legal advisor, I mean. I ought to know how badly you were injured."

We shared a wry smile as I untucked my shirt from my jeans and lifted it up. Kate gave a sharp little intake of breath when she saw the bruising which, admittedly, had developed nicely since last night, from what little I could see without a mirror.

"Oh, Tim! Are there more like that?"

"No, no. That's the worst. There's some bruising to my forearms, obviously, where I was blocking his kicks."

I've never known anyone as able as Kate to give the impression of tapping her foot without actually doing anything so rude as tapping her foot. Sighing, I pulled my shirt off altogether and held out my forearms for inspection.

231

I wasn't quite prepared for her to pull out her phone and start snapping pictures. "For the private album?" I asked drily.

Kate tutted. "For evidence, obviously. Now, tell me—have you found someone? A man, I mean?"

I could feel my mouth stretching into a soppy smile. "Yes. Yes, I have. His name's Matt, and he works at Jay's shop, and he's a really great guy. Actually, he's here now—he wanted to give me time to explain things to you. I'd really like you to meet him—shall I give him a shout?"

Kate put away her phone and smiled a little tearily. "You should see your face right now... Yes—I'd love to meet him."

"Matt!" I yelled up the stairs. "It's safe to come down." I couldn't seem to shift the gormless grin.

"Oh, Tim—I'm so happy for you." Kate sniffed, hugging me a lot more gently this time.

When Matt came warily downstairs, he gave my shirtless, embraced-by-my-not-quite-ex-wife state a pointed look. "Um," he said. "Should I come back later? Or, you know, not at all?"

He let out a startled yelp as a tearstained Kate grabbed him and yanked him into the hug. "I'm so glad he's found you." She sniffled onto his shoulder.

I patted her back. "There, there."

Matt's gaze met mine over the top of her head, and we stayed like that, just looking into each other's eyes, for a long moment.

Then Kate stepped back briskly from the embrace and blew her nose, I put my shirt on and we finally got to sit down and drink our coffee, by now rather lukewarm.

Kate had me run through the events of last night, stopping me to ask questions as I went. I was relieved she didn't see fit to make any comments on my behaviour in front of Matt. Finally, she nodded and stood up. "It's probably best if we go down to the police station and see if Mr. Pritchard has made a statement yet. The way things are at the moment, it's going to very much depend on whether he makes a counter-claim to the effect that you were the aggressor. But hopefully, the most you'll be charged with is battery."

I winced. It sounded all too much like what Pritchard had been doing to Matt. "And what's the sentence for that? And what happens if *hopefully* doesn't pan out?"

Kate took a deep breath. "It's entirely likely you'll just be fined. There is the possibility you could go to prison, but for a first offence, even if you're charged with ABH—that's assault occasioning actual bodily harm—"

"I know what it means, Kate. I just want to know if I'm going to be charged with it."

She sighed. "Honestly, until we've heard from the police regarding the other party's statement, we simply can't speculate."

Matt's hand had crept into mine at the word *prison*, and now he spoke up. "What if someone told the police Ste—Pritchard has a history of violence?"

"They won't," I said firmly. "Not unless they really have to."

Kate's eyes had widened, and she leaned forward in her seat. "I really think—ow! Tim, did you just kick me?"

"Sorry—my foot slipped," I said innocently, wiggling my bare toes at her as if in evidence.

Kate's gaze tracked suspiciously from me to Matt, but she didn't ask any more questions.

Chapter Twenty-One

The drive down to the police station in the centre of town was a nerve-jangling one. We took the BMW, as it turned out Kate had driven down in a brand-new two-seater MG. Seemed like I hadn't been the only one making changes in my life. Matt gave the shiny red sports car a wistful glance as we passed it, and I started wondering about trade-ins.

Only for a moment, though, as I remembered I ought first to see if I'd be at liberty to drive the thing.

When we got to the police station, there was a frustrating wait to talk to someone who actually knew anything about the case. Eventually we were greeted by a young officer I didn't recognise and whose name I was too nervous to catch. Did the fact that he called me "sir" mean I wasn't going to be charged? Or was "sir", in this instance, just police shorthand for "You violent scumbag"?

He took us to an interview room, where he opened up a file and briefly scanned its contents before looking up with a bland expression. "Right, Mr. Knight. We've spoken to Mr. Pritchard—apparently he became somewhat belligerent on being questioned—and we're happy that the statement you gave us corresponds with the truth."

If I hadn't been sitting down, I'd have collapsed with relief. Matt, hovering in the corner as there were only three chairs, gave a huge grin.

"So there's just the matter of the assault charge."

My heart leapt back up into my mouth so fast my head

spun.

"Will you be wishing to pursue the matter, sir?"

"I—what?" I croaked.

Kate rescued me. "He means, do you want to press charges against Mr. Pritchard?"

"I..." I could charge him? Get Prick-tard sent to jail?

"I think Mr. Knight would like a few moments to consider the matter," Kate said smoothly.

"Right." The officer stood up, glancing at his watch. "I'll give you ten minutes and then look back in on you, all right?"

Kate stood too. "That'll be fine. Thank you."

As the door closed behind him, she sat again. I hadn't got up in the first place, sincerely worried I might just fall down. "I think I just aged ten years," I muttered.

"So, are you going to do it?" Kate asked.

I looked at Matt, who'd perched on the edge of the table next to me. "What do you think?"

"It's your decision," he said.

I nodded. "No, then."

"No?" Kate's head snapped round. "Why on earth not?"

"Because...because it's not just about a fight in a car park," I said. "Which, by the way, I won. If this goes to court, there's a good chance a lot of other things are going to come out..." I faltered at the unfortunate choice of words, and Kate shot Matt a shrewd glance. "Anyway, maybe I got a few bruises, but Prick—I mean, Pritchard came off worse. It doesn't seem right to get him fined or sent to jail or whatever as well."

Matt squeezed my hand. I was pretty certain Kate noticed that too.

Stepping out of the police station into the sunshine was like climbing out of a black pit of despair into, well, the sunshine. "Thanks so much for coming down," I told Kate. "Even though it turned out to be a bit of a wasted journey."

"Don't be silly. I got to meet Matt, so it certainly wasn't wasted."

I may possibly have been sporting a soppy grin at her words, as she gave me a fond and almost motherly smile. Matt just took a really good look at his trainers' scuffed toes, and the tips of his ears turned red.

With Jay still in hospital—and with me guiltily aware I hadn't visited him in days—I didn't like to leave my phone off any longer, so I switched it back on. It rang almost immediately. "Sorry, I'd better get it. Just in case."

It turned out it *was* Jay. Calling from his mobile, my phone told me. "Are you allowed to use mobile phones in a hospital?" I asked.

"I'm not in hospital anymore. They chucked me out yesterday. I'm at Mum and Dad's. So what's this I hear about your secret life of violent crime?"

What? "How did you—" I broke off and gave Kate a hard stare. For the first time this morning, she looked unsure of herself.

"Have you been telling everyone about what happened?" I demanded.

"I—well, I told your mum about the fight, and that you were arrested."

"What?" I stared at her in disbelief. "Kate, of all the times to start talking to my mother…"

"I was so worried about you! It seemed you'd been acting totally out of character—I mean, for goodness' sake, *fighting*. In the street! It was just so unlike you—I rang your mum up before I drove down to ask her what was going on, and when it turned out she didn't know a thing about it all, I felt I couldn't *not* tell her. She's your mother, Tim. She cares about you."

I groaned and put the phone back to my ear. "How bad is it?" I asked.

Jay laughed. "Put it this way—you'd better get your arse round here soon as, or Mum's going to come looking for you. Trust me, you don't want that!"

"We should do something to celebrate," Matt said as we stood at the end of Jay's drive and waved Kate off into the distance, a fast-moving little red dot.

"You mean, go for a drink or something? Get a bottle of champagne in?" I sighed. "You know what, after all the stress this morning, all I really feel like doing is going to bed." I certainly didn't feel like driving up to Winchester to explain myself, that was for sure.

"Bed works for me," Matt said with a spring in his step and a leer in his tone.

Suddenly, all the tiredness seemed to drain away, leaving only lust in its wake. "Right. Bed," I agreed, taking his hand.

We practically ran down the driveway and back into the house and barely got the front door shut before heading upstairs to the bedroom. Maybe it was just my imagination, but the room still seemed to smell of sex from our little morning glory session earlier.

"What do you want to do?" Matt asked, tearing off his shirt.

A thought occurred, and I burst out laughing in the middle of undoing my trousers. Matt stared at me. "Sorry," I managed at last. "It's just, I was about to say, *buggered if I know!*" Matt laughed helplessly, nearly falling over as he got out of his jeans.

JL Merrow

I slid my arms around his waist, marvelling anew at the warmth and smoothness of his skin. "Seriously," I said when we'd both calmed down, "I haven't got a bloody clue what I'm doing. But if you'd like to, um..." I swallowed. "If you'd like to er, top, I'd like that. A lot."

"That'd...yeah." Matt seemed to be having some trouble speaking. "Have you, um—did you and Adam—"

"*No*," I interrupted. Grateful as I was to him for all kinds of reasons, I really didn't want Adam intruding at a time like this. "But I've, er, experimented—on my own, I mean." I'd never been more grateful to the friend of Kate's who'd held an Ann Summers party and bullied her into buying a vibrator. If Kate had ever noticed it'd disappeared from her bottom drawer, she'd never mentioned it.

Most people seemed to rate the discovery of America pretty highly; I'd have to say that, for me, it paled into insignificance beside the discovery of my prostate. I hadn't, however, invited Kate to explore this new territory with me. I was fairly sure that in her world, pegging was something that only happened to tents. Or, as it might be, clean laundry.

"Okay—we can take it slow."

"Slow sounds good." I got on with the business of getting naked, my hands shaking a little.

"Have you got any supplies?" Matt asked. "You know, condoms and lube?"

Shit. Why the hell hadn't I thought of that? "I'll see what I can find." I sat on the bed and rummaged desperately through Jay's bedside drawer—coming up trumps with a handful of condoms and a large tube of lube. "Olivia, you kinky devil."

"You don't know that," Matt said with a grin. "And right now, it's not her arse I want to be thinking about," he added with a pointed look at me.

238

My mouth was suddenly dry. "Right," I said hoarsely and stripped off my underwear.

I could have sworn Matt's cock had grown again, now that we were only minutes away from him inserting it into a rather delicate part of me. Now we were so close, I was both excited and terrified. This was it—the final step. Once I'd let another bloke fuck me, all plausible deniability was right out of the window.

"Are you sure about this?" Matt asked softly. "We don't have to..."

What the hell. I was in bed with the man I loved—plausible deniability had undoubtedly packed its bags a long time ago, and good riddance to it. "Yes," I said firmly, suddenly more certain than I'd ever been in my life. "I'm sure. Matt, I..." It was still too soon to tell him I loved him. I knew that. "It means a lot to me, that it's you," I finished.

Matt drew in a deep, shuddering breath and blinked several times, fast. "It means a lot to me too," he said.

He crawled over the bed, naked, his cock bobbing, and kissed me. I couldn't get enough of him, his warmth, his vitality. I pulled him in close, wanting to feel every inch of him against me. Hands roamed over bodies, touching and teasing. When Matt squeezed some lube over his fingers and let one slide down my crack, I arched, willing him inside me. When he breached me, I cried out, it felt so good.

"Okay?" he whispered.

"Bloody okay," I groaned.

He stretched me out slowly—much more slowly than I'd have had the patience for—and used his other hand to tease the rest of me, keeping me at full arousal. I tried to reciprocate but was mostly way too distracted by what his talented fingers were up to. When he crooked them inside me to press on my gland, I gasped. "Do it," I urged him, unable to wait any longer.

"Do what?" Matt asked teasingly.

"Me. Do me," I begged.

Matt sat back on his heels to suit up and slather on some more lube, and I watched him in a lust-filled daze. "How do you want me?" I managed to ask.

"You choose," he said.

It wasn't that easy—on the one hand, I wanted to be able to see his face, but on the other hand my deepest fantasy, the one I'd always wanked to when I'd had a few glasses of wine to lower my inhibitions, was being taken from behind. I hesitated—then shifted onto my knees, laying my head down on my arms.

Nothing happened. I raised my head to look back at Matt.

"Just—just give me a moment," he said, looking incredibly hot and bothered. He took a few deep breaths, then shuffled forward to line himself up.

I could feel the blunt, rubber-clad head of him at my entrance. My hips pushed back without my conscious control as my body tried to impale itself on him. When he pushed forward, there was an incredible feeling of stretching, of invasion. I took a few short breaths.

"I'm not hurting you, am I?" Matt asked.

"No—no, I'm fine; don't stop." Which, okay, wasn't as truthful as it might have been, but God, I really, really didn't want him to stop.

He pushed forward, millimetre by millimetre. I felt overwhelmingly full, and each time I thought my body couldn't possibly take any more of him, he moved again. As the tip of him passed over my prostate, I let out a low, deep groan.

"Okay?" he asked again.

"More than okay. So bloody okay I think I'm going to die from it."

Matt chuckled, but I'd been serious.

He inched forward some more, and I felt his balls nestling against my arse. "That's all of me," he whispered. I felt light-headed, delirious with pleasure. It was everything I'd ever fantasized about and more. I didn't just feel filled—for the first time in my life, I felt whole, complete.

And then he moved. Drawing back a few inches, Matt thrust back into me, his balls hitting my arse with an audible slap. I moaned into the pillow, the stimulation so good it was almost torture. He slammed into me again and again, punishing my prostate, drawing grunts and cries from me I'd probably be mortified to hear played back.

"God, that's so good," Matt gasped, his fingers digging into my hips with bruising force that only seemed to accentuate the pleasure. "Tim, I'm going to—"

I thrust a hand between my legs and pumped myself once, twice—then I was coming so hard I literally saw stars. My orgasm seemed to go on forever, blacking out my vision and tearing through my body so violently I felt it had to leave a scar—and God, I'd wear that scar with pride. Matt let out a huge cry and thrust a couple more times into my oversensitised hole before collapsing, panting, onto my back. I let my knees slide away from me and lay prone on the bed, with him on top of me and inside me, thinking if a meteor struck now, I could die happy.

Then I reflected that was a daft idea, because bloody hell, I wanted to do that again.

As Matt heaved his weight off me, his cock slipping out of my thoroughly fucked arse, I turned over so I could face him. "That..." Words failed me, and I shook my head. "I had no idea," I started again. "I mean, I've never..."

Matt gave me a shaky smile, seeming just as overcome. His

hair was hanging around his face in sweaty straggles as he looked down at me, muscles bulging in those broad shoulders from holding his weight off me, and he was the most beautiful thing I'd ever seen. "No," he agreed. "Me neither."

Chapter Twenty-Two

"Do you want me to come with you?" Matt asked, his face looking worried in the mirror beside mine.

I ran the comb through my hair one last time. I was tempted—but if it went as badly as I feared it might, I didn't want him caught in the fallout. "No—thanks, but I'll be fine. After all, what's the worst that could happen?" I gave a little laugh that sounded horribly fake.

"Your dad isn't a firearms enthusiast, is he?"

"No, but he's got a chainsaw in the shed. And any amount of other power tools." All in pristine condition, because he never actually used the things.

"*The Winchester Driller Killer*... nah, I can't see it, can you?"

"*The Hampshire Chainsaw Massacre* hasn't quite got the same ring, either," I mused. "Do you think this shirt's all right?"

Matt frowned. "I'm not sure anyone's going to care about your clothes, to be honest. I think they're going to be more worried about what you're saying."

He was probably right. I doubted there was an ideal outfit to come out to your parents in.

"You know you don't have to do this, right?" Matt asked one more time.

"Yes, I do. I'm not hiding you." I twisted around to slide my hands round his waist. "And anyway, it's probably as good a time as any. What with the fight and everything. Isn't that what politicians do—try and bury bad news with worse news?"

"Depends what they think is the worse news," Matt said

dubiously.

"Good point. All right, wish me luck—I'm going in."

The drive up to Winchester took half an hour, most of which I spent biting my nails and hoping against hope for a sudden flash traffic jam that'd mean I could put the whole thing off for a bit longer. Needless to say, the roads were clearer than I'd ever seen them.

When I got to Mum and Dad's Victorian semi, I parked at the end of the drive and sat there for a moment, taking some deep, supposedly calming breaths. I could do this. I was twenty-eight, for God's sake, not some confused, hormonal teenager. This was the twenty-first century. *Everyone* knew someone who was gay. It was no big deal anymore.

Yes, right. Tell that to my pounding heart and sweaty palms. I got out of the car, strode swiftly to the door before I could change my mind, and rang the bell.

And waited.

And waited some more. Where the hell was everyone? I could forgive Jay for not jumping up to answer the door, but surely they wouldn't have left him on his own? After all, since he'd retired, Dad hardly even went out anymore—just spent all his time reading the paper or in the garden...

Ah. The garden. It was a bright, sunny afternoon in late June, and Mum had some rather fixed ideas about the health benefits of fresh air. Where else would they be? Huffing a bit at them anyway for making this all even more nerve-racking than it had to be, I trooped around the side of the house.

They were all sitting on the patio, Mum and Dad on their twee little wrought-iron chairs and Jay stretched out on what looked like a brand-new lounger, the Meccano set glinting in the sun. They were sipping PG Tips and nibbling on slices of Mr. Kipling's Battenburg, and the only one missing from the set was Olivia. Birds were twittering, flowers were blooming, somewhere in the distance a neighbour's lawnmower buzzed—the whole scene was idyllically peaceful. Until I stepped into view.

Mum put down her cup of tea the minute she saw me. "Timothy! Now, what's all this nonsense Kate was saying about you being arrested?"

Oh, God. Facing a crazed, violently jealous Steve Pritchard was as nothing to the thought of explaining myself to my mother. "I got in a fight, Mum."

She frowned. "Don't be ridiculous. Why on earth would you do that? You never get into fights. Your father and I have always worried you'd never toughen up and stand up for yourself."

I winced at the implication they were still worrying about it and glanced at Dad. He shrugged and made a face that managed to encompass *sorry, well, a father worries about his son* and *you know what your mother's like* all in one.

"Well, this time I did," I said, hopefully not sounding too defensive.

"I hope this isn't just some silly reaction to losing your job, where you've decided you need to prove yourself—"

"Mum! He started it!" Great. Now I sounded all of six years old. "I mean, we had a bit of a barney—" Mum gave me a sharp look, as well she might. Up until now, the word "barney" as used by me had been merely a generic term for Fred Flintstone's best mate. It seemed Matt was rubbing off on me in more ways than one—and that little image was *not* what I needed to focus on while I was trying to talk to my mother. "A bit of an argument. And then he just went for me."

"But why would he do that? What were you arguing about?

Timothy?"

My throat almost closed up at the thought of telling them. "It was about this bloke..." I swallowed. "Mum, Dad—I've got a boyfriend." I wiped my hands on my jeans, then wondered what on earth I was supposed to do with them now. If I put them in my pockets, I'd come over all sullen adolescent. Folding my arms would look confrontational. Putting them behind my back...

Mum interrupted my frantic mental ramblings. "Don't be silly, Timothy. You're married."

Oops. Had I really forgotten to mention that before now? Had *Kate*? "We split up. Kate's with someone else now. And I'm with Matt. Who used to be with the man I fought. Hence the, er, barney."

"You've split up with Kate? When did this happen?"

"Just before I moved down here. It's fine, Mum—we just weren't really suited."

"It's easy for you to be so blasé about it—what about her? Poor girl, left hanging while you go off and experiment sexually—"

I was fairly sure I was now as crimson as Dad's carefully pruned tea roses. "Mum! She left me! For another man—who, I might add, was a friend of mine."

"Well, I have to say I'm very disappointed in her." She sniffed. "I've held my tongue for a long time—I'm not one to speak out of turn—but I never did like that girl. Coming here, turning her nose up at everything. Thinking she was so much better because she had a *career*—"

"Mum! We're still friends, you know. She came down from London to help me out with the police."

"Well, I hardly see how that was necessary. Anyone in possession of the facts could see you were entirely blameless.

246

Still, I don't see why you felt the need to go off and get yourself a, a *male lover* over it." Mum's eyes narrowed. "I always did wonder when the rebellious phase would finally happen. Don't you think you're a little old for this? Or is it some kind of reaction to being almost thirty?"

"I'm only twenty-eight—and no, it's not a reaction. Mum, I'm—I'm gay." The ground seemed to tilt as I finally said the words, then thankfully settled back. "I've known for a while, all right? I just...didn't want to be."

"Now you're making no sense at all. Either you are, or you aren't."

"He could be bisexual," Jay put in, looking thoughtful, as if it was a matter of purely academic interest. Something inside me curled up and wanted to die quietly at the thought of my whole family actively thinking about my sex life.

Mum was dismissive. "I'm sure I read somewhere there's no such thing. Just people refusing to make up their minds."

"Does it matter?" I asked desperately. "The point is, I'm with a man now. I'm gay." It was easier, saying it the second time.

"Oh, *Timothy!*" And to my utter astonishment, my mother came over and crushed me in a Chanel No. 5-scented hug. "Don't worry, darling. Of course your father and I will support you in everything. You'll have to bring the young man over for Sunday dinner, just as soon as we've got this ridiculous assault charge settled. I'll phone Anna Stephanides from number four right away—you remember Mrs. Stephanides, don't you, darling? Her son's a barrister, very high-flying as I understand it. He'll soon have these charges dismissed."

I don't think I said a word. All these years, when nothing I'd done had ever been good enough to rate a smile from my mother, much less a hug—and suddenly, due to what some parents might have seen as a series of major fuck-ups, I was the apple of her tear-misted eye? I looked helplessly at Jay.

He just shrugged again and mouthed something over my mother's gently heaving shoulder.

I think it was, *She likes to have someone to make a fuss over.*

"Mum," I said, actually feeling a bit reluctant to tell her we didn't need to bother the high-flying barrister, "it's all right. I'm not going to be charged. They've accepted my story."

"And so they should! How dare they accuse my son of lying—" Mum choked up a bit then and squeezed hard enough to give me new bruises. When she finally released me, slightly crushed, a bit damper and a lot more fragranced than I'd been before, I braced myself and turned to face Dad. He hadn't said a word so far. He was looking even older and more tired now, and my spirits sank.

"Dad?" I asked, then swallowed.

"Oh, Tim," he sighed.

"You're disappointed, aren't you?" I managed to keep my voice steady. For a wonder, Mum didn't interrupt.

"Well, I can't say it's what I've always hoped to hear—dreaded, perhaps. It's not most fathers' wish for their sons, is it?"

"Sorry," I whispered, staring at an ant crawling across the patio.

"None of that!" he said sharply.

I looked up. There was something of his old energy showing in those pale blue eyes. "Dad?"

"Your mother's right. Of course we'll support you in everything. You're our son. Nothing could ever change that." He reached out a hand, which shook a little, and I hurried over to take it. "I think I always suspected. You were always so different from Jay—never wanting to play the same rough games."

"Well, I never suspected," Jay put in, sounding annoyed. "I hope you realise you've lost me ten quid."

"Er, how?"

"Olivia. First time she met you, she bet me a tenner you were gay."

"What? How the hell did she know?"

Jay grinned. "Because you're the only 'straight' bloke she's met—present company *not* excepted, and yeah, Dad, I'm looking at you—who can talk to her without spending half the time staring at her tits."

"James!"

"Sorry, Mum. Breasts." He gave Dad a sly look. "Bazoombas. Jugs. Melons. Air-bags. Baps—"

"*James!*"

Mum glared at the three of us, all helplessly giggling like schoolboys.

"Plus," Jay went on breathlessly, "remember that time she turned up when you were letting it all hang out at my place and she pretended you were going grey?"

"What?" She'd only been pretending? I *didn't* have grey pubes?

I was going to murder that woman.

Jay laughed. "Yeah, she said your face fell so fast she nearly dived to catch it. She reckons she's never yet had a straight bloke come in for the old *intimate grooming.*"

"I have not had any intimate grooming!" I shouted, just as Olivia walked around the side of the house.

"If you ask me, more men should," she said, coolly walking up to Jay and giving him a kiss. "Maybe they wouldn't be so keen to insist their girlfriends get a Brazilian, then."

How had my big coming-out speech turned into a discussion on the merits of bikini waxing?

Oh, right. Jay. As usual.

"That's right, laugh at me," I groused, glaring at them both, and Olivia in particular. "When I think of all I've done for you—run your shop, done your books, fed your cat—at, I might add, considerable risk to life and limb—"

"Cat?" Jay said. He and Olivia turned to me with matching frowns. "What cat?"

I wondered what the penalty was for felicide and whether I'd be allowed to serve my sentence concurrently with the one I was about to incur for fratricide and whatever the Latin word was for killing your brother's girlfriend. "Never mind," I said with as much dignity as I could scrabble together, which wasn't much. "I've got a boyfriend to get back to."

I stalked off to the sound of a most un-Olivia-like squeal of triumph.

When I got back home, Matt was sitting on the sofa with Wolverine on his lap, purring gently. By which I mean Wolverine was doing the purring, although Matt was looking pretty content too. He—Matt, that is—looked up at my arrival and gave me a smile that made my heart start doing back-flips. "Did it go all right?"

I leaned against the doorframe. "Well, I was by turns confused, humiliated and treated to the sight of Jay and Dad bonding over women's breasts, and we've got to go round for lunch on Sunday—which if you'd rather break up with me than suffer through, I'd totally understand—but basically, yes, it went all right."

"Brilliant. Gerroff, you," he added, and with total—and, it

turned out, justified—disregard for Wolverine's lethal claws, he tipped the interloping cat off his lap and stood.

I gave the wretched beast a look that said plainly *I'll deal with you later.*

He flicked his tail at me, cat-speak for *Do I look like I'm bothered?*

"Well, I was thinking," Matt said, stretching. "Tomorrow's going to be a busy day at the shop. Maybe we ought to get an early night." There was a mischievous glint in his eyes.

I looked at my watch. It was half-past six in the afternoon.

I gave the worst impersonation of a yawn ever in the entire history of the world. "Good point," I said. "Got to keep our strength up and all that."

Matt nodded, mock-solemn. "Or something."

"*Definitely* or something."

"In fact, something's coming up right now."

"You're right, there. You. Me. Bed." I grabbed Matt by the hand and pulled him towards the stairs. "And Wolverine?" I threw over my shoulder. "You are *not* invited."

"Is he ever?" Matt asked with a laugh.

"Good point. We're locking the door. I'd like to see him get round that one without opposable thumbs."

"You know, there's a lot of things you can do with opposable thumbs..."

"Less talking, more doing," I said and kissed him.

About the Author

JL Merrow is that rare beast, an English person who refuses to drink tea. She read Natural Sciences at Cambridge, where she learned many things, chief amongst which was that she never wanted to see the inside of a lab ever again. Her one regret is that she never mastered the ability of punting one-handed whilst holding a glass of champagne.

She writes across genres, with a preference for contemporary gay romance and the paranormal, and is frequently accused of humour.

Find JL Merrow online at: www.jlmerrow.com.

A stranger could light up his world...
or drive him deeper into darkness.

Wight Mischief
© 2011 JL Merrow

Will Golding needs a break from his usual routine, and he's been looking forward to a holiday helping Baz, his friend-with-benefits, research a book about Isle of Wight ghosts. When an evening beach walk turns into a startling encounter with Marcus Devereux, Will can't get his mind off the notoriously reclusive writer's pale, perfect, naked body. And any interest in ghostly legends takes a back seat to the haunting secrets lying in Marcus's past.

Marcus, painfully aware of his appearance, is accustomed to keeping to himself. But the memory of tall, athletic Will standing on the beach draws him out from behind defenses he's maintained since age fourteen, when his parents were murdered. While his heart is hungry for human contact, though, his longtime guardian warns him that talking to anyone—particularly a journalist like Baz—is as dangerous as a day in the sun.

As Baz gets closer to the truth, the only thing adding up is the sizzling attraction between Will and Marcus. And it's becoming increasingly clear that someone wants to let sleeping secrets lie...or Will and Baz could end up added to the island's ghostly population.

Warning: Contains perilous cliffs, elusive might-be ghosts, a secret tunnel, and skinny-dipping by moonlight.

Available now in ebook and print from Samhain Publishing.

When the boat's a'rockin', don't come knockin'!

Barging In
© 2011 Josephine Myles

Out-and-proud travel writer Dan Taylor can't steer a boat to save his life, but that doesn't stop him from accepting an assignment to write up a narrowboat holiday. Instead of a change of pace from city life, though, the canal seems dull as ditchwater. Until he crashes into the boat of a half-naked, tattooed, pierced man whose rugged, penniless appearance is at odds with a posh accent.

Still smarting from past betrayal, Robin Hamilton's "closet" is his narrowboat, his refuge from outrageous, provocative men like Dan. Yet he can't seem to stop himself from rescuing the hopelessly out-of-place city boy from one scrape after another. Until he finds himself giving in to reluctant attraction, even considering a brief, harmless fling.

After all, in less than a week, Dan's going back to his London diet of casual hook-ups and friends with benefits.

Determined not to fall in love, both men dive into one week of indulgence...only to find themselves drawn deep into an undertow of escalating intimacy and emotional intensity. Troubled waters neither of them expected...or wanted.

Warning: Contains one lovable tart, one posh boy gone feral, rough sex, alfresco sex, vile strawberry-flavoured condoms, intimate body piercings, red thermal long-johns, erotic woodchopping, an errant cat, a few colourful characters you wouldn't touch with a bargepole, and plenty of messing about on the river.

Available now in ebook and print from Samhain Publishing.

SAMHAIN

PUBLISHING

www.samhainpublishing.com

Green for the planet.
Great for your wallet.

SAMHAIN
PUBLISHING

It's all about the story...

Romance

HORROR

www.samhainpublishing.com